THE HANGING GARDEN

By the Same Author

Green Trigger Fingers
Flowers of Evil
The Mantrap Garden
A Botanist at Bay
Menacing Groves
A Bouquet of Thorns
The Sunflower Plot

THE
HANGING
GARDEN

JOHN SHERWOOD

Charles Scribner's Sons
New York

Maxwell Macmillan Canada
Toronto

Maxwell Macmillan International
New York   Oxford   Singapore   Sydney

Copyright © 1992 by John Sherwood

Charles Scribner's Sons
Macmillan Publishing Company
866 Third Avenue
New York, NY 10022

Maxwell Macmillan Canada, Inc.
1200 Eglinton Avenue East
Suite 200
Don Mills, Ontario M3C 3N1

Macmillan Publishing Company is part of the Maxwell Communication Group of Companies.

ISBN 0-684-19429-5

Printed in the United States of America

For J.H.
Who showed me the real Madeira.

The church and square of São Lourenço
will not be found on maps of Funchal.
They are as imaginary as the characters
in this story.

ONE

The narrow lane ran steeply uphill between high garden walls. The woman who called herself Maria Silva tackled the climb with springy, determined steps. She was in her thirties and tall, with a mass of dark curly hair and handsome, rather hawklike features. They were set in a look of fierce concentration. No one seeing her could have guessed that behind this confident mask she lived in a state of mental insecurity bordering on panic.

Still striding along firmly, she came out into the square at the top of the hill. On one side of it, a little garden overlooked the view down to the centre of Funchal and the harbour. On the opposite side, with the mountains in the centre of the island rising behind it, stood the eighteenth-century church of São Lourenço, whose interior was a masterpiece of elaborate rococo plasterwork and one of the architectural wonders of Funchal. On Sundays in Lent the square was the scene of grim ceremonies of self-abasement by penitents. On ordinary days, tourists photographed each other against the background of the view, for the square and the church were on one of the taxi-drivers' standard sightseeing runs, which also took in the Botanical Gardens, the Boa Vista orchid houses and the much-hyped toboggan run down a steep cobbled lane.

But it was still early. The only people about were three starved-looking British students, lounging outside the little café, who seemed to be a permanent feature of the square. Maria ignored them, as she ignored everyone she passed on her appearances in public. In her situation it was wise to keep herself to herself. Her aloofness probably stirred up curiosity, but unsatisfied curiosity was safer than having to invent lying answers to the neighbours' questions.

With the morning sun hot on her, she turned her back on the

church and crossed the square to the little garden. Her resolve had suddenly sagged into despair. Leaning on the railings, and ignoring the view over the city below her, she stared out into space with unseeing eyes and tried to collect her thoughts. Should she go into the church? What was the point? No one could relieve her of the frightful burden she had to carry. She would get the same old story from Father Rodrigues. It would give her no real comfort. But she would feel even worse if she turned tail without making her confession. Screwing up her courage, she went in.

After the fierce heat outside, the interior struck chill into her despite the sunlight streaming through the high windows. She knelt in a pew and made her preparation, a confused mental process which tailed off into an absent-minded repetition of familiar prayers. She was filling in time, for she was early. Confessions did not start till nine.

Presently Father Rodrigues appeared in the doorway of the sacristy. He was short and tubby and brisk in his movements, unmistakably the sort of priest whose ministry relies heavily on common sense. He nodded to show that he had seen her, and went into the box. She took her place in it at once, and said: 'Bless me, Father, for I have sinned. It is two weeks since my last confession.'

An improvement, Father Rodrigues thought. At least I have discouraged her from coming once a week.

'I confess,' Maria began, 'that I have harboured hatred against the elderly person whom it is my duty to care for. I have answered him harshly when I should have been patient. I have not always attended to his needs as quickly as I should. I accuse myself, and repent of my sin.'

Always the same story, Father Rodrigues thought. She has this urge to confess. So she invents some trivial sin because the real one, the sin she confessed months ago when she first came to me, is too frightening to be thought about; it has to be choked down out of the way and something silly put in its place.

Wearily he played along with her obsession. 'Are you sure you do not exaggerate your fault, my daughter? Caring for the elderly is testing work, we often have impatient thoughts which we dismiss at once.'

'No, Father. Yesterday he spilt his tea, and I refrained with difficulty from hitting him.'

'Maria, for months you have been confessing to trifling sins, torturing yourself about them. Is it because that other, more grievous sin still troubles you deeply? You confessed it, and have received absolution. God has forgiven you.'

'I cannot forgive myself.'

'God does,' he insisted.

'But many people came to their deaths because of me. I am in torment.'

'Listen, Maria. God tested you and you were weak, you committed a great sin. But you do penance for it all the time.'

'No, Father!'

'Yes, all the time. You are young, you have many talents. Why are you acting as nurse to a helpless, crotchety old man to whom you owe no tie of family? Because that is your penance.'

'It is *not* a penance,' Maria burst out. 'It is my refuge from the world I have betrayed, my hiding-place from my enemies who are searching for me. My guilt is all the greater because I am safe.'

Just as she clings to her guilt, he thought, she clings also to her safety as the nurse-companion to an invalid. Sheer fright was probably her basic trouble. If she was found and her alias penetrated, there would be extradition proceedings in the Madeiran courts, followed by far from comfortable confinement in a Latin American prison.

There was a priest attached to the cathedral who was supposed to have special talents in dealing with difficult cases. Father Rodrigues decided to ask him for advice about the best line to take with Maria. Meanwhile, he asked her if she sincerely repented of her unkindness to Sir Adrian, gave her a penance of two sets of Our Father, Hail Mary and Glory be to God, and sent her away.

Maria stumbled out of the confessional box feeling vaguely comforted, and settled in a pew near the high altar to say her penitential prayers. Then she set off home. The square was filling up as the first tourists began to arrive. As always she stared straight ahead to avoid eye contact. She walked across the square, then on down the lane, with a banana grove on one side and on the other the high garden wall of the Quinta Coulson, where her employer lived.

9

Like many of the old houses in Madeira, the Quinta Coulson presented a blank face to the outside world. Its front entrance, a postern door in the high wall, gave no hint of what lay within. Maria unlocked the door, and let herself into a luxuriant garden. A short path of patterned cobbles, flanked by Canary palms underplanted with Madonna lilies led up to the elegant façade of a gracious old white-painted house with green shutters, surrounded by lawns and shrub borders in full flower. Maria skirted round the house to the back door, intending to ask Mrs Hanbury to buy her father some more pyjamas. Then she remembered: it was Saturday, when Mrs Hanbury drove down early to the city centre for an operation she called 'having my wiggie washed'. This consisted mainly of ensuring the uniform blondness of her hair, which was a very different colour when new growth emerged at the parting.

Abandoning the quest for pyjamas, she crossed the lawn on the garden side of the house, which commanded the view over the old town. Beyond it the garden fell steeply downhill in terrace after terrace, and she plunged down the slope on flights of steep stone steps. On the bottom terrace but one stood what had once been the gardener's cottage, yellow-washed under the curving eaves of its pantile roof.

In it, Sir Adrian Morton was still in bed. Maria had given him his breakfast there before she left. When she appeared in the doorway of his bedroom he gave her a lop-sided smile and made the cheerful neighing sound which was his way of expressing affectionate welcome. The main casualty of the stroke had been his speech, but he had evolved various methods of making himself understood and there was plenty of evidence of a mind still active. Another pang of guilt hit Maria. In successive confessions to Father Rodrigues she had built him up as a demanding, crotchety patient. But in fact he was a sweet-tempered old man, enormously grateful to her and keen to save her trouble as far as his condition allowed. Though still distinguished looking under his shock of white hair, he had a paralysed arm and one rather unreliable leg. And as he had had two quite serious heart attacks she had to discourage him from overstraining himself. But he was not bedridden and could shuffle about the cottage without support.

However, he could no longer manage the climb up and down

the terraces. At his daughter's suggestion he had moved down from the main house to the cottage to be near his collection of rare orchids, set out at the other end of the terrace under a plastic shelter which protected them from the hot sun. They were his pride and joy. Apart from reading, which he still enjoyed, contemplating them was his main pleasure in life.

She took away his breakfast tray, wiped a little snot from his face and helped him into the shower room that Mrs Hanbury had installed for him. While he washed she busied herself with domestic chores, then helped him to dress. But at the most awkward moment in his toilet, when she was getting him into his trousers, there was an interruption. Up the slope above her, the bread van was hooting to warn the locality that it had arrived.

It was Saturday, when Mrs Hanbury kept her weekly date at the hairdresser's and Teresa, her daily woman, did not come. The arrangement was that on Saturdays Maria was to collect the bread for both households.

If she had spent less time at the confessional, Sir Adrian would have been dressed before the bread van arrived. The timing was unfortunate. He would have to be left half in and half out of his trousers while she collected the bread. Unless she attended to it now, the van would have moved on to its next hooting-point and she would be in Mrs Hanbury's bad books. She tried to make him understand the problem, but he was too deaf to hear the van's siren message and the concepts of Saturday, the need for bread and the absence of Mrs Hanbury and Teresa were obviously too much for him. Leaving him sitting on the bed with a bewildered expression, she hurried up to the top of the garden.

The van was parked up in the square at the top end of the lane. People from all the surrounding houses were buying their bread. True to her policy of avoiding local contacts, she waited till most of them had finished, then bought supplies for herself and Sir Adrian as well as for Mrs Hanbury. But when she went back to the quinta to put Mrs Hanbury's loaf in the kitchen, she found that the back door was locked.

The back door was Mrs Hanbury's normal access route to the car. She went across the yard at the side of the house to the garage. A glance through the window showed that the car was still there. Mrs Hanbury had not gone to the hairdresser's after all. Had she overslept? The shutters of her bedroom windows on the garden side of the house were still closed.

Down at the cottage Maria had a spare key, kept there in case of emergencies, such as having to telephone the doctor if Sir Adrian had one of his 'turns' in the night. She decided to fetch the key, let herself in to deposit the bread in the kitchen, and investigate discreetly to make sure nothing was wrong.

But the key was not on its nail in the little entrance lobby.

Its absence was a nuisance and rather puzzling. So was the fact that Mrs Hanbury had shown no sign of life, not even opening her shutters. But she refused to dramatise. If anything was wrong, the consequences for her would be too awful to contemplate, so she blocked the possibility out of her mind. She would deliver the bread later, when Mrs Hanbury had woken up and unlocked the house.

Sir Adrian had managed somehow to get into his trousers and was struggling to zip up his flies with his one good hand. She helped him, and was rewarded with a neigh of embarrassed gratitude. Having settled him with his newspaper under the trellis in front of the cottage, she went about her household chores. By the time she had finished them it was half-past twelve. Willing herself to expect a return to normal up at the house, she decided to deliver Mrs Hanbury's bread before she cooked Sir Adrian's lunch.

But nothing had changed. The back door was still locked, the bedroom shutters were still closed, the car was still there. Panic set in, and it was a purely self-centred panic. If Mrs Hanbury was, for example, lying dead in bed, the household would cease to be viable. Sir Adrian would have to be put in a home and she would have to find a fresh refuge from danger, a difficult task for anyone like her, condemned to a furtive life underground. Someone must help her to get into the house and find out what was wrong.

She ranged round the garden looking for Agostinho Correia, the gardener, having forgotten in her agonised confusion that he and his wife Teresa did not come on Saturdays. But they had a key, and they lived in a flat just down the main road in a new block put up by a speculative builder. She found them about to sit down to lunch. When told about her worries, Agostinho suggested that

Mrs Hanbury had gone away to spend the night with friends, and had forgotten to tell anyone.

'Without taking the car?' Maria objected.

'She is impulsive and absent-minded,' said Teresa dismissively.

Agostinho grimaced. 'Perhaps she makes one of her jokes.'

'But it is midday,' cried Maria, 'and her shutters are still closed.'

Suddenly the Correias caught her alarm. Leaving their meal on the table, they started up the road with her to the Quinta Coulson. She did not let them break into a run because that would be an admission of panic. Forcing herself to believe everything was still normal, she wondered on the way up about her relations with the Correias. They obviously thought her odd. She knew she neither looked nor behaved like the stereotype of an old man's paid nurse-companion. Her speech, the Brazilian variety of Portuguese, marked her out as a stranger to Madeira, and the first name of the alias she had adopted was all wrong. Having been christened Maria-José, she had kept the Maria for simplicity, but had not bothered to invent a substitute for the José. But all the Marias in this part of the world were Maria-Teresas or Maria-Natálias or Maria-Joãos, anyway Maria-somethings, and a plain Maria was an oddity. The Correias were probably agog with curiosity, but did not seem to disapprove of her. They had worked for years for Sir Adrian, and their loyalty was to him. They probably approved of her because she cared for him. How far they approved of his daughter, with her taste for silly jokes and stupid nicknames, was another matter. Occasional hints suggested that they regarded her arrival as an intrusion and a necessary evil.

Up at the quinta, Teresa unlocked the kitchen door and let them in. Apart from a dripping tap the house was silent.

'Mrs Hanbury?' Maria called.

There was no reply. Making enough noise to establish a non-emergency atmosphere they walked through into the hall and called again. There was no reply.

On the far side of a screen of pillars the staircase rose in an airy curve to the bedrooms above. Something was lying on the half-landing, barely visible from below. Maria hurried up the stairs till she could see round the curve, then stood stock still in horror, fighting back nausea. Antonia Hanbury lay on her back on the half-landing, with her head hanging down over the top step of the lower flight. Her upside-down eyes were wide open and her face was livid.

The Correias peered over her shoulder, crossing themselves and muttering a prayer. Maria rushed up to Mrs Hanbury. Her shoulder, bare above the skimpy nightdress, was cold to the touch. She had been lying there for hours.

Maria tried not to feel cross with her employer for being dead. Why do I think only of myself? she asked herself guiltily, but it was hard to do otherwise. The break-up of the household, leaving her without the shelter of a job, was a disaster, and it was not the only danger she faced. There would be some kind of inquiry, she would be under a spotlight, have to answer questions. She had an instinctive Latin American distrust of all police forces, and although her residence papers were in order she had urgent reasons for not drawing attention to herself. Were the circumstances suspicious, would the police have to be called in? There was no sign of a bruise or a wound on the body, no suggestion of violence. But she had to be sure. Stepping gingerly past it, she went on up the staircase to investigate. To her relief, there was no disorder in Mrs Hanbury's bedroom. The bedside light was still on. A half-full bottle of whisky and an empty glass were on the night table, and also a bottle of sleeping pills. She returned to the landing. The light there was off, and it was quite clear what had happened. Some time during the night Mrs Hanbury had risen from bed stupefied by whisky and soporifics, and had made for the lavatory by the head of the stairs. Having failed to find the switch of the light on the landing she had missed the lavatory door and plunged down the staircase to her death. As she had been alone in a locked house, there was no question of foul play, and no reason why bullying policemen should invade the house and ask a lot of pointless questions.

Having reached this satisfactory conclusion, Maria left everything as it was and went back downstairs. The Correias were standing in the hall, as if paralysed. She told them what she had seen and the conclusions she had drawn. In shocked whispers they made it obvious that they were looking to her to take charge of the situation and deal with the authorities.

The responsibility that they had thrust on her had to be pushed

14

off on to someone else as soon as possible. The proper person to telephone, she decided, was the family doctor, who, finding nothing suspicious, would issue a death certificate, and that would be the end of that. She rang Dr Mendes. According to his receptionist he was out on his rounds, but she would get a message to him as soon as possible.

Only now did she realise that Mrs Hanbury's death was a disaster for Sir Adrian as well as for herself. Leaving the Correias to wait for Dr Mendes, she set off down the terraces to the cottage to tell him what had happened. She was sincerely sorry for him, but even her compassion was tinged with self-interest. He had already suffered two fairly serious heart attacks. If, confronted with the news, he had a fatal one, she would be out on the street within hours with nowhere to hide.

He was standing among his orchids at the far end of the terrace, smiling and mumbling happily to himself as he gazed at a huge purple cattleya. She would wait till it was time for his siesta, the strain on his heart would be less if he was lying down. Till then everything must seem to be normal, and she went inside to prepare the lunch.

On fine days they had it outside, under the shade of the trellis. As she carried it out, she caught sight of the nail just inside the entrance door on which the key to the back door up at the house normally hung. How long had it been missing? She could not remember. She had last used it about a fortnight ago to phone the doctor when he had a mild heart attack and Mrs Hanbury was dining out. No doubt someone had borrowed it and forgotten to give it back. If it had been missing for all that time, there could be no connection between its disappearance and Mrs Hanbury's death. The house was locked up, there were no suspicious circumstances, the doctor would issue a death certificate, there would be no police spotlight on Maria who found the body, she would not be questioned.

But to be absolutely safe she would have to take one precaution: nobody, but nobody, must know that the key was missing.

After lunch she settled Sir Adrian down on his bed for his siesta and broke the news to him. His grief was alarming as well as pitiful. Twice, she had to give him oxygen from the cylinder that stood by the bedside ready for emergencies. She could see the fear in

15

his eyes as he foresaw a future with no daughter to keep the household running, for he clearly knew as well as she did that he would have to be transferred to some kind of home. She spent the rest of the day seeing him through the worst of his grief, and had to persuade him to take a sleeping pill when she settled him down for the night. Only then could she slip away to keep the rendezvous which was the high spot of her week and her only consolation in her nightmare exile. Every Saturday night, after Sir Adrian was asleep, she crept out to the phone booth at the café in the square to make a phone call to her mother.

Santa Teresa is a hilly inner suburb of Rio de Janeiro, settled early in the history of the city by wealthy people taking refuge from the noise and bustle below. It was late afternoon, and shadows were lengthening among its gracious colonial houses when Cristina Beleza left home to walk through the narrow tree-lined streets to the house of her sister-in-law. She went there every Saturday to receive her daughter's weekly phone call.

She was quite sure now that her own phone was tapped and the house watched. For reasons which she understood only too well the surveillance, which had been desultory in earlier months, had been stepped up suddenly. But anyone watching her movements would conclude that her weekly appointment to drink English tea and eat little cakes with a rather deaf old lady was a work of charity. In fact, her sister-in-law Angela was full of racy conversation and utterly reliable when it came to keeping a family secret.

Drinking the tea and chatting, she waited eagerly for the call to come through. Her husband and her only son were dead. Maria-José was all she had and she lived for their weekly phone call.

'My darling, how are you?' she cried when the call came through.

'I am well, but a disaster has happened, a thing which will cause me much trouble. My employer has died.'

Maria-José never mentioned names, in case they gave an eavesdropper a clue to her whereabouts.

'The old gentleman?' Cristina asked.

'No. His daughter. She was a wicked, cruel woman and I ought

16

to be glad that she is dead. But without her to keep the house we cannot continue as we are. He will be put in a home and I shall have nowhere to go.'

There was a sob of panic in her voice, which went straight to Cristina's heart. 'Listen, my darling. Go to the friend who helped you before. She will find you a place where you can be safe.'

'No. She has become afraid. She helped before because she knew nothing about my trouble. Now she knows the truth and it terrifies her. She will do nothing for me, I am utterly alone.'

'My angel, have you money?'

'Not much. My unkind employer paid me very little.'

'I shall give you money.'

'No, mama. You have only papa's Army pension, barely enough for yourself. And you have given me so much. I cannot take more from you.'

'Listen, my pigeon, this is no life for you, we must arrange something better and this is my plan. I shall give you great-grandmother's diamond necklace. Sell it, and you will have enough to build yourself a new life, somewhere safe.'

'The necklace? No, mama, please. The sacrifice is too great.'

'It is nothing. What is jewellery, compared to your unhappiness? How can I be easy knowing that you are caught like a rat in a trap and cannot escape?'

'There is no way to get the necklace to me. The post is not safe.'

But Cristina, swept up in a great wave of yearning, had decided on a desperate measure. 'I shall bring it to you, my angel.'

'Impossible! You must not, that is madness.'

The necklace was partly an excuse, a pretext for a reunion which would spell frightful danger for them both. Maria-José saw that at once and her mother's next words confirmed it.

'It is a year since we met. You are my daughter, my only child. Do not turn me away, I long to see you again.'

'But the risk is too great. For you as well as me.'

Cristina knew that. Her movements were being watched because she might lead the watchers to her daughter.

'They will follow you,' Maria-José moaned.

'No. I shall watch for them with all my wits, I shall trick them,

17

put them off the track. Trust me, I shall be as wily as a serpent. If I see that I am followed I shall turn back.'

'When you have led them to me,' Maria-José added, 'they will kill us both. I beg of you mama, no.'

'It is better for both of us to die than to live in this fear.'

There was a long silence at the other end.

'Come, mama, come,' Maria-José burst out. 'I long to see you. If we die, we die together.'

'I come, my pigeon, I come.'

One of the attractions of Rio for visiting businessmen is the provision of service apartments which offer not only living accommodation but also a fax machine, a photocopier and all the other necessities of business life-support. It is an ideal solution for people who are not staying long enough to bother with setting up an office, but want to avoid the confinements of life in a hotel. It is also ideal for visitors who do not want their activities observed too closely.

In one such apartment, set back a few blocks from the Copacabana beach, Fred Barton stood staring gloomily out at the view. He was an overweight American with straw-coloured hair cut in a pudding-basin style which made one suspect, wrongly, that it was a wig. He was not a cheerful-looking fat man. His red, congested face and bulging angry eyes suggested that he hated the burden of his extra weight. He also hated most of the human race, including his sidekick Ricardo Fernandes, who sat at the desk lugubriously filing his fingernails.

Fernandes was a sad-eyed, dark-haired forty year old with a blue shave, wide shoulders and narrow hips, a sharp dresser in boldly patterned shirts. Fortunately the apartment had two bedrooms, but when they shared a room on one of their trips out of Rio, he had infuriated Barton with his snores. Worse still, he used scent. But Fernandes had to be kept sweet, because this operation called for someone who spoke Spanish and Portuguese and could feed in local knowledge. Fred Barton despised him as he did all Latin Americans, but imagined, wrongly, that he had managed to hide it from him.

The hassle from head office grew worse every day. Since the crisis broke they had kept up a barrage of increasingly bad-tempered phone calls demanding quick results. Clearly, their controllers at the other end had no idea of the difficulties. Admittedly the need for results was now urgent, but there was a limit to what could be done. The surveillance on Mrs Beleza's movements had been stepped up, but the watchers had not reported anything significant and the tap on her phone had yielded only the small-talk to be expected from a middle-aged widow of independent means.

'Boring old cow, kick her in the crutch, shall we? Wake her up,' Fred Barton had commented as he ruffled through some transcripts of her telephone gossip.

'It is a miracle,' said Fernandes, 'that such a placid woman of no interest should have produced such a poisoning little viper of a daughter.'

'Maria-José gets it from her dad, Rick. He was a general, didn't you say? Trust a soldier to fight dirty.'

Three weeks ago Ricardo Fernandes had let fall another casual piece of information. Mrs Beleza's Saturday visits to her sister-in-law were not, as Barton had assumed, an act of charity towards an elderly and even more boring unmarried relative. Angela Beleza, a beauty in her day, had been the mistress of one of Brazil's most respected presidents, and a leading figure in several decades of political intrigue. Brooding on this information, Barton had found himself wondering whether her appetite for intrigue might not have survived intact into old age, in which case Mrs Beleza's regular Saturday visits might well be a cover for something else, for instance a chat with her daughter on a phone other than her own.

Tapping it had proved the hunch correct. But even on a phone they thought secure, mother and daughter were very careful what they said. The tap had produced results of a sort, but so far nothing really useful. They knew only that somewhere in the world, but probably not in Brazil, the girl they were after was looking after an elderly invalid.

'So what do we know, Fred, about wicked little Maria-José?' Ricardo Fernandes grumbled. 'Only that she looks after this old man in his house, and never goes out unless she must.'

'Where's this lousy rat-hole of a house? Not here. Portugal?'

'Why? Why not America, England, Spain, Venezuela? She is speaking fluently in English and Spanish. Luis says there was on the tape another voice, very faint, speaking in the background. I tell him to amplify it, then we know what language was spoken.'

'OK, but where the hell does that get us?'

'It narrows a little the field.'

'Oh ha ha, Rick, very helpful. It don't even tell us which continent. She trained as a nurse, right? You can nurse people any damn where. Looking after an invalid at home, that's a bloody good rat hole to bolt down. No tricky questions from the personnel manager or the tax people. No having to exchange girlish confidences with her fellow-slaves in the factory toilets. Head office doing its nut won't change things, Rick. We're beat.'

There was nothing more to be said, nothing that had not been said twenty times over in the last few weeks. As they fell into a gloomy silence, Ricardo Fernandes avoided looking at his superior, whom he had come to loathe. The angry face under the ill-cut thatch of hair was bad enough, even without the fact that he needed, but did not use, a deodorant. Even worse was his Anglo-Saxon lack of sophistication about alcohol. Evening was coming on. Any minute now, Barton would reach for the whisky bottle. Drinking himself into a stupor was his normal way of seeking relief from his frustrations.

But even as Fred poured himself two fingers of bourbon the fax machine sprang to life. They ambled over to it, expecting nothing more exciting than another instalment of Mrs Beleza's telephone gossip. What they read astonished and delighted them. They were out of the doldrums at last. The report was a transcript of a telephone conversation an hour ago on the sister-in-law's supposedly secure line. Maria-José, in great distress, had agreed to let her mother join her.

Fred, wishing to celebrate their breakthrough with a friendly gesture, jumped at Rick like a footballer after a goal, in a passionate full frontal embrace which disgusted him. 'At last!' he crowed. 'Constipated old cow. She's on the move.'

'But she will lead us to her calf only if we are careful, Fred. See what the wicked little Maria-José says here to her. "They will follow you," she says.'

'Too right. We will.'

'And "When you have led them to me they will kill us both," '

20

Ricardo quoted from the transcript, and added with relish: 'That also we will do.'

'Check. The old cow's scared shitless. Eyes in the back of her head and up her arse and all over her, right?'

'So she sees that she is followed. What then?'

'She aborts the operation. Head office is furious, and so panic-stricken that it disappears up its own arsehole. We get fired.' He poured the two fingers of whisky back into the bottle. He never drank when there was work to be done.

'So we use all the people we can hire,' he added, looking grim. 'And we knock seven different kinds of shit out of anyone who lets her spot them tailing her.'

'And we do not show this fax to head office,' said Fernandes.

'Why not, Rick?'

'If we do not, and all goes well, only you and I will know that beside her corpse there was found a valuable diamond necklace.'

For the first time they looked at each other without mutual loathing.

TWO

'Celia? Margaret here. Bad news, I'm afraid.'

Celia Grant steeled herself. Margaret was the headmistress of a well-known West Country girls' school and the sister of her dead husband, Roger. When she telephoned with 'bad news' it almost always meant a death in the family and an inconveniently timed funeral to attend in some inaccessible corner of the British Isles.

'Antonia's died,' said Margaret bluntly.

One of Celia's legacies from Roger was a widely scattered family of elderly in-laws. Who was Antonia, one of the Inverness-shire maiden aunts? Uncle Claude's half-mad widow in Torquay?

'Antonia . . .' she echoed vaguely.

'Our niece. Yours and mine. Antonia Hanbury.'

Light dawned. Antonia Hanbury was quite young, the daughter of Roger's elder sister Julia, who had married a Whitehall grandee called Adrian Morton. Julia had been dead for some years. Antonia was their only child.

'Where's the funeral?' Celia asked nervously.

'In Funchal, for obvious reasons.'

Without a context, Celia could not place Funchal. 'Is that in Scotland?'

'Funchal,' Margaret rasped, 'is the capital of Madeira, an island in the Atlantic which is part of Portugal.'

'Oh, *Funchal*! Of course.'

This began to make sense. After a distinguished public service career Adrian Morton had retired to a house he had inherited in Madeira. When he had his stroke, Antonia went out there to look after him. Fortunately there was no question of attending the funeral.

'Thanks for letting me know, Margaret. I'll send some flowers.'

'That isn't the really bad news. I had a phone call from her lawyer there. Antonia's will names you and me as her executors.'

Celia was horrified. 'Oh really! Without asking us? What impertinence, can't we refuse to act?'

'Not with any decency. One of us will have to go out there.'

Celia knew at once which of them it would be. Margaret could always produce a pretext for doing nothing about family crises. If it was not the beginning of term, or the middle of term or the end of term, it would emerge that she was tied up in London, chairing a Royal Commission on juvenile delinquency. She seemed to think that Archerscroft, Celia's thriving nursery garden business, could be left to look after itself at the drop of a hat.

'I can't possibly spare the time,' said Margaret firmly. 'I've got fifty girls leaving. They all want me to advise them what university course to go for. I'm sure you can manage, Celia. It will only be for a day or two.'

No it will not be for a day or two, Celia thought. Alternative care arrangements for Antonia's stricken father would have to be cobbled together. Someone on the spot would have to be persuaded to attend to the household bills as they fell due. And as if that did not take up enough time, there was another complication. 'Antonia had some children, didn't she?'

'That's right, Sarah and Peter. Sarah's in the first year here and Peter's at a prep school for Winchester. They ought to attend the funeral, I thought they could travel out with you.'

And what do I do with them after that? Celia asked herself. Leave them there for the summer with the old gentleman and whatever hired help I have managed to arrange? Bring them back to Archerscroft and keep them amused till it's time to send them back to school? Yet another problem occurred to her. 'Did Antonia have any money?'

'I doubt it. Adrian's been paying their school fees. Antonia couldn't afford it. One of the Inverness-shire aunts left her a little, but that crook of a husband probably had it off her before the divorce.'

'Oh, him,' said Celia. 'D'you think he'll want custody of the children?'

23

'I doubt if he'd get it. He's only been out of prison for a month.'

Gerald Hanbury was a shady financier who had played for high stakes and lost, one of five men whose management of a dubious investment trust had fallen foul of the law. His marriage to Antonia had disintegrated during the long, much-publicised trial at the Old Bailey.

So on top of everything, Celia thought, I shall have to settle the children's long-term future. 'Damn Antonia,' she exclaimed. 'How dare she?'

'She always had a strong sense of family. And she couldn't appoint her father. Apart from him not being in a fit state for it, she didn't expect to predecease him.'

Celia remembered Antonia as a healthy jolly-hockey-sticks schoolgirl. By now she must be in her late thirties. 'Did the lawyer tell you what she died of?'

'He says it was a stupid accident. She got up in the night to pee and fell downstairs in the dark, breaking her neck.'

No, Celia thought, that is the last straw. I am having nothing to do with this business, because I know exactly what will happen, it always does. I shall arrive to find the police pulling long faces because she didn't fall, she was pushed, and there will be a splendid selection of suspects with guilty secrets, and I shall shove in my oar as I always do. By the time I extricate myself and get back to Archerscroft there will be red spiders in all the glasshouses and angry noises from the bank because we're overdrawn again.

'Give me that lawyer's phone number,' she demanded. 'It may be just a matter of signing things, in which case neither of us need fly out to Madeira.'

'You're forgetting poor old Adrian and his stroke. By all accounts he's far too helpless to be left where he is without Antonia to look after him, he'll have to be moved to some kind of home. Have you got a pencil? I'll give you the lawyer's phone number. I said you'd ring him and say when you're arriving, so that he can fix the funeral.'

Celia argued fiercely, but lost. It was a foregone conclusion that she would. According to Roger, Margaret had always been a bully, even in the nursery.

* * *

24

Fred Barton began to look slightly less angry as he and Ricardo Fernandes followed Mrs Beleza's preparations for making a furtive exit from Rio de Janeiro. Ten watchers were on the job, including the three engaged in tapping the two relevant phones. In the apartment high above the waterfront the faxed and telexed reports came in thick and fast. Everything was going well, the silly bitch was taking every possible precaution against being followed, and all of them were in vain.

On leaving her sister-in-law, Mrs Beleza had gone home and used her own phone to call a niece who lived in São Paulo, two hundred miles away along the coast. For the benefit of eavesdroppers, she had invited herself to stay for a day or two. Sounding surprised, the niece had agreed, whereupon Mrs Beleza had sallied forth downtown to a travel agency, and booked herself on to a morning flight to São Paulo. Barton and Fernandes saw no reason to believe that she intended to visit her niece, for the fax machine had already delivered a transcript of the next intercept on the sister-in-law's supposedly secure phone. Angela Beleza was on the move too, it seemed. She had rung the airport to ask about flights to Caracas in the morning, and had expressed interest in one which left shortly before the São Paulo plane. On learning that there were seats available on it, she had taken a cab to a different travel agency from the one patronised by Mrs Beleza, to make her booking. Unaware that her phone was tapped, or that anyone was interested in her movements, she took no notice of the young woman standing behind her at the desk and waiting to be served. The watcher was able to confirm that as the much-wooed ex-beauty had refused to marry any of her numerous admirers, both the ticket to São Paulo and the one to Caracas were booked in the name of Beleza.

In the morning both ladies rode in their respective taxis to Rio's Santos Dumont airport, down near the city centre on land reclaimed from the sea. A fleet of watchers took turns to tail them in inconspicuous cars, and reported later that both of them glanced nervously out of the rear window from time to time, making sure they were not being followed. But on arrival in the terminal building, Mrs Beleza did not spare a second glance for the young man waiting in the queue for the payphone on which, the watchers presumed, she was calling the niece in São Paulo to say she had changed her plans and would not be visiting her after all. She then checked in for her internal flight to São Paulo, while Angela went to the international area of the terminal and checked in for Caracas. Both ladies then repaired to a ladies' lavatory. The middle-aged woman who watched them lock themselves into adjoining cubicles had herself avoided recognition by putting on a different jacket and a chestnut wig since her previous confrontation with Mrs Beleza at the travel agency, and was therefore amused to see them exchanging various articles of clothing with each other over the top of the partition.

When Angela emerged to catch her plane to São Paulo, whence she would return on the next available flight, she was wearing a light overcoat in an arresting shade of scarlet, a pair of gold-framed sunglasses and a tulle headscarf, all of which had been worn into the airport by Mrs Beleza. Similarly, when Mrs Beleza emerged to catch her plane to Caracas, she was wearing Angela's buff-coloured linen overcoat, floppy face-concealing hat and quite ordinary dark glasses. As she boarded the Caracas plane, she was very satisfied with her arrangements. She even had her own suitcase, Angela had checked it in for her. Leaving their baggage trolleys unattended for a moment and switching them had been child's play.

Faced with these satisfactory developments, Fred Barton had begun to grin with fierce satisfaction and had stopped scratching irritably at his straw-coloured hair. But he was still tense because of all the things that could go wrong. The Caracas flight was fully booked, and massive bribery had been needed to get two Japanese businessmen thrown off it to make room for him and Fernandes. But head office was still breathing down his neck and interfering. They suspected, as he did, that Caracas was not Mrs Beleza's final destination. Rather than engage in airborne hide and seek, he and Fernandes were ordered to stay where they were and await developments. Four of his men were to fly to Caracas in their place and report back when they knew where she had booked to next. When they knew the final destination he and Fernandes could fly there direct. That would enable them to get there first and make whatever local arrangements were necessary to continue coverage.

In due course, the operatives who had flown to Caracas reported in. Before leaving the airport for her hotel Mrs Beleza had booked on a flight to Lisbon next day.

'Portugal. What did I tell you?' Barton grunted, digging Fernandes in the ribs.

Fernandes reeled back from the blow. 'So now at last we get our hands on the neck of the wicked little Maria-José.'

Seats were available on a night flight from Rio which would get them to Lisbon six hours before Mrs Beleza arrived from Caracas. That would allow plenty of time to arrange coverage with a local agency and get her followed to wherever she went in Portugal. But at this point, everything began to go wrong. The take-off from Rio was delayed by engine trouble, and they arrived at Lisbon with only half an hour to spare before the Caracas flight came in. In desperation they had phoned from Rio to arrange coverage by a local detective agency, and it had a representative waiting at the exit from customs to pick up Mrs Beleza's trail. But an unwelcome surprise awaited them. Having claimed her suitcase from the carousel and gone through customs she went straight to the desk where Air Portugal checked in internal flights.

Barton made himself known to a senior detective from the agency, who was displaying a board with his name on it. 'Can you find out where she's booking herself on to?'

'Of course, Mr Barton.'

Presently a young woman who had been standing behind Mrs Beleza at the Air Portugal desk came over to them. 'She already has her booking. To Funchal.'

This was the worst shock yet, and it was due to culpable negligence. In due course the operatives providing cover in Caracas were destined to be half murdered by head office for not having observed that an obliging hall porter at Mrs Beleza's hotel there had booked her on to the connecting flight from Lisbon.

'Are you represented in Funchal?' Barton asked the detective.

'I'm sorry. Not enough people in Madeira are curious about each others' affairs to justify it. We send operatives from here if necessary.'

'We shall need some. Can you manage to let us have half a dozen?'

'Not today, unfortunately,' said the girl. 'The flight is fully booked.'

Barton's gloom deepened. 'Mr Fernandes here and I must get on to it. Expense no object, can you fix it?'

The detective went over to the desk and murmured something to the two girls on duty. They fetched a man, who listened to his proposal, but seemed to dislike it and referred him back to the girls.

'I'm sorry,' the detective reported. 'There's been a big scandal about this, they have to watch their step. But I've arranged with them to put you on stand-by.'

Barton waited, in agonies of apprehension. By the time a double cancellation came in and made room for him and Fernandes, they had had plenty of time to reflect on the awkwardness of their situation. When they arrived in Funchal they would have to do all the shadowing themselves. Anyone speaking the Brazilian brand of Portuguese would automatically be conspicuous, and a fat American with badly cut straw-coloured hair would stick out from the surrounding landscape like a sore thumb. Moreover, Mrs Beleza would be on the lookout for them.

Far too early in the morning for comfort Celia Grant presented herself at Gatwick airport and waited near the desk where a flight to Funchal was checking in. Thanks to vigorous organisation by Margaret, Antonia's children were to be delivered to her there by emissaries from their respective schools.

'Mrs Grant?' said a voice behind her. 'Here's Sarah. I'm Dame Margaret's secretary. Oh what a relief. I was terrified of missing you in the crowd, but I recognised you at once from her description.'

('Nonsense, you can't miss her,' Margaret had said. 'She's tiny, not much more than four feet tall, with silver-grey hair and a perfect complexion and the figure of a twenty-year-old, and why she doesn't give up that ridiculous nursery garden and marry a millionaire I can't imagine.')

Sarah, the elder of the two children, was a distressingly plain thirteen-year-old, with a tendency to puppy fat. Peter, delivered a few minutes later by a louche prep-school master who treated Celia to a sexy ogle, was a raving beauty, though his looks might not survive puberty unscathed. To Celia's relief, the pair were not in floods of tears. Either the first shock of bereavement was past, or the reality of it had not sunk in yet.

While she checked in they talked to each other in low tones. In the departure lounge she bought them suitable reading matter for the journey, and a small plastic car for Peter which he seemed to covet. As they sat waiting for their flight to board he clutched it tightly and withdrew into some fantasy connected with it while Sarah, despite her unfortunate looks, proved to possess the elements of poise.

'It's sporting of you to come with us to the funeral, Aunt Celia. I hope it's not too much of a drag.'

'Oh no. It's nice to have company. I'd be going anyway, because I'm one of your mother's executors.'

Peter looked up for a moment from the toy car. 'Will you be staying in Funchal, Aunt Celia, to look after us and grandfather now that mum's dead?'

Celia did not believe in being vague to children, it alarmed them more than being told unwelcome truths. 'Oh dear, I can't. I'm sorry but I have to get back. I have my business to run.'

'Actually, you won't need to stay,' Peter decided on reflection. 'Vampire-Eyes can look after us when you've gone back to England.'

'Vampire-Eyes?' Celia queried.

'Her real name's Maria,' Sarah explained. 'She's a sort of nurse who looks after grandfather.'

Peter giggled. 'Mum called her Vampire-Eyes because she stares at you and looks as if she wants to suck your blood. Mum had funny names for people.' He paused, then blurted out with tears near the surface: 'Holidays in Funchal won't be the same now.'

He wandered off disconsolately, running the toy car along the back of the bench.

'Peter's very upset,' Sarah confided.

'I expect you are too, Sarah.'

'Yes, but I'm trying not to show it, so as not to make it worse for him. The thing is, we don't know what will happen or where we'll land up in the holidays. Are you terrified of us being dumped on you to look after?'

Celia thought about this. 'It would be all right for a bit while you're still small. But my cottage at Archerscroft is tiny, I rather blench at the thought of two hulking great teenagers having their adolescent crises in it. Perhaps I could share you with Margaret.'

'Horrors no, we spent Christmas there once and she made us play writing games. It was dire, like doing intelligence tests non-stop. Let me see, who else is there that would do? Mum took us once to stay with some weird old women in Scotland, but that was dire too, the house was freezing cold and there were stags on the walls, it would be awful.'

A silence fell. When Sarah spoke again, her voice had an undertone of tears. 'The real nightmare scenario would be having to go and live with Dad. He was brutal to Mum, and you know he's been in prison for fraud? Juvenile delinquency in six easy lessons, that's what we'd get from him.'

'I expect his prison record rules him out as unsuitable to be your guardian.'

'Are you sure? He's very cunning, I know he'll try to get us in his clutches. Don't tell Peter this, he'd have a fit, but as soon as Dad came out of the prison he phoned Aunt Margaret at the school asking to see me, and Aunt Margaret said not without Mum's permission and Mum said no.'

This was a new and unwelcome element in the situation. She's right, Celia thought, Gerald will certainly try for custody. So on top of everything else, I shall have to referee what the tabloids call a tug-of-love between my dead niece and an ex-convict, with two terrified children pulling at my skirts.

She decided it was time for some plain speaking. 'Peter, come here, there's something I want to say to both of you. I know you must be very worried about what's going to happen to you and I wish I could give you some firm answers. But I can't, till we know what's in your mother's will and what the lawyer says and whether . . . Maria, is that her name? is willing to stay on and look after your grandfather. I know it's difficult for you, but you're being very sensible and brave, so please be patient for a little longer.'

Sarah shot her a look of panic. 'But you won't let Dad have us, will you?'

Peter looked down at the toy car he was clutching, which seemed to have become his talisman against the shocks of reality.

But it had lost its power to shield him from them, and he began to cry.

'Mum called Dad Satan,' said Sarah.

The shortish runway at Funchal's Santa Cruz airport has mountains on one side and a steepish slope to the sea on the other. Except in bad weather it is far less dangerous than it looks, but a safe landing is always a matter of surprise to the passengers and they often applaud the pilot. Having only cabin luggage, Barton and Fernandes were among the first to get into the arrivals channel, but Barton insisted on loitering by the baggage carousel, to give Mrs Beleza time to catch up with them.

'You want to tail her?' Fernandes murmured. 'No, it will be a disaster. She will see that she is followed and warn her daughter and head office will strangle us when we tell them that the naughty little Maria-José has escaped from us.'

'You mind your own business, I know what I'm doing,' Barton growled.

'But listen, there is another way. Why is she having a panic and sending for her mother? Because the daughter of the old man, the one she looks after, is dead. She died on Saturday, that we know. So we buy the newspaper and we look at the necrological notices. Perhaps we have to make some inquiries, but presently we find that among the women who died on Saturday there is one whose invalid father was looked after in her house, and in that house we find Maria-José. Simple, isn't it?'

Fernandes had worked this out during the flight, but had not been able to share the idea with Barton because they had been sitting separately.

'Of course we do bloody that,' Barton snapped, having thought of it independently. 'We don't tail her too close, we don't scare her. But knowing which way she goes from the airport will help a bit.'

This made no sense to Fernandes, but he kept his peace for fear of making Barton's bad temper worse.

Mrs Beleza had reclaimed her suitcase and was heading for the taxi rank. Barton grabbed the cab behind hers and told it to follow her. 'Most of these cabs will be heading for town,' he explained. 'She heads for town, that's OK. She turns off and goes some other way, we go straight on so the silly cow doesn't panic. Saves us time if we know the general area she's making for.'

They followed Mrs Beleza's cab towards Funchal along a twisting coast road spectacularly trapped between the mountains and a deep drop to the sea. Under terse instructions from Barton, their driver kept his distance, and there were three other vehicles between the two cabs when they reached the outskirts of the city. But the traffic circuits in the centre disposed of all three, and deposited pursuer and pursued one behind the other in a tailback held up by an unloading truck.

'Oh-oh,' Barton muttered. 'Paying off her cab, bugger her.'

Taking advantage of the traffic block, Mrs Beleza had reclaimed her case from the boot of the taxi, and was standing on the pavement with it beside her. 'Don't look as we go past,' Barton hissed as the line of cars began to move. But Fernandes gave the suitcase a longing look. Perhaps the diamond necklace was inside it.

'Excuse, please,' said the driver. 'Where do we go now?'

'To a hotel,' Barton growled. 'Any damn hotel. What is there here?'

After inquiries about the hostelries on offer, he settled for the Savoy.

'Can she have spotted us tailing her?' Fernandes asked nervously.

'Nope. Routine precautions. She'll arse about a bit, go into shopping arcades with two entrances, play peek-a-boo round corners. Then she goes on to where she's meeting her daughter. So we lose a lot of time, not knowing where.'

'Why, Fred? You say this, but I do not understand.'

'If we don't know the area, how long will it take us to go through scores of death notices in the papers and eliminate the duds?'

Fernandes ceased to be puzzled. He had underestimated Anglo-Saxon ignorance of Iberian geography, that was all. 'Listen, Fred. This island is not so big, you know what is its population? Only three hundred fifty thousand, thereabouts. Of these perhaps sixty thousand are children. Of the rest how many are women? Half? Perhaps a little more, but how many of them died on Saturday? Two? Three? So we buy a newspaper and we eliminate quickly the two which are without an elderly

32

relative who is looked after at home by a nurse, and we find Maria-José.'

'OK, but what if the women of Madeira are dying like flies in an epidemic?' Barton growled. 'If they are, it would be just our luck.'

'So viperish little Maria-José dies too, Fred, and we have no problem.'

At the Savoy, they booked into separate rooms by mutual consent. Head office would grumble about the extra expense, but Barton's failure to use a deodorant was as offensive to Fernandes as his own raucous snoring and fragrant male toiletries were to Barton.

Down in the hall, Fernandes had bought a copy of that morning's *Diário de Notícias*. He sat on the bed to study the death notices. There were so few of them that the paper had had to throw in some advertisements to fill the page, and only three were for women, a Maria-Graça, a Maria-Teresa and the one in English that caught his attention at once.

> The death is announced of Antonia Mary Hanbury, dearly loved daughter of Adrian Morton and mother of Sarah and Peter. The funeral will take place on Tuesday 27th of May at 11h00 a.m. at the British Cemetery, preceded by a service at 10h30 a.m. in the cemetery chapel.

Below was a Portuguese version of the same information. Fernandes knocked on Barton's door and showed it to him. 'See, Fred. This is the one we look for.'

'You sure? What's wrong with the others?'

'The other two concern big families with nephews and cousins and grandchildren. They can care themselves for their old people, they would be ashamed to hire a stranger for that. Also, there is no husband mentioned in the *participação* for this Mrs Hanbury. If a husband existed, he would carry on the household after her death, and our little viper would not be fearing that it would break up.'

'OK Rick, I'll buy that. Where do these people live?'

Fernandes looked up Morton, Sir Adrian, in the telephone directory by the bed. 'The Quinta Coulson, in the Caminho do Dr João Rodrigues.'

'A quinta? Then it's a farm?'

'In Madeira a quinta doesn't have to have land. Just an old house in a big garden, rather grand.'

'OK, tomorrow we go to the Hanbury woman's funeral and hope Maria-José's there. After that, we stake out her quinta.'

'That we could do tonight,' Fernandes suggested.

'No, Rick. Too late. Let's have a night off, we deserve it.'

Fernandes knew what that meant. Barton intended to spend the evening getting unpleasantly drunk. After sitting through the initial stages he would tell Barton he was tired and wanted to go to bed early, then ask the hall porter to recommend a respectable brothel.

As Celia emerged from customs at the airport the children ran ahead towards a tall man who stood waiting for her, shouting 'Hallo, Smelly!'

He greeted them cheerfully, then transferred his attention to Celia. 'Mrs Grant? I'm Carlos Bettencourt, I've no idea why Antonia used to call me Smelly.'

Bettencourt was Antonia's lawyer. Celia had phoned him before leaving, and the clipped upper-class English in which he offered to meet her flight had made her assume that he was a British resident in Madeira with a slightly odd name. In the flesh he was a surprise, a thing of beauty in an exotic Latin style, with a clear olive skin, dramatic coal-black eyes and a neatly trimmed little beard, all of which contrasted oddly with the strangled aristocratic vowels which emerged from him. He had noticed, or perhaps guessed at, her surprise, and grinned. 'I know it sounds odd, but I was educated in England, you see.'

Celia was anxious not to upset the children by discussing their mother's death and problems arising from it in front of them. She discouraged this by putting Peter in front beside Bettencourt. Installed in the back, she settled down to enjoy the spectacular coastal scenery of the drive into Funchal. It was on one of her journeys with Roger that she had last seen the kind of subtropical flora which was on display by the roadside, and renewing her acquaintance with it was an uncovenanted treat. As they sped past gardens ablaze with silk trees and jacarandas in full bloom, she had to remind herself that this was strictly a business visit.

She must resist the temptation to go in search of plants that were native to Madeira. There was a scylla and an orchid, she remembered, and two cranesbill geraniums and probably a lot of other tempting things besides.

Plunging steeply downhill into Funchal, Bettencourt threaded his way through dense traffic on to a boulevard skirting the harbour, then on beyond the town centre into the suburbs, where a side road climbed steeply uphill between houses and banana groves in a series of hairpin bends. From this he turned off again into a narrow lane with high walls on either side, and stopped opposite a door in the wall, set in a vaguely classical stone frame with a pediment. A plaque labelled it as the Quinta Coulson. The children, who had talked a little during the journey, had fallen silent as they approached their motherless home.

Bettencourt pushed the bell and waited. Presently it opened, to reveal an elderly couple whom he introduced as Teresa Correia, the cook-housekeeper, and her husband Agostinho, the gardener. In further evidence of their mother's idea of fun, the children shouted 'Hullo Tillie, hullo Gussie,' submitted uneasily to the couple's condolences and escaped through the door as soon as possible. Celia followed. Nothing in the secretive frontage on to the lane had prepared her for what lay within: a luxuriant garden with spacious lawns and jacarandas and huge grandiflora magnolias in full bloom. Along the inside of the wall were beds of exotic shrubs fronted by drifts of white and yellow marguerites and . . . yes, it was, *Geranium maderense*, one of the endemic Madeiran cranesbills.

A cobbled path flanked with Canary palm trees and Madonna lilies led up to the front door of the house. Celia was alarmed by her first sight of its restrained colonial beauty. It was far larger and more imposing than she had imagined, and therefore a major problem. What was to happen to it if Adrian had to be settled elsewhere?

In the pillared entrance hall, the white-painted staircase mounted to the first floor in an airy curve. She checked back a cry of admiration just in time, realising that this must be the staircase that had broken Antonia Hanbury's neck. An archway opened from the hall into the finely proportioned drawing-room. The furniture was mostly eighteenth-century. Sir Adrian had inherited it with the house from his mother, a descendant of one of the British trading families which had made their fortunes in Madeira. Again the problem arose. What was to happen to all this?

While Sarah made herself agreeable to Teresa, Peter followed her into the drawing-room, like a lost dog attaching itself to a friendly stranger.

'Let's go and say hello to your grandfather,' she suggested, looking round. 'Where is he?'

'He doesn't live here,' said Peter. 'He's down the hill in his burrow with Vampire-Eyes and his plants. Mum calls it his burrow, but actually it's quite a nice little house.'

Bettencourt explained about the separate establishment which allowed Sir Adrian to go on enjoying his orchid collection, and suggested that they should go down there to see him. As the children raced on ahead down the terraces, Bettencourt said: 'I must get back to my office now, Mrs Grant, but I've arranged for Teresa to feed Peter and Sarah and see them into bed, and if you'll come and eat with us, my wife will be delighted and we can talk things over then.'

Celia said that she too would be delighted. Refusing to let herself be distracted by the tecomas and tibouchinas flowering around the lawn behind the house, she set off after the children down flight after flight of stone steps, flanked with strelitzias and clivias. On one of the lowest terraces stood a small building: a cottage in yellowish stucco with a pantiled roof which curved gracefully at the eaves in a vaguely Chinese manner. Sir Adrian Morton was sitting under a trellis in front of it, nodding and smiling and neighing an inarticulate welcome to his grandchildren. Celia approached, and he shot a puzzled look at her. She explained that she was his brother-in-law Roger's widow, and was neighed and smiled at in her turn. With an enormous effort he managed to produce an approximation to the vowel sounds of the word 'Celia'. But the tears which come easily to stroke victims made him weep a little when he remembered the reason for her coming.

Maria was hovering in the background with a tense expression on sharp, alert features. Antonia's name for her, Vampire-Eyes, though unkind, was accurate.

36

Celia made suitably cordial overtures. But the grim, concentrated look did not relax.

'How's he taken it?' she asked in a low voice.

Maria shot a gloomy look at Sir Adrian. 'Badly. He no longer eats, he has no appetite. His heart is bad. He looks at his orchids and weeps, and sometimes the weeping makes him breathless and I have to give oxygen.'

'I suppose the orchids are his main consolation now.'

'No! They remind him of Mrs Hanbury. She cultivated them for him, therefore he weeps because she is not here.'

'Who's looking after them now?' Celia asked.

'No one, it is a problem. Yesterday I called Agostinho, thinking that it was work for a gardener. But Agostinho is not knowing enough about the orchids. He gave too much water or too little, and the senhor became enraged and wept and I gave oxygen.'

As Celia wondered who on earth was going to look after the collection, Adrian, who had been staring fixedly at Celia, rose unsteadily from his wicker chair. Gripping her by the arm, he started off towards the plastic-covered greenhouse at the other end of the terrace. 'No, senhor!' shouted Maria in a bullying tone. 'The senhor must not go to the orchids, he knows how it upsets him.'

Treating her to a mocking gesture of impatience, Adrian continued on his way to the orchid house at the far end of the terrace. Its door opened on a long vista of greenery and hectic bloom. Celia knew very little about the *Orchidaceae*, and had not succumbed to the fascination of their contorted shapes and over-vivid colours. Out of flower they were ugly, with excrescences called pseudobulbs designed to store moisture and nourishment through the dry season like the humps on camels, and in some cases they insisted on growing on bits of wood or cork dangling ridiculously from the roof on wires, with their roots waving in the air. It seemed to her that only slightly mad people would be prepared to pander hourly to their tyrannical requirements about humidity, ventilation and temperature, only to see them rot and die if fractionally overwatered, and sulk if they were allowed to get too dry.

She had assumed that Adrian was going to show off his treasures to her, but she was wrong. His speech might be impaired, but he had his wits about him. Having remembered who she was and realised that she was clued up horticulturally, he was pointing imperiously at a garden tap and watering can. Under his instructions, conveyed by grunts and gestures, she administered minute quantities of water to the thirsty and gave liquid fertiliser to the starving. This is not what I'm supposed to be doing in Madeira, she thought as she scraped dead roots off a dormant *Catasetum pileatum* and repotted it. And what was to happen to all these plants if the household broke up, as it surely must? Many of them were rarities, it was the wide-ranging collection of an expert. Visiting it had not brought on the paroxysms of grief at the loss of Antonia which Maria had led her to expect. Perhaps his distress had been lessened by his discovery of someone competent to take her place with the watering-can.

Presently they came to a row of three plants with spectacular flower spikes. The labels showed that they were all *Miltonias*; a dark purplish *spectabilis* var. *moreliana* with a paler lip, and a reddish-brown *clowesii* barred with yellow. Between them stood a plant in which the deep purple of the *spectabilis* was faintly tinged with the brown of the *clowesii* but on the shorter stem of the *spectabilis*. There was no specific name on its label, only a series of figures.

When they had received their meed of water, he struggled to explain something about them. Presently Celia grasped what he was trying to convey.

'The middle one's a hybrid, is that it, between the others? And the yellow bar is recessive?'

He nodded vigorously.

'You bred it? You did the cross?'

He wagged a mischievous finger. Celia was puzzled. Did that mean, 'Yes, I'm a clever old so-and-so, aren't I?' Perhaps. But it might also mean that there was something more to the story, she had not got it quite right.

'How long did you have to wait to flower it? Three years? Five?'

He did not reply. But there was a surprising glint in his eye of glee and low cunning.

The children, bored by Maria's absent-minded replies to their chatter, had gone back to the main house, leaving her brooding

38

by the cottage. As Celia tried to find out more from Adrian about the hybrid *Miltonia*, she presented herself in the orchid house and addressed Celia with a false-friendly smile. 'Please, senhora, the senhor must not stay here, it tires him, he will have an attack.' She turned to address Sir Adrian. 'The senhor must come, it is time for him to have his rest.'

Celia was prepared to argue, but Adrian hung his head like a scolded child, reviving her suspicion that Maria bullied him mercilessly when they were alone. Though he had not previously needed support, he meekly took Maria's proffered arm and let her lead him back along the terrace to the cottage. Having settled him indoors on his bed, she addressed Celia in an undertone.

'The senhora will stay? She will look after the house and the senhor and the children?'

This was not the moment for blunt truth-telling, which would surely encourage Maria to leave her in the lurch and go in search of another job.

'Nothing's been decided yet, Maria. I've been in Madeira for less than an hour, and I don't know what's in Mrs Hanbury's will.'

Maria scowled. 'Please, I must know quickly what is to happen.'

'Of course, but do give me a chance. As soon as I've talked to the lawyer and so on, I'll tell you.'

Maria turned away with a despairing shake of the head, as if dismissing her as a hopeless imbecile.

As Celia climbed the steps to the main house, she faced the fact that this tense, sullen woman had taken an instant dislike to her, and that it was mutual. Of the many problems she would have to tackle, the knottiest would be coping with angry, enigmatic Maria.

THREE

Under a jacaranda tree on the lawn by the main house, Celia found Sarah slumped in a garden chair with a book by Beatrix Potter.

'I always read my baby books when I'm sad,' she explained. 'But this one's horrible, I can't think why I liked it.'

She held it up. It was *The Tale of Peter Rabbit*. 'It's really sadistic, the way the gardener chases that wretched little creature around.'

Celia dispensed sympathy for a moment, then asked: 'Where's Peter?'

'Playing with his trains, I expect.'

She found him in an attic bedroom, shutting out the harsh world by concentrating fiercely on an elaborate layout of model trains. How long would these anaesthetic devices go on working? Not very long. The children would need firm assurances about their future very soon.

In due course Bettencourt arrived to escort her to his house for dinner. They walked, for it turned out that he lived near by. On the way she discovered that he had an English law degree as well as his Portuguese qualification, which was why he had a large practice among the British community.

His house was a sumptuous modern bungalow clinging to a steep slope, just below the main road to town. It contained good pieces of English and Portuguese antique furniture, obviously inherited, and some gilt-framed family portraits dark with varnish. His wife Freda was a thin, almost emaciated blonde whose languid upper-class accent matched his and suggested that she had been acquired in England as a sequel to his well-heeled education there. Her thin cheeks and stringy neck were in strange contrast with his ornate southern good looks, as if the pair belonged to some natural species in which the female is dowdy and the colourful plumage is reserved for the male. There was no sign of children and no mention of any.

Over their pre-dinner drinks Bettencourt paid a warm tribute to Antonia. 'You have to hand it to her for the way she coped, organising the household marvellously and battling with her money troubles and looking after Sir Adrian and the children. And of course she was a bundle of laughs, she had this marvellous sense of fun.'

This surprised Celia, who had assumed that he was too sophisticated to enjoy Antonia's 'fun'.

'She had a peculiar sense of humour,' said Freda languidly.

Bettencourt shot her a haughty look of reproof, then got down to business, explaining the arrangements he had made for the funeral next day at the British cemetery down in the town centre. Celia wondered if there should be some kind of reception afterwards with refreshments.

'Absolutely not, by Madeiran standards that would be ultrashocking,' said Freda. 'Last year a Swedish woman laid one on after her husband's funeral, and was almost drummed out of town.'

'There'll be quite a crowd,' Bettencourt predicted. 'The old-established British families will turn out because Sir Adrian ranks as one of them on account of his mother. Her forbears owned one of the great Madeira wine houses in the days when the whole British Empire downed the stuff in bucketfuls.'

'Some non-establishment British will come too,' said Freda. 'People who haven't been here long enough to rate socially and don't live in quintas.' Her tone suggested that she sympathised with these underdogs.

'You don't approve of the Madeira establishment?' Celia asked.

'Not really. But Carlos and I have to play along because we're part of it.'

'A good many of the neighbours will come,' Bettencourt predicted. 'It's a bit of a British enclave round here.'

'But not all the neighbours, I hope,' said Freda with emphasis. 'With any luck George Whiting and his groupies will stay away.'

He thought for a moment. 'If they have any decency, yes.'

41

Who, Celia asked, was George Whiting.

'He lives in a bungalow up behind the quinta. He and Sir Adrian don't get on.'

'It's a crashing bore,' said Freda languidly. 'There are two camps, like the Montagues and the Capulets in Shakespeare. If you're seen consorting with the enemy by having a drink at the Quinta Coulson, you're excommunicated by George Whiting and his cronies, and vice versa.'

'And this still goes on, even after Adrian's stroke?' Celia asked.

'Oh yes,' said Freda. 'I think it appealed to Antonia's odd sense of fun.'

'My dear, you're in a very bitchy mood this evening,' said Bettencourt, only half in joke.

A moment of tension followed. To ease it Celia asked what had started the Whiting–Morton feud. According to Freda there were several versions of its origins. 'All different and very complicated, and all dating from the distant past.'

Celia forced herself not to be interested. She was here to execute Antonia's will, not to investigate the squabbles of an inbred expatriate community. She asked Bettencourt what Antonia's will contained.

'She's left everything to the two children, but unfortunately the estate doesn't amount to much, apart from the house. Sir Adrian made it over to her a year ago, to avoid inheritance duty.'

'Is that heavy here?'

'Not really. If the house stays in the family, you only have to pay on what they call the patrimonial value.'

'The duty's chicken-feed, I don't know why she bothered,' commented Freda with a rather odd laugh which made her husband wince. 'But Antonia was funny about money, scraping together pennies one minute and splurging out the next. Look how she behaved over the gardener's cottage.'

Bettencourt explained that Teresa and Agostinho Correia had lived in the cottage till Sir Adrian had his stroke. Antonia had turned them out so that he could move down there and be near his orchids.

'Poor Antonia, that little operation cost a fortune,' said Freda.

'She had to pay them to get out of the cottage, and then buy them the flat they're living in now.'

The bitter edge to her mockery set Celia thinking. Far from sharing her husband's admiration for Antonia, she was doing a not very subtle job of character assassination. Moreover, she was right about Antonia's absurd behaviour over the gardener's cottage. It would have been much cheaper to move the orchids up to the level of the lawn by the main house, and install Sir Adrian in ground-floor quarters from which he could get at them easily. Why had that not occurred to Antonia? And what had she done to make an enemy of Freda?

With stern self-control, Celia dismissed these mysteries from her mind as irrelevant, and asked where Antonia's income had come from if she owned nothing but the house.

'She didn't have a regular income,' said Bettencourt. 'Everything went west when her husband's business crashed. It worried her a lot and she tried various wheezes for making money, a boutique for instance and for a time she had a half-share in a market garden. But none of them brought in much, so she and the children have been living on Sir Adrian's pension which dies with him, and on the dividends from his few stocks and shares.'

'She wasn't getting anything from her ex-husband?'

'I understand Hanbury's more or less destitute. Incidentally, he'll be at the funeral.'

Celia was startled. 'Gerald will? Damn. Why has he come? Does he want custody of the children?'

'To judge from what he told me, he'll certainly try for it.'

'Will he get it?'

Bettencourt hesitated. 'I suppose he's got a fifty-fifty chance.'

Celia digested this unwelcome news. 'How tiresome of him. But if you're destitute, how the hell do you find the fare to fly out from England and attend your ex-wife's funeral?'

'I can't imagine, but he's the sort of impressive-looking businessman who can always scrape together money from somewhere. Actually, he didn't fly out for the funeral. He's been here for over a week.'

'You mean, Gerald was here when Antonia was still alive?'

'That's right, Mrs Grant. According to him, he came to try for

43

a reconciliation with her. But I think what he really wanted was access to the children.'

But why was that so urgent, Celia thought, why rush here straight from the prison gates, there is something queer about this. For a moment she let sinister fantasies flit across her mind, then dismissed them with an inward giggle. She was here to execute a will, not to sniff out wrong-doing and stumble yet again into lurid adventure.

Pulling herself together she asked what had happened at the inquest. 'They brought in accidental death, of course?'

'There aren't any inquests here,' Bettencourt corrected. 'When someone dies in an accident the police have to be informed as a matter of routine, and the doctor concerned does an autopsy. If he finds nothing suspicious he issues a death certificate, and that's the end of that.'

'But if he is suspicious?'

'The usual procedure under the Code Napoléon, which applies here just as it does in France. An investigating magistrate takes over and the judicial police move in.'

'But the circumstances weren't suspicious.'

Bettencourt looked at her sharply. 'Good heavens no. She was alone in the house, the doors were locked, there was no sign of a break-in.'

'But what an extraordinary thing to happen. Why didn't she turn on the light?'

'Apparently she takes sleeping pills, and there was a whisky bottle and an empty glass on the bedside table. If she'd had a tot of whisky and taken a sleeping pill, she could have been too confused to find the switch.'

It would have to be more than a tot, Celia thought. 'Was she a secret drinker, then?'

'I wouldn't know,' said Bettencourt, looking sheepish.

Freda threw him a strange, mocking glance, and went to attend to the dinner.

As Celia wondered what the look meant, Bettencourt said: 'Antonia's landed you with a shocker of a problem, hasn't she?'

'Yes. It would be a pity to sell the house, the children can decide what to do with it when they're of age. I thought we'd let it, to provide an income for their education.'

'OK, but aren't you forgetting Sir Adrian?'

'I've been thinking about that. He and Maria can't stay where they are with no one in the main house to give moral support. I thought we'd try to find someone prepared to look in there on a day to day basis, someone that Maria can turn to in a difficulty. Could you fill the breach, or would that be asking too much?'

He hesitated. 'I'll take care of the money side of things, of course. But . . . I'm sorry. I have a very busy legal practice to look after.'

'Would your wife take it on? For a consideration, of course.'

'Oh dear. I'd better tell you. Freda and I are on the verge of getting divorced.'

Not altogether surprised, Celia said that this was sad for him and unfortunate from her own point of view. 'But is there anyone you know of who would fill the bill, think about that, will you?'

'Certainly, but my mind's a blank at present.'

'If there's nobody, Adrian will have to go into some kind of home, preferably one where his orchid collection could be tucked away for him to look at in a corner of the garden. I expect you know of suitable places, but his pension would have to cover the fees. D'you remember how much it amounts to?'

'No, Antonia dealt with his finances under a power of attorney. His bank statements will be in her desk. Mrs Grant, may I say what a relief you are. I was afraid you'd turn out to be a wimpish female who'd collapse in despair when she saw the problem, and expect me to do all the thinking and provide all the answers. It's wonderful to be dealing with someone decisive.'

'Well, I do run quite a flourishing business back home. And do remember, I want to get back to it as soon as possible.'

Over dinner, Celia made civilised conversation, but could not stop her mind working. Why had Antonia banished her father to the bottom of the garden at great expense? So that he should not get in the way of her private life, in other words a lover? What lover? Bettencourt? He was a very attractive man married to a very plain woman, and his marriage was on the rocks. His wife detested Antonia, and had made a face which called him a liar when he claimed not to know whether Antonia was a secret drinker. Did he have good reason to know her drinking habits? And was Freda fully aware that he did?

45

Jealous wife pushes husband's mistress down staircase, she thought frivolously as she spooned up her soup, but sobered up in time to deal judiciously with a question of Bettencourt's about the political situation in England. There were no suspicious circumstances about Antonia's death. The doors of the Quinta Coulson had been locked.

Back in the living-room while Bettencourt loaded the dishwasher and made coffee, Freda made a suggestion. 'Mrs Grant, when you've a moment you ought to find out what's happening about Adrian's memoirs. Antonia was arranging to get them published, and by all accounts they're pretty hot stuff.'

Celia could believe this. It was well known in the family that his official activities had to do with counter-intelligence and were unmentionable, which was why works like *Who's Who* were evasive about him. But it was news to her that he had written his memoirs. And how was she to investigate?

'There's probably some correspondence about them in Antonia's desk,' Freda suggested as Bettencourt came in with the coffee.

At the end of the evening he walked her back to the quinta, and began repeating his praise of Antonia. 'It was such a *stupid* thing to happen, Mrs Grant, such a waste of a super person . . .' The theme lasted him all the way up the hill till they parted at the door in the wall of the quinta. Walking up the path to the house, Celia wondered if he had wanted to divorce Freda so that he could marry Antonia. If so, why was there still talk of divorce now that she was dead?

Inside, Teresa was in the kitchen, embroidering a white tablemat with ultrafine stitches while she baby-sat for the children. After they had exchanged lamentations about the tragedy of Antonia's death and commiserated about her orphaned children, Teresa embarked on a series of queries about the domesticities. Did the senhora wish her to do the marketing? The senhora did, she had no intention of going shopping in Portuguese. Lunch after the funeral for the senhora and the children would have to be cold, there was a ready-cooked chicken. But what about supper? Should she buy espada?

'Espada, it is fish,' she explained.

'Do Peter and Sarah like it?'

'Everyone like the espada, it is very good fish.'

As more questions followed, Celia realised that Teresa was trying to entangle her in a network of long-term domestic arrangements and install her forcibly as the permanent mistress of the household. Escaping from this trap on the excuse of tiredness, she dismissed her, looked in on the children, who were sound asleep, and went on to the room that Teresa had prepared for her.

It had obviously been Sir Adrian's room. Men's suits lingered in the wardrobe and there was an old-fashioned trouser press. In a tarnished silver frame on the dressing-table was a carefully posed studio portrait of Antonia wearing a frilly blouse and an elaborate hair-do, quite unlike the no-nonsense fun-lover whom Bettencourt had described. She had kept her looks, but they had hardened a little. Her expression struck Celia as, to put it crudely, rather bossy.

On the way to the lavatory at the head of the stairs, she took casual note of the relative positions of the light switch, the lavatory door and the staircase, and decided that it would be easy for a sleepy person to make a fatal mistake and tumble headlong down. But it depended to some extent on which bedroom they had come from. Antonia's was probably the one opposite hers, on the other side of the landing. Out of curiosity she went in to check.

It was a chintzy room, with vaguely French-looking furniture; not Antonia's girlhood bedroom because it contained an enormous double bed. Perhaps it had once been the guest room. There was nothing on the bedside table, Teresa must have removed the bottle of whisky and the glass. Some morbid impulse made Celia wonder if she had also removed Antonia's sheets from the bed. It was an elaborate affair, with a headboard and footboard formed from a mesh of cane framed in carved and painted wood. She drew back a corner of the counterpane at the foot of the bed. There were no sheets to be seen and the blankets were folded neatly.

Leaning forward, she began to push the corner of the counterpane back down the crack between the mattress and the footboard. But there was something down there; a shiny object a long way down, trapped between the footboard and the old-fashioned box mattress which lay on the iron frame of the bed. Kneeling at the foot of the bed, she peered through the mesh of the cane, trying to see what it was. But the light was bad and the mesh interfered with her view. She fetched a wire coat-hanger from the

47

wardrobe, noticing incidentally that Antonia's taste in dress ran to hectic patterns in very bright colours. Having bent the coat-hanger into shape, she pushed the hook down the crack. After a few false starts she fished up a gold-plated wrist-watch.

There was no question of it being Antonia's. It was large and masculine looking, and the gold-plated strap was much too big for a woman's wrist. It was a flashy affair, with blobs of something cheap-looking and black marking the hours. For a moment she stared at it, fascinated. Then ingrained habit took over and made her thrust it back into its hiding-place. Good detective practice forbade interference with evidence.

So Antonia *had* a lover. Bettencourt? Possibly, she had not noticed if he was wearing a wrist-watch or if so, what it was like. Whoever the man was, it was no business of hers. A divorced and unattached woman was perfectly entitled to take a lover.

How long had the watch been in the bed? The sweep second hand was still moving, but it was a quartz watch with a battery. It could have been there for months. Antonia had died alone in a locked house.

But as she dropped off to sleep Celia reflected idly that women who had lovers sometimes gave them a key.

The day of Antonia Hanbury's funeral dawned bright and clear. For some of the neighbours the question of whether to attend posed no problem because they were on visiting terms with the Quinta Coulson, on the strict understanding that they had nothing to do with the disreputable clique of second-raters led by George Whiting.

In the opposite camp, George Whiting had ruled against attendance. 'I see what you mean,' he told waverers who rang to ask his advice. 'You think we should show solidarity among the expatriates and all that. But they're not burying Morton, the old bastard will be there, alive and kicking and as full of his venomous nonsense as ever. He's quite capable of making a scene at his own daughter's funeral, we don't want him roaring at us like a demented bull and turning us out of the chapel. I think we should all send him a letter of condolence that he'll be too gaga to read and leave it at that.'

Three couples living outside the immediate battle zone had a

48

real problem because they had managed, by behaving rather deceitfully, to frequent both camps without being excommunicated by either. Was it safe to go? They had found out by devious means that the Whiting party line forbade attendance. He was known to have an informer in the opposite camp, who would probably be infiltrated into the cemetery to report on defaulters. One couple decided to risk it, the others did not.

The hillside round the Quinta Coulson was in a state of social transition. Modern villas, inhabited by foreigners attracted to Madeira by its favourable climate and low cost of living, had invaded an area of peasant holdings, each consisting of a small cottage hidden in a lush grove of banana trees. In one of the surviving peasant houses, an argument was going on. Lúcio Freitas was in favour of attending the funeral. His wife Jacinta was not.

'She was our neighbour,' he argued. 'We owe her respect.'

'The Santos and the Gonçalves will not go. Only the English, who would look at us down their long noses and despise us.'

'Teresa and Agostinho will go.'

'Because they worked for her. Let us send a wreath and stay away.'

Lúcio rebuked one of the children for making too much noise, then returned to the charge. 'Yesterday Agostinho told me that an aunt of the children is arriving from England to attend the funeral.'

'So?'

'Agostinho says she is given powers under the will. If she stays to keep house for Sir Morton, she may be useful to us.'

'How, useful?'

'There is the matter of the water rights.'

Jacinta was astonished. 'You want to start that business again? But it is settled, her lawyer convinced us that we have no claim.'

'No. He said only that he thought the claim weak, but if we wished we could pursue it in the courts.'

'So?'

'The aunt from England may be willing to settle the matter amicably.'

At this, Jacinta snorted scornfully.

'It is possible,' Lúcio argued. 'When I see her, I shall be able to judge if it is worth making the attempt. Therefore I shall go to the funeral.'

'Then you will go alone,' said Jacinta firmly. 'I shall stay here.'

Over breakfast at the Savoy hotel, Ricardo Fernandes faced a delicate problem. At all costs, Barton must be persuaded to stay away from the funeral. He had tried to tone down his appearance and look more like a tourist. The hotel barber had made his curious head of hair look less like a wig, but it was still a very odd colour. Even if he put on his jacket, his sweatshirt and white slacks, bought as part of the tourist disguise, would be out of place at a funeral. A strangely dressed stranger whom no one recognised, with an American accent and an aroma of stale sweat and hangover, would be the centre of attention at once, with everyone wondering who he was.

'It's better if I go alone,' Fernandes argued. 'I shall not be conspicuous, I am just another dago.'

'But would you recognise Maria-José if you saw her?' Barton objected.

'Of course, I have her photo in my pocket.'

Still queasy from his hangover, Barton agreed.

At the quinta, Celia was having difficulty in assembling the mourners. As a search of the children's wardrobes had revealed that they had outgrown the only garments suitable to the occasion, she had rashly told them to wear what they liked. But Peter's choice of a spaceman T-shirt had outraged Sarah's sense of propriety, and her attempt to veto it had led to a quarrel, complete with screams and floods of tears for two. Meanwhile Sir Adrian, coaxed into his best suit by Maria, had refused at first to get into the carrying chair with poles back and forth, in which Bettencourt and Agostinho were scheduled to carry him up the terraces to the gate, and put him in the large black taxi which was the nearest approach to a funeral limousine that Madeira could manage. When this difficulty had been overcome Maria, who appeared to be in blooming health, suddenly pleaded a stomach upset and said she must stay behind. This hardly mattered, but meanwhile Agostinho and Teresa, also in their best clothes, were having an agitated discussion in Portuguese about some emergency whose nature they would not explain. Celia, fearful of being late for the obsequies, urged them into the car, but they were still muttering ominously as it set off downhill.

Threading through narrow streets in downtown Funchal, it negotiated a pair of massive wrought-iron gates and deposited the party in the forecourt of the chapel at the British cemetery, an oasis of quiet among high buildings. Under the shade of its trees lay British soldiers of the Napoleonic wars, Victorian tuberculosis sufferers whose hopes of a cure in a mild climate had proved vain, miscellaneous 'strangers' who, not being Catholic, could not be accommodated elsewhere. Among all these were the burial plots of the British merchant families which had made fortunes in Madeira, the Cossarts and the Leacocks, the Blandys and the Coulsons.

Some of their descendants were among the mourners who had assembled in the cemetery chapel, along with the Honorary British Consul, humbler friends of the family and enough sympathising Portuguese to allow Fernandes to take his place among them without feeling conspicuous. There was no sign yet of Maria, but he assumed that she would be among the family mourners when they arrived.

The Bettencourts were also surveying the congregation, and noted with satisfaction that the Whiting camp was not represented.

'Sensible of them,' Carlos murmured. 'Naughty old Adrian would have kicked up a fuss.'

Antonia's coffin, surrounded by potted plants and wreaths and candles, was already standing on its bier in front of the altar. Presently the bereaved family filed in, led by Sir Adrian. But instead of taking his allotted place as chief mourner he paused in the doorway of the chapel, looking distinguished but frail, and made a frowning scrutiny of the assembled company.

'What did I tell you?' Bettencourt whispered to Freda. 'He's looking for Whiting and Co. Thank God they aren't here.'

But trouble had not been avoided, Sir Adrian had seen a mourner he disapproved of; a well-dressed man in his forties with coarse, overblown good looks and an air of great importance, sitting in one of the nearby pews. Grunting with annoyance, Sir Adrian fixed him with an icy glare and made firm gestures towards the door, as if wielding the flaming sword which barred Adam and Eve from the Garden of Eden.

51

Freda looked at her husband and mouthed the word 'Who?'

'Gerald Hanbury,' he whispered. 'Antonia's ex-husband.'

She nodded. Sir Adrian had good reason to hate the son-in-law whose dishonesty had made Antonia a pauper.

When Hanbury did not react at once, Sir Adrian let out a wild bellow of rage and pointed at him accusingly. Hanbury half rose to his feet. His air of importance collapsed.

Sir Adrian seized him by the lapel and made a noise which sounded vaguely like the word 'out', which he repeated loudly several times. Hanbury stumbled noisily out of the pew and left the chapel.

After the stresses of her departure from the quinta, Celia had been looking forward to the funeral service as an oasis of ecclesiastical calm. But Peter had burst out into terrified boo-hooing on catching sight of his father, and Sarah had turned very white for the same reason and said she felt sick. Sir Adrian, still standing in the aisle, seemed to have fallen into a trance after the enemy's retreat and had to be coaxed into his place at the front. Some time passed before order was restored and the clergyman, who had waited patiently for the tumult to subside, was able to begin the burial service.

In due course the undertakers' men carried the coffin out on to a perambulating wooden bier, arranged the wreaths around it, and trundled it down a path lined with double poinsettias to where a grave for Antonia had been dug beside her mother's and grandmother's in the Coulson burial plot. Sir Adrian followed the coffin on Celia's arm, with the two children, both crying quietly behind them. The other mourners followed, and stood a little apart while the chaplain went through the committal service. There was no sign of Gerald Hanbury.

The children burst into loud lamentations when they saw earth being thrown on to their mother's coffin, and she tried to comfort them. When the committal was over the chaplain found out who she was and said, disconcertingly: 'Bless you for coming to the rescue. These motherless children need your care.'

True, she thought. But how, when and where were they going to get it?

The mourners edged forward to shake hands and express their sympathy. Some of them began lavishing dramatic expressions of sympathy on Sarah and Peter, who had obviously had as much emotional public attention as they could take. She decided to get them out of harm's way by taking them to sit in the hire car till it was time to leave, but the Bettencourts intercepted her. 'I'll go with them,' Freda offered. 'You go back and look after Adrian.'

As she went back to the group of mourners, a Portuguese in a very formal dark suit stood blocking her path and treating her to a bold-eyed stare. He was chunkily built, but with muscle rather than fat, and a face which was striking without being handsome. His fixed stare puzzled and also frightened her, as if it implied some kind of threat. She turned aside to avoid him, but he followed her with his eyes. This went on as she shook hands with people who clearly wondered who she was and what she was doing there. She was careful not to look in his direction, but could not help being acutely aware of him.

After the majority of mourners had taken their leave a few close friends remained behind, including a very old lady, beautifully turned out in a grey silk suit, who drew Celia aside. 'Hullo, my dear, I'm Winifred Fuller. Do tell me how you fit into the family?'

'I'm only an in-law, the widow of Lady Morton's brother.'

'Ah yes, the clever botanical brother who worked at Kew. Julia told me a lot about him. Such a splendid woman, I miss her abominably.'

'You knew her well?'

'Yes, because Adrian and I are related through our mothers, they both married into the family wine business. Come out from England to tidy the situation up, have you? I don't envy you the job.'

'Everything here's a mystery for the moment, but I suppose my foggy brain will clear.'

'I doubt it, my dear. Madeira's full of very sinister wheels within wheels churning away, no one from outside can understand them. So do let me know if you want advice or moral support.'

'Thank you. How very kind.'

'What will you do about poor Adrian?'

Celia explained that she hoped to keep him where he was, provided someone could be found to look in on him and Maria and trouble-shoot if necessary. 'Perhaps you know of some-one?'

'Not offhand. I'd do it myself but I'm too old and I live too far away, but there must be somebody. I'll cudgel my poor old wits about it, and let you know in a day or two.'

She turned to go, then caught sight of Bettencourt and added in an undertone: 'I should watch out for that feller if I were you. One hears funny things about him.'

She went. The bold-eyed man in the dark suit had been hovering near Celia with his eyes still fixed steadily on her, as if waiting for a word. He lost no time in closing in.

'Hullo there, I'm a neebour of yours, Lúcio Freitas,' he began. 'Do please accept my sinceerest sympathies for your sad loss.'

She replied suitably without pointing out that she would be his neighbour for only a few more days, and wondered about his accent. It was Portuguese, overlaid with a dialect of English that she had heard somewhere before. Where? The thin *e* of 'neebour' and 'sinceerely' were very familiar.

Asked if this was her first visit to Madeira, she replied that it was. 'But you will be stayeeng on to keep house for the poor old gentleman?' he asked.

'Nothing's been decided yet,' she prevaricated.

'But unless you stay, poor Sir Morton cannot reemain at the queenta, isn't it so?'

'As I say, we haven't taken any definite decisions.'

He looked as if he wanted to ask more questions, but she gave him no encouragement. Still exuding menace, he turned to go.

'Who on earth was that?' she asked Bettencourt.

'Lúcio Freitas? Emigrated to make some money and came back when he'd got some, like they all do. He has a little house and a banana patch up behind the quinta.'

'Where did he emigrate to?'

'South Africa, I think.'

Of course. That was where the accent came from. 'Why does he think it necessary to make his number with me?'

'He must know you're the executor, news spreads like wildfire here. I expect he has an axe to grind.'

'What makes you think that?'

'A few months ago he made a bit of a nuisance of himself over

54

the levada water, claiming that the quinta was getting more than its share. There was nothing in it, it was just an excuse to be awkward.'

What on earth was levada water? Adding this to her lengthening list of Madeiran mysteries she helped Adrian dispose of the few remaining mourners. When the last of them had gone, the whole party embarked in the big hire-car to go back to the quinta.

Ricardo Fernandes had left earlier, foreseeing an angry reaction from Barton when he was told that Maria-José had not been among the mourners. Perhaps they were on quite the wrong track. He was not even sure that the old man with the stroke was disabled enough to need a nurse, and had hung around on the fringes of the group near the grave to have a good look before he left to make his report.

They had arranged to meet at a café round the corner in the Rua da Careira. Barton's reaction to his news was even more violent than he had expected. 'What d'you mean, she wasn't bloody there? Why the hell not, Rick?' He brooded for a moment. 'I'll tell you why not. Because she and her cow of a mother were on a flight out early this morning.'

'No, Ed.'

'Taking our lovely diamond necklace with them.'

'No, Ed. If they have gone already, why did mama risk coming to Madeira? She could have sent her little poison-pants the fare and met her in Lisbon.'

'OK then, why the hell wasn't poison-pants on parade at the funeral? Rick, I could break both your legs, you deserve it. Leading me down the wrong track on a wild-goose chase and wasting my bloody time.'

'Perhaps it is the right track.'

'If so, she's the old bastard's nurse, the Hanbury woman's his daughter and she's got to be there at her funeral. Murdering little bitch, why wasn't she? Tell me that.'

'Please, Ed, try to be calm, there is a reason, I have just thought of it. She is scared to appear in public. She says to herself, this Morton, he is an important personality, there will be many people, perhaps photographers from the newspapers. So she says "No, this is dangerous for me," and she makes the excuse.'

Barton calmed down a little. 'What excuse could she possibly give?'

'She can say, "I suffer with the belly, I vomit, it is impossible for me to leave the house." No one can contradict her.'

Barton pondered. 'How bad is the old man's stroke?'

'He cannot speak, only make noises. And he has a bad leg and arm.'

'Does he really need a nurse?'

'Yes, because his mind is disturbed. I told you how violently he behaved in the chapel.'

Barton hesitated. 'What d'you think, Rick?'

'It seems to me that we should investigate further this possibility.'

'Can't you find me a more promising corpse in that damn paper?'

'No, Fred. I told you.'

'OK then. Let's go and have a look at this quinta.'

Silent after the traumas of the funeral, the passengers in the hire car disembarked at the Quinta Coulson. Adrian was obviously exhausted, and made no objection when Bettencourt and Agostinho put him into the carrying chair to take him back down the terraces to the cottage. Celia went with them to hand him over to Maria, but she was not at the cottage. She called, and presently heard a crackling sound among the brushwood in the neglected vegetable plot on the terrace below her, the bottom one of the garden. Maria came into sight, looking shamefaced, at the foot of the overgrown steps.

'We're back, and Sir Adrian's very tired,' Celia told her.

As she wondered what Maria had been doing down there among the brambles, Teresa and the children came running down to meet her, shouting something in horrified tones.

'Ladrãos! Thieves!' cried Teresa.

'Oh Aunt Celia, it's dire,' Sarah shouted. 'We've been burgled, everything's all over the place.'

FOUR

Viewing the broken pane in the window beside the back door, Celia cursed herself for her carelessness. If she had thought about it she would have realised that Madeiran burglars were just as capable as English ones of noting the time of a funeral announced in a newspaper and taking advantage of their knowledge. But it had not occurred to her to organise any precautions.

She hurried into the house and found chaos everywhere. Cupboards and desk drawers in all the downstairs rooms had been emptied on to the floor, and the disorder upstairs was almost as bad. When she rang Bettencourt in his downtown office he sounded astonished by her news. 'I don't understand this. Teresa's cousin was going to sit in and guard the house. Let me speak to her.'

After an agitated exchange with him in Portuguese, Teresa handed Celia back the phone. 'She says her cousin didn't turn up,' said Bettencourt. 'She and Agostinho didn't know what to do, but you more or less forced them into the car, so they decided to trust to luck.'

Celia remembered now, and blamed herself bitterly. Agostinho and Teresa had been desperately worried about something as they were leaving for the cemetery. Plagued by the quarrelling children and Adrian's objection to the carrying chair, and fearful of being late, she had failed to find out what the trouble was.

'I'll get on to the police and ring you back,' said Bettencourt. 'Meanwhile, go round the house with Teresa and get her to tell you what's been stolen, so that we can make the insurance claim.'

A tour of the wrecked rooms revealed that though desks, drawers and cupboards had been ransacked, obviously valuable china and silver had been left untouched and even the television set had survived. 'The thieves, they search only for the money,' Teresa explained. 'They must have it for the drugs.'

Was that the explanation? Possibly. But another one had occurred to her.

When Bettencourt rang back he was hugely apologetic. 'I'm desperately sorry about this, it's all our fault. Freda was going to arrange for Teresa's cousin to sit in, but he couldn't make it for some reason. She was going to fix it with someone else, but at the last moment, what with one thing or another, she forgot.'

His inflection of the word 'forgot' was a masterpiece of restrained sarcasm at Freda's expense.

'It was partly my fault, Mr Bettencourt. I should have made Agostinho stay and mount guard.'

'Oh no. He couldn't have missed his employer's funeral without a tremendous loss of face.'

'Teresa says it was probably drug addicts in search of money.'

'She's probably right, Mrs Grant. There's a teenage drug problem here.'

'But are they really stupid enough to expect to find money bags under the mattress in a house like this? There are lots of obvious valuables lying about, and they didn't touch a thing.'

After quite a long pause, Bettencourt said: 'You must remember that the typical drug addict's mentality is very odd.'

Why the long pause before he answered? Celia was sure he was wrong, the burglar was not a drug addict. The drawers and cupboards which had been ransacked were all places where a document might be found. Suppose that was why the house had been broken into, what document would the thief have been looking for? Adrian's unpublished memoirs? Possibly, Freda Bettencourt had described them as 'very hot stuff'. All sorts of sinister people might be interested in them, including gung-ho security men from London.

According to Freda, Antonia had been arranging for the book to be published, presumably as one of her ploys for raising money. Freda had asked what was happening about this, with a note of suppressed anxiety in her voice. Moreover it was Freda who had forgotten to have the house guarded during the funeral. Had she 'forgotten' on purpose? If so she was someone's accomplice. But whose?

58

Having spun this elaborate web of suspicion, she dismissed it abruptly as fantasy. Bettencourt was right, drug addicts were the obvious answer.

The policeman who arrived to view the damage was of the same opinion, and seemed disgusted when neither Celia nor Teresa could tell him how much cash Antonia had left lying about the house before dying. On learning that Maria had been in the cottage at the time of the burglary, he insisted on interviewing her and extracted a series of near-hysterical denials: no, she had heard nothing, she had seen nothing, no she had not left the cottage all morning. Asked why it had not occurred to her to go up there and see that all was well, she took refuge behind her alleged stomach upset. Seeming gravely dissatisfied with her answers, he made it clear to Celia that he was resigned to leaving the crime unsolved, and withdrew.

There was one matter which he had not investigated, but which troubled Celia: how had the burglar got in? Not through the front entrance, which was kept locked. Not over the wall flanking the lane, it was too high to climb without a ladder. She summoned Agostinho and put the problem to him. 'Come, *minha senhora*, I will show you,' he said, and led her to a border on the uphill side of the house. Half hidden behind a tangle of jasmine and bignonia and plumbago, a stone retaining wall separated the quinta's garden from the property behind and above it. The stems of banana trees were visible on the far side of the wall, where the ground was obviously much higher.

'Easy, *minha senhora*,' said Agostinho. He was right, a burglar would have no trouble slithering down the retaining wall, and there were enough toe-holds in it to make scrambling back up just as easy.

'Who does the banana plantation belong to?' she asked.

'To Lúcio Freitas. He is the neighbour who spoke with you at the funeral, you remember perhaps.'

She did indeed remember. He was the man whose compelling stare had unnerved her.

'But his house, it is on the far side,' said Agostinho. 'A thief could come among the bananas and he would not see.'

As she went indoors, she wondered again what the burglar had been looking for. A document, almost certainly, but was that all? Suddenly she decided that perhaps there was something else. Feeling that she was being slightly absurd, she went up to Antonia's room and delved in the bottom of the bed with the coat-hanger. She was wrong. The watch was still there.

She stared at it for a moment and was about to put it back in its hiding place when Sarah appeared in the doorway. 'Peter's up there with his trains. I'm sure all this escape into toyland is bad for his psyche but he won't come down. Oh. What's that?'

Celia showed it to her. 'A watch.'

'But it's a man's watch, Aunt Celia.'

'Yes.'

'Where did you find it?'

Celia showed her. 'Down there.'

'Oh well,' said Sarah after a pause for thought. 'I know sex is supposed to be part of the youth culture, but I've never believed that nothing goes on between mothers and fathers below the waistline.'

'Not fathers in this case, I imagine.'

'Ugh. No fear, she'd have preferred to bed down with a rattlesnake. I expect that thing belongs to Smelly Bettencourt. He was her steady, they used to do it in the afternoon.' She lowered her voice conspiratorially. 'Don't tell Peter. He's too little, he wouldn't understand.'

Celia thought for a moment. 'Have you seen Mr Bettencourt wearing this watch?'

'No, but I wouldn't have noticed. Aunt Celia, d'you think Smelly pushed Mum down the stairs and killed her?'

'Sarah! What a dreadful idea. Whatever put that into your head?'

'It could be him. They were having frightful quarrels last holidays, yelling and screaming at each other, just before we went back to school. Anyway, someone must have given her a push.'

'Listen, you mustn't say things like that without a good reason. Tell me at once what this is all about.'

Instead of answering, Sarah put another question. 'Did Mum have a whisky bottle when she was found?'

'Yes, I believe she did. How did you know?'

'I eavesdropped at the funeral. Afterwards, when Peter and I were sitting in the car, and the windows were open, two weirdo old women came past on the way out, and one of them said Mum was drunk when she fell down the stairs in the night. And the other one said oh how dreadful, dear, is that really so? And then the first one said yes, she was lying there clutching an empty whisky bottle.'

'Oh really, that was just naughty old women's gossip. She wasn't clutching the bottle, it was on the bedside table and it was half full. But there were some sleeping pills there too, and I think she'd taken some. I'm sure she wasn't drunk, but the two in combination, a tot of whisky plus the pills would have made her drowsy and confused.'

'But she never drank whisky! She never drank anything much, not even wine unless it was a party.'

Damn, Celia thought, sick with shock. Is this child telling the truth? If so, all the silly things I've been forbidding myself to fantasise about have got to be taken seriously: Gerald's unexplained rush to Madeira; the rift in the Bettencourts' marriage and his obvious admiration for Antonia; the watch left in her bed by her lover – had he pushed her downstairs, then let himself out with his key? Unless Sarah is wrong, she thought, there's no escape, here we go again on the Miss Marple trail, which is an abominable nuisance because I've quite enough to worry about without that.

After a moment of panic, sanity prevailed. Antonia must have been a secret drinker, clever enough to hide her addiction from her children. Or perhaps she restrained herself while the children were at home for the holidays, and broke out into drunken orgies in their term-time.

Sarah was still watching her, waiting for a reaction. Instead of providing one, she began searching the room.

'Oh, Aunt Celia, what are you looking for?'

'Bottles.'

'Oh, why?'

'She'd have had to drink quite a lot to make her drunk enough to miss the light switch and fall downstairs. If she was swigging quantities of whisky she'd have to hide the bottles somewhere. Let's make sure there aren't any.'

The chest of drawers yielded none. Nor did a suitcase under the bed, so she opened the doors of the wardrobe and pushed the dresses aside. Half a dozen empty whisky bottles were ranged along the back of the wardrobe behind them.

'Oh no!' Sarah shouted fiercely. 'Mum didn't drink. Those aren't hers. Someone pushed her downstairs and put the bottles there to make it look like an accident.'

Was this possible? Yes, just. Say Bettencourt was the owner of the watch. He would have had access to the house after Antonia's death. He had made a great carry-on about his admiration for her, persisting in it tactlessly in front of his acidulous wife. Did he really admire Antonia? Or had the affair turned sour? If he hated her, he could be lying to cover up the murderous truth.

After playing for a moment with this lurid scenario, Celia dismissed it firmly from her mind. Antonia was a secret drinker. Lots of divorced women were. Sarah had been watching too much television.

Teresa came upstairs to say that lunch was ready. Finding them in Antonia's bedroom seemed to shock her, as if they had no right to be there. Puzzled by this reaction, Celia was even more puzzled by Teresa's blurted remark: 'You look for something?'

Before she could answer, Sarah broke in eagerly. 'Mum didn't drink whisky, did she?'

Teresa's face expressed shock. 'No, little one. Never the whisky, never the gin. Sometimes perhaps the Madeira, when the guests came. When they find the whisky bottle by her bed, I say to myself this is strange.'

Sarah opened the wardrobe and pulled the dresses aside to display the whisky bottles. Teresa put both hands to her mouth in dismay. 'This I do not understand,' she said, and gave Celia a long, searching look.

'There, what did I tell you?' cried Sarah.

Thoughts crowded in on Celia which were too complicated to share with a thirteen-year-old child. With an effort of self-control she dismissed them as nonsense, the imaginings of a feverishly suspicious mind. No one had pushed Antonia downstairs. For reasons best known to herself, she had gone on a bender while the children were away, and had managed to do so without Teresa's knowledge. The need for a sitter-in during the funeral had genuinely slipped Freda's memory. Or perhaps she had seen no reason to oblige a husband she disliked by attending to this tiresome chore. The burglar was a drug addict in search of money.

Teresa had laid lunch under the jacaranda tree on the lawn, for the dining room was still littered with the aftermath of the burglary. When it was over, Peter retired to the attic to commune with his trains and Sarah volunteered to help Celia restore order in the house. It was in chaos, with the spilled contents of drawers and cupboards lying about everywhere. As they put back the debris where it came from, Celia kept a wary eye open for papers which ought to be looked through. The cupboards and drawers in the dining and drawing rooms had housed only the sort of family possessions one would expect to find in such places. But the study floor was a sea of paper, obviously the fall-out from an elegant mahogany desk.

It had clearly been used by Antonia, who proved to be a hoarder of paper. The drawers had housed a jumble of invitations to parties months ago, correspondence with lawyers about her divorce, documents bearing on her various attempts to make money, including the market garden venture and the boutique, and letters from friends. Mixed up in all this were bills, receipts, bank statements and insurance papers for her house and car. But if the manuscript of the memoirs had been among the hoard, the thief must have taken it, and there was no trace of correspondence connected with it.

With Sarah helping her she started sorting everything into date order and reconstructing a picture of Antonia's business life. There were three sets of bank statements, two of them Sir Adrian's which she operated under the power of attorney. His account at a London bank covered the children's school fees and other sterling expenses, and the one at the Espirito Santo bank in Funchal obviously bore the brunt of the household bills. The balance in both was substantial, thanks to a lavish four-figure monthly payment on account of his civil service pension. As long as he lived, there would be no problem about meeting the children's school fees. But what would happen if he died?

The third set of statements, belonging to Antonia's personal bank account, told a different tale, of small and irregular sums scratched together. Celia began comparing the entries with the records of the successive business ventures with which Antonia had tried to shore up her precarious finances. As Bettencourt had said, none of them had brought in very much, and the last of them had folded well over a year ago. But surprisingly, monthly payments into her account continued. Why? If the amounts had varied from month to month, they could have been explained as the fluctuating takings of some trading venture which had left no trace in the hoard of paper. But the figure, paid in on or near the first of the month, was always the same, fifty thousand escudos, and it had started just after the last of the commercial ventures folded. What did it represent? Not a remittance from home; entries involving foreign exchange had 'Cam' opposite them, presumably standing for 'Cambio'.

Of the other entries, some were labelled 'Dep', while others had nothing against them. What was the distinction? Going back to the earlier records she established that when the entry was unlabelled, the sum deposited corresponded roughly with the takings of one of the businesses. Did that mean that Antonia had paid the money in herself, whereas 'Dep' meant a deposit by a third party? She decided instantly not to find out. The pattern, with fifty thousand escudos paid in each month, bore a horrid resemblance to the one that would be thrown up by the proceeds of blackmail, but she choked back the thought. She was in Funchal to execute a will, not to start a criminal investigation.

But she was neglecting her duties as an aunt. Peter's solitary confinement in the attic worried her and Sarah was getting bored. 'Let's all do something more amusing now,' she proposed. 'What sort of thing would tempt Peter away from his trains?'

Sarah thought. 'He's very fond of ice-cream. I quite like it too, actually. There's a place just down the hill where they have scrumptious ones.'

Sarah was right, ice-cream proved a more powerful attraction than the trains in the attic. 'Yippee!' cried Peter as they emerged from the garden into the lane. 'I shall have a chocolate one and a vanilla one and a strawberry one and lots of nuts and Melba sauce.'

'Greedyguts, you're only allowed two,' Sarah shouted, and they began to quarrel noisily.

Someone was working in the banana grove on the far side of the lane, to judge from agitated movements among the fronds.

'Hey, children, stop that noise,' Celia ordered. 'Or no one will get even the smallest vanilla cone.'

They set off down the lane, then turned off it on to a footpath running along above the back gardens of houses farther down the hill. On the uphill side of the path was a low wall surmounted by a tall fence of wire mesh supported on angle irons bedded in concrete; the lower boundary, Celia realised, of the quinta's garden. Once more, she found herself puzzling over Antonia's curious arrangements for Adrian. He obviously hated being hauled laboriously up to the front entrance in the carrying chair. Why had she not had a gate made, opening from the bottom of the garden on to the path? That would have made it possible for Adrian to get out of his cramped territory into the wider world without an enormous carry-on.

The path emerged into a street with a small row of shops, including an ice-cream parlour in which she let the children order lavishly. 'This is what mum used to call a "rich lick",' said Sarah, spooning it up. Inspecting her colourfully heaped bowlful, Celia decided that for once, Antonia's erratic sense of humour had found the *mot juste*.

Back at the quinta, she left the children to their own devices and went down to the cottage to begin sorting out the domestic situation. Her first task was to find out what Adrian wanted. Was he content to stay where he was if she could arrange for Maria to stay and look after him? She put this to him under the trellis while Maria was getting his tea. He thought for a moment, then nodded gravely.

Had he hesitated a little? She suspected that Maria bullied him. Was he opting for an unsatisfactory *status quo* from fear of something worse?

'You're sure?' she asked. He nodded again emphatically, and managed a smile.

Reassured, she went into the cottage to tackle Maria. 'You wanted to know what arrangements I'm thinking of making,' Celia began. 'Nothing's settled yet, but I can tell you what I'm aiming at.'

'Thank you, senhora,' said Maria, looking tense. 'I shall be happy to know.'

'The main house will have to be let, but there's no reason why

65

Sir Adrian shouldn't stay on here, provided proper arrangements can be made to look after him.'

Proper arrangements, she explained, included finding someone to pay the household bills, look in frequently to see that all was well, and trouble-shoot in emergencies. Supposing such a person was found, would Maria be willing to stay on and look after Sir Adrian?

During this, Maria's face had changed by degrees from scowling tension to radiant happiness. Celia was no longer in her doghouse. 'Oh thank you, thank you, senhora. I shall be very happy to accept.'

'I thought we'd look for someone who could give you a regular day off,' she said, 'and perhaps a longer holiday sometimes.'

'No,' Maria protested, still wreathed in smiles. 'The holiday, it is not necessary. Here is quiet. I like it.'

Celia tried without success to argue her out of this appetite for nun-like seclusion, and wondered what tensions and hang-ups underlay it. Even if Maria was not a bully, perhaps it was not quite fair to subject Adrian to her concentrated attention.

He fidgeted as they drank their tea. As soon as it was over he rose to take Celia along with him to the orchid house, where his pampered and capricious treasures awaited her attention.

'No, senhor! Not the orchids, not today. The senhor is too tired after the funeral, he will exhaust himself.'

Adrian dismissed this with a mischievous smile and a friendly but impolite gesture which reassured Celia that he was holding his own. They went into the orchid house and worked their way along the benches, with Celia wielding the watering can. What was to happen to all these rarities if despite her efforts Adrian had to leave the quinta and they were orphaned? She disliked the *Orchidaceae*, but they were plants and therefore had a claim on her. She would feel guilty if she failed to find them good homes.

Suddenly Adrian startled her with a cry of rage, and pointed indignantly at a pot containing an orchid which was not in flower. It was labelled *Oncidium varicosum*. His expression suggested that it had misbehaved in some way.

There were no signs of disease, so what was wrong with it? To judge from his gestures, the offence had been committed by the two ugly green excrescences which grew out of the rhizome. After more gesticulation she grasped what the trouble was. 'Are the pseudobulbs the wrong shape for *varicosum*?' she asked.

He nodded vigorously and gestured again.

'They're too big, is that it?'

Even more emphatic nods were followed by a complicated mime. Celia deduced with some difficulty that there ought to be three pointed leaves growing out of the top of each pseudobulb. There were other things wrong with them, but his struggle to explain resulted only in frustrated noises which she could not interpret.

He went on to point an accusing finger at the label. It was clear now what was wrong. The thing was mislabelled. Someone, presumably Antonia in her capacity as orchid-minder, had made a mistake. Celia was puzzled. Pseudobulbs did not appear on an orchid overnight, the wretched plant must have been maturing them for months. But to judge from his reaction, he had only just noticed that something was wrong. Why had he not spotted it long ago?

He had begun to hunt furiously along the benches, apparently in search of further errors, and soon fixed with a roar of anger on a small epiphytic plant growing on a raft of tree-fern which dangled on a wire from a high bench. Again, it was not in flower. According to its label it was a member of the *Epidendreae* called *Leptotes bicolor*. He waggled a reproving finger at it, and frowned forbiddingly. To judge from his gestures, the pseudobulbs were again at fault, but there was also something wrong with the plant's general habit of growth.

Farther along the bench, he detected two more mistakes of labelling. Suddenly some thought seemed to hit him, perhaps the memory of Antonia who had looked after his collection for him. Staring fixedly at a *Laelia purpurata* in full and glorious bloom, he burst into frustrated tears.

Maria had heard him sob and came flying along the terrace with a determined expression. Seeing Celia's startled look, she suppressed the determination and substituted anxiety for her patient. 'Please, senhor, you have had much distress today, you are exhausted.' She took his arm to lead him away. 'Come, please, it is better if you sit quietly under the trellis.'

When he had been settled there Celia climbed back to the main house with her conscience still uneasy. If Adrian was prepared to put up with Maria it was difficult to say no. But to put it as charitably as possible, she was very possessive about him, and clearly suffered from a mass of neuroses. Moreover there had been something shifty about her behaviour that morning. When they came back from the funeral she was down on the bottom terrace by the boundary fence, looking guilty. What had she been doing there? Had she really seen and heard nothing during the burglary?

Celia summoned Teresa and Agostinho, and told them that she hoped to arrange for Sir Adrian to stay where he was, and to let the main house till the children came of age. 'And if we can find some nice tenants, I'm sure we can arrange for you both to go on working for them.'

Agostinho murmured something indistinct and Teresa made no comment. Unnerved by this semi-hostile reaction she withdrew to the drawing room and waited for Bettencourt, who was to collect her and take her downtown to start the legal processing of Antonia's will.

'I haven't seen it yet,' she said when he arrived. 'It's at your office?'

'No, that's not the system here. The notaries have huge books in which everyone's will is entered. When someone dies you produce the death certificate and the notary gives you a certified copy of the entry in the book. It's a sensible system really. Wicked relatives can't destroy a will, and if the testator has made several wills one after another it's impossible to pass off one that isn't the latest as valid. As your representative I've already given the notary Antonia's death certificate. What we're going to do now is to get the certified copy.'

As they walked to the entrance, it occurred to her that he had probably come up specially from his office to collect her and that using him as her driver was probably adding greatly to her legal costs.

'It's kind of you to ferry me about,' she said. 'But it's not as if I was the Queen Mother on a State visit. I could drive myself around in Antonia's car.'

He looked doubtful. 'The roads here are narrow and winding, and the accident rate's hair-raising.'

'I've driven in London and Paris. I can probably manage.'

'If you really want to risk it I'll look at the insurance cover and extend it if necessary. You have your British driving licence? Good.'

His own car was outside in the lane. He drove her down into the crowded town centre, and parked outside a Mussolini-type neoclassical building fronted by a gesticulating bronze lady symbolising justice. Bettencourt led her in and halted outside a door with a brass plate on it. 'Now, Mrs Grant. When we've got our copy of the will I shall explain to the notary that you don't live here and want to get back to England, so will he please fix a date as soon as possible for the next stage.'

'Which is probate?'

'No, they don't bother with such Anglo-Saxon complications. The next stage is called *habilitacãoes*, which means that whatever the testator has left is handed over to the beneficiaries for them to do what they like with. Here we are, let's go in.'

The notary was an elderly man with a sleepy expression and slow movements. Bettencourt shook hands with him and introduced Celia, then addressed him in Portuguese. It sounded at first as if the request for an early hearing was unwelcome, but after further argument by Bettencourt the notary's face cleared and a date early in the following week was agreed.

Out in the corridor Bettencourt said: 'So that's that. They don't like being hurried, but I pointed out that the beneficiaries were both minors, which means that the court has to appoint what they call here a *tutor* to look after things till they come of age. We may not get *habilitacãoes* next Tuesday, but we have to put up a proposal for a *tutor*, and they'll pronounce on it then.'

But what proposal? Celia thought.

'Would you be willing to act, Mrs Grant?'

'I suppose so, if there's no one else.'

'One couldn't ask Adrian to take it on, and I doubt if they'd accept a man of his age in a poor state of health. The only other possibility is their father.'

'But the children hate him.'

'Antonia hated him,' Bettencourt corrected, 'and they took their attitude from her. It could change.'

'But he's a convicted criminal, Mr Bettencourt. You're not suggesting that we should ask the court to appoint him?'

'No. But he has a claim, and I think he will press it. However, the law says that the person appointed as *tutor* has to be "reputable". If you want to block it, you can object that he's disreputable, and they'll probably listen. It's up to you.'

What a choice, she thought. Do I saddle myself with massive responsibilities on this outlandish island miles from home? Or do I hand everything over to a city slicker who swindled investors out of millions, and let him do what he likes with two children who are terrified of him?

Seeing her hesitate, Bettencourt said: 'Would you be willing to meet Hanbury?'

'If you think it's advisable, but why?'

'There's nothing to be gained by keeping him at arm's length. He'll want to see the children, and you'd find it difficult to stop him. If they dislike him as much as you say, and show it when they meet him, you may be able to talk him out of applying for custody.' He paused, then added very casually: 'Hanbury wants to meet you, as a matter of fact. He asked me to tell you that he's waiting for you now in a café down by the cathedral, on the off-chance that you'll agree to see him.'

I am being manipulated, Celia thought. This wily young lawyer has fixed up for Gerald to be in the café because he's decided that as their father he will get custody in the end. So the sooner I see what I'm up against and cave in, the better. However, there was no way she could refuse to meet Gerald Hanbury, so she steeled herself for an unpleasant encounter and let Bettencourt guide her into a pedestrianised street near the cathedral, flanked by open-air cafés.

'There he is, Mrs Grant. I think it will be best if I leave you to talk to him on your own.'

And I know why you think so, she decided. You're convinced that I'm not tough enough to fight my own corner, and you have no intention of fighting it for me. Well, we shall see.

Gerald Hanbury was sitting at a table in one of the cafés. His good looks had coarsened with middle age, and he had put on weight. He was overdressed in a sharply cut tropical suit and his brilliantined hair was off-putting. So was the disquieting fact that he was not wearing a wrist-watch.

'Ah, Celia, this is nice, it's been far too long,' he said, giving her an impressive company chairman's handshake. His manner to the waiter as he ordered Celia's drink made it clear that he was accustomed to instant service, and when he brought himself up to date with her recent history his attitude to her nursery garden business struck her as patronising. Having devoted the regulation five minutes to what the salesmen's manual called 'establishing a personal relationship', he got down to business.

'Bettencourt's told you, I suppose, that I shall be applying for custody of the children?'

'Yes. He did mention it.'

'Well? You're not going to oppose it, I hope?'

'I might.'

'But my dear girl, you haven't got a leg to stand on.'

'I'm not so sure, Gerald. The law here is that custody is only given to a person of good character.'

'So?'

'It would be open to me to suggest that in view of recent events, you don't qualify.'

There was a long silence. 'Would you really do that?'

'It depends.'

'On what?'

'Partly on whether the children are willing to accept you as their guardian.'

'But you know as well as I do that Antonia did everything she could to poison their minds against me.'

Celia refrained from saying that Antonia had been abetted in this task by his own poisonous behaviour.

'Do you propose to continue dishing out the venom and prevent me from seeing them?' he asked. 'Because if so I shall obviously have a fight on my hands.'

'Keep your hands under control for the moment, and let's talk about the financial problem. As you know, Antonia has no income. The children's expenses, including some quite heavy school fees, are being met by Sir Adrian. That won't continue if you get custody, he made his feelings about you obvious at the funeral. Moreover he's got a bad heart and gets his whole income, almost, from a pension which dies with him. How d'you propose to support Peter and Sarah?'

'I shall earn. I started from nothing once, I can do it again.'

And end up in prison again? Celia wondered.

'I've got a lot of irons in the fire,' he volunteered. 'Job applications and so on.'

'But there's nothing definite yet?'

'My dear girl, give me a chance. I've been out of prison for less than a month. I came straight out here to try to come to an arrangement with Antonia.'

What sort of an arrangement? Only for access to the children, or had he hoped for a full reconciliation? It would be worth it from his point of view, Antonia owned the Quinta Coulson, a valuable asset on which money could be raised. She looked again at his wrist. Did the watch in Antonia's bed belong to him?

'How did your negotiations with her go?' she asked.

'I don't think that's any business of yours,' he said angrily. 'You've obviously made up your mind against me, I'm getting nowhere.' He stood up. 'There's no point in carrying on with this conversation, I'm going.'

'Without hearing various conclusions that I've reached?'

He sat down again.

'That's better, Gerald. Now. I accept the obvious fact that you have every right to see the children, and I suggest that you come up to the quinta for lunch tomorrow.'

'With you breathing down their necks and making sure they stick to the hate-daddy party line? No, damn you, I want to have them to myself.'

'No. I don't trust you to bring them back, and they'll be less terrified of you with me there. Even so, you'll have a difficult time with them, so let me give you some advice. Ditch that idiotic car salesman's suit and put on a short-sleeved shirt and slacks. And stop this dreadful pompous act. It doesn't impress me, and the children will see through it at once.'

'I am *not* pompous!' he roared.

'Yes you are. You're behaving like a grand panjandrum of international finance who's suffered nothing worse than a temporary business setback in what still promises to be a successful power-grabbing career. No, Gerald. To keep the flag of tycoonery flying after a prison sentence you have to have money stashed away in a tax haven, and it's public knowledge that you haven't. You're down on your uppers, you can't even afford to pay your defence lawyers' bill. I even wondered if you were running away in a tantrum to avoid having to pay for our drinks.'

Muttering angrily, he slapped some money down on the table and stood up. 'Good night, Celia. You always were a tight-arsed upper-class bitch.'

'Well, you are entitled to your opinion. But are you coming to lunch tomorrow or not?'

'Yes, damn you, I am.'

FIVE

Barton and Fernandes had had a frustrating day. An inspection of the high garden wall of the Quinta Coulson had added nothing to their knowledge of what went on inside, and the unfrequented lane in which it stood was no place for a watcher to mingle unnoticed in a crowd. An army of casual passers-by would be needed to maintain proper surveillance, but head office had vetoed the use of agency operatives flown in from Portugal. Reinforcements from headquarters across the Atlantic would not arrive for twenty-four hours at least. Till then they were on their own.

They had done their best, despite the odds against them. The gate of the banana grove opposite the quinta was padlocked, but this posed no problem, it was easy to lift it off its hinges and slip inside at the hinge end. Armed with a Polaroid camera, and camouflaged with banana fronds, they settled down to photograph everyone who came in or out of the door in the quinta's wall. But their bag was meagre. The first person to fall victim to their hidden camera was, puzzlingly, a policeman. Later, they were able to add a couple who looked like servants going off for their lunch hour. After another long wait, a family emerged consisting of a tiny silver-haired woman with the complexion of a Dresden shepherdess, accompanying two children whose shouted remarks suggested that this was an expedition to an ice-cream parlour. Fernandes, who was sensitive to feminine beauty at all ages, wondered why she had passed on her looks to her son and not to her lumpy, unattractive daughter, and speculated on the frightful tensions which this maldistribution of beauty must have set up in the family. Barton, for whom beauty had to be blonde, big-bosomed and under twenty-five, merely cursed the silver-haired lady for not being Maria-José.

In mid-afternoon there was another burst of activity. A strikingly handsome Portuguese with a neatly trimmed beard had driven up to the door in the wall. Having rung the bell, he was admitted by the servant and emerged soon afterwards with the silver-haired woman, now minus the children.

When the pair had driven off, the two watchers consulted gloomily. There was still no sign of Maria-José, and the tableau of settled domesticity presented by the woman with the two children suggested strongly that they had come to the wrong house. As dusk fell they abandoned their vigil and went back despondently to the hotel. Fernandes was gloomily convinced that Maria-José's late employer had lived somewhere quite different, and that her death had so disorganised the surviving members of the household that they had forgotten to put a notice in the paper. But Barton insisted perversely on investigating the less unlikely of the two other women listed in the paper as dying on Saturday, and they spent the evening making themselves conspicuous at Ribeira Brava along the coast, as they enquired about the circumstances of a dead widow who proved to be too old to have an invalid father.

Maria, meanwhile, had given Sir Adrian his supper, settled him in bed and told him she was going out for a walk. This did not surprise him, for she often went out for a breath of air under cover of darkness, when she felt safe. But this time was different. For the first time for a year, she was going to meet her mother.

The first news she had of Mrs Beleza's arrival had come that morning, and it had not come direct. While the rest of the household was at Mrs Hanbury's funeral a furtive visitor had brought her the news that her mother had booked in at a small hotel away from the tourist area, and would like Maria-José to phone her there.

The visitor was her mother's Cousin Isabel, who lived near by. Appealed to by Mrs Beleza to find Maria-José a job on the island, she had fixed her up with Sir Adrian. But instead of trusting her cousin with the truth, Mrs Beleza had fed her a cock-and-bull story about Maria-José having to go into hiding to shake off a persistent but undesirable suitor. When Cousin Isabel discovered the far more sinister truth she was furious, and she had delivered Mrs Beleza's message with very bad grace.

'And tell your mother I do not wish to see her, already I have enough trouble because of this affair. It is bad enough that she telephoned me with her message, why could she not approach you direct?'

When Maria-José telephoned her mother, the reason became clear. Mrs Beleza was terrified. Convinced that she had been followed to Madeira, she insisted that there was no question of her coming to the quinta in case she led their pursuers to her darling Maria-José. Even elsewhere it was too dangerous for them to meet openly by daylight. They had agreed a rendezvous not far from her hotel, after dark.

The bus from the stop in the square deposited Maria by the statue of Henry the Navigator in the centre of town. She walked up the steps into the Santa Catarina Park, lit by the underwater floodlights of a dozen enormous fountains in its lake, and waited in the shadows for her mother to appear. Presently Mrs Beleza joined the strollers on the path round the lake, and gave a barely perceptible nod as Maria passed her going the other way. This meant that as far as she could tell she had not been followed. With Maria keeping her distance behind her, she struck off the path into the shadows.

All the dark corners in the park proved to be infested with pairs of lovers. But they could stay apart no longer, and fell into each others' arms, ignoring the whispered conversations around them. When the first endearments were over, Maria asked whether she really believed she had been followed from Rio.

'I am sure of it, my pigeon. There are two men, brutes with loose jackets to hide the guns under their arms. When I was checking in for the flight from Lisbon they sent a woman to stand behind me and find where I was going, and afterwards they were on the plane. I cannot be sure, but one of them, dark-haired and thin, is very like a man I saw watching the house in Rio.'

'But you could be mistaken?'

Mrs Beleza became tearful and agitated. 'If I am wrong, why did they wait at the carousel for me to collect my case, though they had only cabin baggage? Why did they take the taxi behind mine in the queue and follow me into town?'

'To the hotel?' Maria asked. She was really alarmed now.

'No. I gave them the slip. But my darling, it is not safe for you if I stay here longer. It breaks my heart, but for both our sakes, I must go. Here is the necklace, take it. With the money you can leave the island and make yourself a new life.'

'No, Mama. The aunt from England is a good woman and practical. She says she will arrange matters so that I can stay here and look after the old gentleman as before.'

'And you accepted? My darling, this is no life for you.'

'I cannot face the world, I am ashamed. It's better if I stay hidden here.'

After a lot of argument, Mrs Beleza persuaded her to accept the diamond necklace. Till long after the lovers whispering under the trees had gone, they talked on, not knowing when they would be able to meet again, and making the most of their few short hours together. When the time for parting came, Maria watched in tears as her mother walked away past the floodlit fountains, then hailed a late-prowling taxi and drove back to the quinta. To avoid alerting the sleeping household, she made the driver drop her in the square, let herself in through the door in the wall and hurried down the terraces to the cottage.

But as she tiptoed towards her bedroom, panic hit her. Groans of distress were coming from Sir Adrian's room. She went to look at him, fearing the worst, and saw that the worst was happening. The strain of the funeral had brought on a heart attack, and she had not been there to help. She fetched his pills, and slipped one under his tongue. But his groans grew louder, and when she produced the oxygen mask and cylinder he brushed them away. She was appalled. Was he having another stroke?

Dr Mendes must be summoned. The key to the back door of the house was not on its nail. It was still missing, as it had been on the morning when she found Mrs Hanbury dead. She would have to bang on the door and ring, till someone let her in to get to the telephone. She hurried up the terraces, reproaching herself bitterly. She should not have stayed away so long. And now that the damage had been done, she should not be thinking only of the consequences for herself. But she could not help it. If Sir Adrian died she would be left without a refuge.

Up at the house Celia was being attacked by her standard nightmare: she was a saxifrage, and pot-bound. But this time she was on a bench in an orchid house, surrounded by the ghosts of orchids which she had abandoned to die a lingering death from neglect and thirst. Presently Gerald appeared, picked her up in her pot and threw her to the ground.

She woke to find someone shaking her shoulder.

'Aunt Celia, Aunt Celia, wake up,' Sarah shouted in her ear. 'Peter's having a nightmare.'

Telling herself that Peter was not the only one, Celia switched on the bedside light. It was two in the morning. Screams were coming from Peter's room along at the end of the passage. She hurried along and, after a time, managed to wake him. 'I dreamt Dad was banging on the door and ringing,' he sobbed, 'and trying to get at me and take me away.'

Peter's room was at the side of the house, over the kitchen door. Sarah opened the shutters and leaned out. 'You didn't dream it, it's happening,' she reported. 'But it's Maria banging at the door, not Dad.'

'The senhor is having an attack,' Maria shouted up. 'I must telephone to the doctor.'

Celia went down to let her in. While Maria telephoned she hurried down to the cottage to give any help she could, and found Sir Adrian on his knees in the bathroom, vomiting neatly into the water-closet. By the time she had helped him back to bed and made him comfortable Dr Mendes arrived, and confirmed that his patient had suffered nothing more serious than a stomach upset.

After the alarms of the night everyone except Maria slept late, and it was mid-morning before Celia went down to the cottage to inquire about Sir Adrian. He was not in his usual chair under the trellis, for a sharp wind had sprung up and driven him indoors. Maria, who was also there, defended herself tensely against any suggestion, though Celia had not made one, that she should not have caused a false alarm by summoning Dr Mendes in the middle of the night. Celia said at once that there was no need for apologies, since there were special problems when looking after a patient who could not tell one which of many possible ailments he was suffering from.

'And I'm sorry you had such trouble getting in to phone,' she added. 'Didn't Antonia give you a key to the house?'

After hesitating for a moment Maria said: 'Certainly, I kept it on a nail, out in the entry. But it has gone.'

'What d'you mean, gone? Who took it?'

78

Maria gave a wide-armed Latin American shrug. 'It disappeared.'

Celia was aghast. 'Since when?'

'Since . . . perhaps a week or a little more.'

In other words, since before Antonia's death. Who had stolen it? Gerald Hanbury? Perhaps, he had been on the island when it went missing. Bettencourt, if he was the lover who had left his watch in Antonia's bed? Possibly, unless she had given him a key. If she had, and Gerald was the thief, two people were in possession of keys to the house at the time when Antonia was supposed to be dying in it alone.

The wind was blowing fiercely through the garden and shaking blossom from the trees. But that was not why Celia shivered as she climbed back to the house. The theft of the key horrified her. Coming on top of the seemingly pointless burglary, it was the last straw, which broke the back of her ability to shrug off events which had struck her as vaguely sinister. They had all been capable of an innocent interpretation, and up to now she had dismissed her suspicions as the product of an over-developed sense of evil. No longer. Evil, probably murder, was in the air.

But there was no proof, no hard fact that one could take to the police and say: 'Here you are, this is murder. It's your job, get on with it.' Once, long ago, she had gone to the police with an accusation that she could not substantiate. She had been proved right in the end, but not before she had been charged with wasting police time, while her neighbours in the village muttered darkly about delusions brought on by the change of life. That episode had left a deep scar. It was an experience that she was determined never to repeat. Till she could prove she was right by producing solid evidence, she would have to slog on alone.

Her uneasy meditations were broken by a telephone call. 'Celia? Gerald here, I'm sorry about last night. I'm ringing to apologise.'

'And so you should, Gerald.'

'I've got slacks on and a T-shirt that says California Lido Beach.'

'Sackcloth and ashes would be more appropriate.'

'Metaphorically I am wearing them. Am I forgiven for the business suit and the pomposity and calling you a bitch?'

'I suppose so, if you intend to mend your ways and behave like a normal human being. You propose, then, to come to lunch and charm the children with winsome behaviour?'

'Yes please, but I'd like to talk to you again before I meet them. Not at the house, I don't want them to feel we're discussing them behind their backs. There's a little bar in the square where the church is, how about that? At twelve?'

How did he know about the bar in the square? Had he and Antonia met there because she refused to have him in the house? Had he sat there alone, thinking out ways of seducing and perhaps killing her?

Both children were eyeing her accusingly as she put down the phone. 'He's coming to lunch? Satan is? You actually *asked* him?' cried Sarah angrily.

'Yes, but listen, both of you. He wants to see you, in fact he insists, and as he's your father I can't stop him. He wanted to take you off somewhere by himself—'

'Oh no!' cried Peter, terrified.

'But I wasn't having that, so I asked him to lunch here. He can't eat you.'

'I wouldn't put it past him,' said Sarah gloomily.

'Nor would I,' cried Peter, 'but I hate him so much, I'd make him sick me up.'

'Don't be such wimps. I'll be there all the time, you won't be left alone with him. So put a brave face on it. Let him see you have nice table manners and don't spill soup over him in your agitation.'

After a lot more discussion they accepted the inevitable. But they were still very alarmed, and when she announced that she had to go out, but did not confess that it was to meet Gerald, they panicked. 'Shush, do calm down,' she told them. 'Don't worry, I'll be back before he comes.'

Meeting Gerald again in the bar in the square, she was surprised to see that the slacks and gaudy T-shirt did not look incongruous on him. He had washed out the brilliantine and allowed his hair to flop about. There was still no sign of a wrist-watch.

When they had settled down at a table he broke into a grin. 'Oh God, Celia, I was an idiot to try it on, I ought to have remembered what a wide-awake cookie you are. You're right,

I'm on my uppers. I'm squatting in a grotty little time-share flat lent me by one of the few friends I've got left, and eating in cheap snack bars, and praying the money won't run out before I've made my peace with the children. I must have been mad, putting on that act. You saw through it at once, didn't you?'

Yes, Celia thought, I did, and if this bid for sympathy is also an act I shall see through that too.

'I saw you gaping at my wrist,' he went on. 'You don't miss a thing, do you? I sold my watch to buy my air ticket, it was a solid gold Omega that I managed to hold on to when the vultures moved in.'

Was it really an Omega? Or was this a cover story? Was he the owner of the cheaper and flashier watch reposing at the bottom of Antonia's bed at the quinta? And had he realised that he had lost it there?

'Why did you come when you're broke?' she asked. 'Did you think you could patch things up with Antonia if you met her face to face?'

'I wanted to get some arrangement about the children. I'd thought about them a lot while I was in prison.'

'You could have written. You didn't nourish hopes of a happy reconciliation in a double bed?'

He looked at her sharply and reddened. 'Celia, when you make shrewish remarks like that, I have to suppress an urge to hit you.'

'Shrewish? I am all innocence. What have I said?'

'Surely you knew? I thought everyone did. Antonia kept open bed for all comers, except me. When I insisted she made a disgusted face, as if I still smelt of my uncle's fish and chip shop in Bolton, where I worked when I left school at fifteen. I used my brains and my elbows and made a lot of money, and that was what she married me for. Her big turn-on was having the flat in Belgravia and the place in Sussex and inviting important people to dinner and going to grand parties in chauffeur-driven cars. According to her I was still a barrow-boy from the slums and damn lucky to be married to the daughter of a Whitehall panjandrum with a knighthood; and if I wanted more from her than I was getting I could damn well think again.'

Was this portrait of the marriage true? It sounded more like a glib invention by someone who had read too many cheap novels. This was the first she had heard of the fish and chip shop. Till now he had given out that his family background was northern middle-class. Antonia had always figured in the family as an efficient and respectable tycoon's wife. Was this talk of their strained relations a legend, to establish that he was a sexual non-starter as far as Antonia was concerned, and could not possibly be the owner of the watch he had lost in her bed?

'I still don't understand,' she complained. 'If things were as bad as that between you, what was the point of coming?'

'It was because of the children,' he said in a strained voice. 'I tried to arrange to see them at their schools, but Antonia put a stop to that. I came because I had to do something about it.'

Was this the real reason, or a pretext? If Antonia was as promiscuous as he said, he could not be sure that the children were his, so why make such an issue of them? Perhaps he had come to Madeira for some quite different reason.

'I wanted Antonia to see that I wasn't a threat any more,' he explained. 'I'd changed, and if we shared the children the way other divorced couples do, it would work out OK.'

'Would it? How have you changed?'

He looked her straight in the eye. 'Being in prison turns your world upside-down, things that used to seem important like power and fast cars and hob-nobbing with eminent people seem rather futile compared with what really matters.'

'What does really matter, Gerald?'

Still staring hypnotically at her, he said: 'Being at peace with myself. Not being frightened because I've fought dirty with someone who's going to fight dirty back. Not wondering if the Office of Fair Trading will torpedo a big deal that isn't quite legal. Not having to cover up about the fish shop and the gaps in my education. Wanting to make sure my children have a better start in life than I did, and don't make a mess of things by grabbing at things that aren't important.'

If this is an act, it's a good one, Celia thought. Aloud she said: 'Let's talk about the children. It sounds as if you have plans for them.'

'Yes. While I was in prison I took an Open University degree in maths. They're desperately short of mathematics teachers in the schools, I'll have no difficulty in getting a teaching job, but the salary won't be brilliant. I certainly won't be able to afford boarding school fees for the children, and anyway I don't want them to be brought up in that sort of cocoon of privilege. They can live with me and go to state day schools and learn what life is about.'

It sounded fine. But did he really mean it, or was schoolmastering to be a temporary refuge till something less humdrum turned up? 'Are you sure you won't miss the excitement?' she asked. 'You won't try an occasional flutter on the stock exchange? Buy a tobacconist's shop and put in a manager? Then buy another shop till it develops into a chain?'

He gave her an irritated look. 'My poor Celia, you haven't taken on board what I've been saying. I've put all that rabbiting for money behind me, it doesn't mean a thing to me any more.'

He was staring into her eyes with the blazing sincerity of a salesman dealing with a gullible customer. Till a few moments ago, she had been inclined to give him the benefit of the doubt. But now she was not so sure. Perhaps that look was simply a habit he could not shake off, a mannerism ingrained by years of putting dubious propositions across to people. But was it merely a dislikable mannerism? He was just out of prison with no job and no money, why was access to the children so desperately urgent? Had he come to Madeira to murder Antonia? Alternatively, was he the burglar? Perhaps Antonia was holding some document he needed to get himself started again in business. Failing to get it from her before her death, he had broken into the house in search of it, and left chaos behind.

They had been talking against the background of bustle over on the far side of the square, which was a regular stopping point on the taxi drivers' sightseeing circuit. Tourists were being deposited there all the time, to wield their cameras in the ornate rococo church and photograph each other in the little garden overlooking the view of Funchal. Three young people in jeans were active among them, a tall dark boy, rather handsome, a shorter youth with red hair and a pink face, and a plump, jolly-looking girl. They were accosting the tourists and seemingly importuning them to buy something, but what? They were not carrying their wares, or even a leaflet to hand out, and seemed to be having little success.

The tall youth with dark hair was crossing the square towards the bar. He halted at the table where Celia and Gerald were sitting, inside and not on the terrace because of the wind. 'You're English, aren't you? Nice to meet someone from home. I'm Jonathan, mind if I join you for a moment?'

Without waiting for permission he sat down and began to rattle off a sales pitch which sounded well worn with repetition. 'See that apartment building up there, to the left of the church? Marvellous flats with great big balconies, swimming pool, restaurant, and the garden will be fabulous when it's been laid out. Really exclusive, not like those grotty places down on the coast. They're time share, cost you less for a fortnight every year than the return fare from the UK. Have a look, why don't you?'

'I can think of lots of reasons why not,' growled Gerald.

'But it's a brilliant offer, you can't refuse.'

'I can, very easily,' said Celia.

'I know what you're thinking. Time shares have a bad reputation, there are a lot of cowboy firms in the business, but these people are exceptional, they've done marvellous developments in half a dozen countries.'

'We're still not interested,' Gerald growled.

The young man leant forward and became confidential. 'Look, you don't actually have to want one of their horrid little flats. All you have to do is inspect one of them and sit through a demonstration video and drink some rather sweet wine. Come on, it won't do you any harm.'

'Why should we?' asked Celia, intrigued.

'Because I'm doing this on commission, dear. We're three students from Leicester Polytechnic trying to earn our keep, but what they pay us wouldn't keep a rabbit in lettuces. You've got a kind face, dear, have a heart and do us a favour.'

An ingenious idea occurred to her. Here was a way of sparing the children their father's presence for a little longer. 'Why don't you go, Gerald? I must get back, but there's plenty of time before lunch.'

Gerald scowled furiously. Before he could refuse, she added: 'If we arrive at the house together, the children will realise that we've met and discussed them behind their backs.'

He shrugged, and followed the young man across the square

with very bad grace. Celia went back to the house and found that Teresa had taken a telephone message: Lúcio Freitas wished to discuss a matter of business with her, and would call, if that was convenient, late in the afternoon.

'Oh, very well Teresa. Would you be very kind and phone him back? Say I'll be happy to see him if he comes at six.'

Presently the children emerged giggling from the attic bedroom. They had found paints somewhere and painted their faces with cats' whiskers and aggressive markings round the eyes. 'We're tigers,' Peter explained defiantly.

He added that they intended to be tigers during lunch. Celia sympathised with this throwback to the primitive use of warpaint as a ritual defence against evil influences, but wondered how Gerald would react.

He returned from his timeshare experience with a very sour face. 'Celia, that wasn't fair of you. The incompetence of the sales presentation was even worse than the horrible little flats. Where are the children?'

She called them.

'Hullo, you two,' he said when confronted with their stony but bedizened faces. 'What are you, lions? Going to eat up your naughty old father, are you? I don't blame you for wanting to, after I left your mum in the lurch with no house and no money, and got myself sent to prison. I deserve to be torn to pieces by lions, I do really.'

The children did not react. 'I think they're tigers, not lions,' said Celia, trying to ease the tension.

But Gerald seemed to need no help. He was putting up a front of perfect ease, chatting away to the children and assuming the responses that they refused to give. A very funny reminiscence about an invasion by the neighbour's goats at the house in Sussex fell flat. So did his rueful self-reproach for the loss of their home, and with it Sarah's pony and the swimming pool. But he chattered on, in a superbly confident performance which lasted well into lunch. If he can put on a show like this for the children, Celia thought, how do I know he wasn't putting on a very deceitful one for me?

Towards the end of lunch, Sarah broke silence for the first time. Staring at him hard, she said: 'Why did you do it?'

He considered. 'That's a question I've often asked myself. I think towards the end I got a very swollen head. You know, mister big can do anything he wants, he only has to rub Aladdin's lamp and no one can touch him, even if he does something very dodgy it will turn out OK.'

'But why did you get a swollen head?' Sarah persisted.

'You see, when I was very young I thought I was a failure and would have stoogy jobs all my life and earn very little money. But suddenly one thing came right for me and then another, and soon I was making a success of everything I touched. It was like a dream, we had lots of money and you had your pony and there was the swimming pool and that lovely house, and I thought it was all because I'd been very clever. I see now that a lot of it was luck.'

Sarah brooded. 'Was the thing you got put in prison for the first dodgy thing you'd done?'

'No. The others weren't so serious, but when you've done one dodgy thing without being caught, you try again. I did, and things began to go wrong. The magic didn't work, I was afraid of losing the lot and having to give up the house and your pony and nice clothes for your mum and all the fun we were having. I didn't want that to happen, I wanted the dream to go on. That was why I did the pretty awful thing that landed me in prison.'

'I see,' said Sarah, and fell silent.

'Why did you want to know?' he asked.

'I just wondered. Aunt Celia, can we get down now and go and play with Peter's trains?'

Before she could reply Gerald said: 'Yes, but would you do something for me first?'

'What?' Sarah asked, wooden-faced.

'Wash that stuff off your faces and come back and show me. I'd like to see what you and Peter really look like. Will you, please?'

The children consulted each other mutely.

'No!' Peter shouted.

'Let's go and play with your trains, shall we?' said Sarah.

They went, leaving an awkward silence behind them.

Gerald did his best to ignore the setback. 'Sarah's marvellous, isn't she? Straight to the point and no punches pulled.

Peter looked terrified all the time. What's he like when I'm not here?'

'Withdrawn. He plays with his trains to shut the world out. D'you want to join them up there and continue the campaign?'

'What do you think?'

'I'd leave it, if I were you.'

He frowned. 'Keeping me away from them, are you?'

'No, I'm neutral. You can go up there if you want to but I don't advise it. Rushing at them will only make them worse.'

'But I've so little time. Can I stay on for a bit in case they come down?'

Celia considered, then agreed. Unless she found herself having to unmask him as a murderer or a burglar, she was not prepared to block his access to his children, so she settled down to a strained conversation with him.

It had not gone on very long before Bettencourt appeared, taking advantage of his lunch hour at home to bring her papers to sign, and to extend the insurance cover so that she could drive Antonia's car.

'Lúcio Freitas phoned,' she reported. 'He's coming to see me at six. To discuss a matter of business, he says.'

'He probably wants to have a go at you about the levada water. Receive him politely, give him a glass of Madeira and refer him to me.'

'Very well, but what is "levada water"? I may as well know.'

'The levadas are irrigation channels that collect water from the springs up in the mountains and distribute it to farms and gardens lower down. The main ones skirt along the contours of the mountainside almost on the level, and have maintenance paths that a lot of tourists walk for the sake of the views. Leading downwards off them are levadas which fork over and over again to deliver water to a mass of gardens and smallholdings. Each of them has the right to receive water regularly for a certain length of time, and the levadeiros see that they get it by putting stones or clods of earth or old nylons in at the forks to divert the water.'

'And Freitas thinks he's getting too little and the quinta's getting too much?'

'That's right, but the details are very complicated, don't let him bore you with them.' He glanced from her to Gerald and concluded, rightly, that she had had enough of him. 'I'm going back downtown to my office now, Hanbury, if you'd like a lift.'

Gerald could be seen to be wondering whether or not to sit it out and hope the children would come down again. Celia waited, keeping studiously neutral. After a long pause, he admitted defeat and accepted the lift. 'Thanks for the lunch, Celia. May I come back tomorrow?'

'Of course. Lunch again, if you like. You may have better luck.'

When Bettencourt had removed him, she went in search of the children. They were in the attic bedroom with the trains, looking glum. 'Well, that wasn't too awful, was it?' she asked.

'Yes, frightful,' said Sarah. 'He was disgusting. How dare he try to suck up to us after swindling all those people out of their money? Creeping and crawling and wagging his tail at us like a dog saying it's sorry it peed on the carpet.'

'I told you, Mum's name for him was "Satan",' Peter shouted angrily, 'and she was right, that's just what he is.'

'Oh surely,' Celia objected. 'Isn't Satan supposed to be a bit fiercer than that?'

'Not necessarily,' said Sarah. 'The chaplain at school says the devil appears in all sorts of subtle disguises to snatch people's souls. I bet he'd pee on the carpet if he thought he could get our souls that way.'

'You won't make us go and live with Dad, will you, Aunt Celia?' Peter pleaded.

'Not if you don't want to. But I think he's fond of you.'

'We're not fond of him,' Sarah objected. 'So why should we? We'd much rather come and live with you.'

'I expect you can, if you're good,' said Celia, who had already decided that this was the only viable solution to the problem of their future.

To celebrate this announcement they rushed downstairs and out into the garden, where they worked off energy catching the flowers which the wind was blowing to the ground from the silk trees. Celia went into the study for another attack on the papers in Antonia's desk. She had an uneasy feeling that Antonia had left bills unpaid, and after an hour spent poring over bank statements this suspicion was amply confirmed.

The wind was blowing from the north. It was funnelled along the gullies running from the mountain-peaks down to the sea, gathering force all the time. In one of these gullies it bore down with such strength on the western approach to the runway at Santa Cruz airport that it could have caught the tail of a plane coming in to land and blown it off course. Shortly after dawn, the air traffic controllers had closed the airport and stranded hosts of returning package tourists. According to the hall porter at the Savoy, the north wind was capable of keeping the airport closed for days on end.

This was bad news for Barton and Fernandes. It meant an indefinite delay in the arrival of the reinforcements promised by head office. When they protested that this made their task impossible, head office had blown its top. Did they not realise how urgent the operation had become? They were to stop bellyaching and get on with it. If necessary, they were to recruit local talent as a temporary measure to help them out.

But what local talent was there?

For lack of any other lead to follow, they had resumed their vigil in the banana plantation opposite the entrance to the Quinta Coulson. They had made only one addition to their portrait gallery, a shot of a middle-aged man in slacks and a T-shirt, who arrived at the quinta at lunch-time. But there was still no sign of Maria-José, and Barton was becoming increasingly foul-mouthed and restive.

'So we make some inquiries among the neighbours,' Fernandes suggested, 'and they tell us if she is here.'

'No. Fucking yakking neighbours. They'd talk, she'd get to know and take fright.'

'If she is not here she does not take fright and we waste our time.'

They argued about it. Fernandes pointed out that their activities were already attracting unwelcome interest. Several passers-by had eyed them curiously as they loitered in the lane, waiting to lift the gate of the banana plantation off its hinges as soon as the coast was clear. A small boy, hearing noises among the banana trees, had peered in through the gate, fortunately without seeing them. But he called several other boys, who also craned their necks through the gate and shouted rude remarks in Portuguese. Persuaded that their observation post was becoming untenable, Barton agreed in the end to adjourn.

They had left their hire-car in the square, which was in a state of even more bustle than usual as tourists driven from the lidos and swimming pools by the wind took to sightseeing instead. Three young touts, two men and a girl, were peddling something among them. As Barton crossed the square with Fernandes in tow, the taller of the two men accosted him. 'Hi, you're American aren't you? I'm Jonathan, nice to meet someone from the States.'

Barton was too out of temper to confirm or deny that he was American, though the passports he possessed under various false names all boasted the bald eagle. Jonathan embarked at once on his sales pitch. 'See that apartment building up there to the left of the church? Marvellous flats with great big balconies, swimming pool, restaurant, and the garden will be fabulous when it's been laid out. They're time share, very good value, but you'd need to hurry, there are lots after them. Why don't you come up and have a look?'

'Go away, we're busy,' said Fernandes coldly.

'It won't take a moment. You'll be missing a marvellous bargain if you don't.'

The words 'fuck off' hovered on Barton's lips, but he had had an idea and suppressed them. 'How much do they pay you, Jonathan, for each punter you bring in?'

'Five hundred measly escudos. The developers' rep in London said it was money for jam in the sunshine, but it's starvation, mister.'

'You here in the square every day?'

'Every damn day. It's a bad pitch, the time share public wants to be down among the noise and exhaust fumes on the coast road where the action is.'

Barton produced a snapshot from his pocket book. 'You seen this girl around here?'

'Sure. Lots of times.'

'That on the level? This is important, don't feed me crap.'

'It's not crap, mister. The cat that walks by itself, that's her. If you wolf-whistle at her she takes no notice, walks straight on

90

with a face like murder, as if she'd seen the devil. We think she's half mad.'

'She live round here?'

'Down that lane somewhere.'

He was pointing in the direction of the Quinta Coulson. Barton and Fernandes exchanged triumphant glances. They were on the right track after all. Another thing. Head office had told them to hire local talent to help them out, and here, surely, was local talent right on the spot where it was needed.

'Want to earn some real money, you and your mates?' Barton asked.

Jonathan's eyes lit up. 'Tell me more.'

'OK, call them and we'll go sit in the car, talk about it.'

Lúcio Freitas arrived punctually at the quinta to keep his appointment. As if to mark the fact that this was a formal business occasion, he was in the Sunday best which he had worn at the cemetery, and there was the same note of menace in his black boot-button eyes. As advised by Bettencourt, she offered him a glass of what she hoped was Madeira from a decanter on the dining-room sideboard. When they had settled down in the grand drawing-room, he inquired into her impressions of the island. When she had invented some for him, he said: 'So you like our countree. But you will not stay here in this beauteeful house, that's sad.'

'How d'you know I'm not going to?'

'I am friends, you see, with Agostinho and Teresa. They tell me you have business in England, and cannot stay.'

'That's quite correct, I have to get back there as soon as I can. So shall we get down to business now? Mr Bettencourt says you have some query about the levada water.'

He looked shocked. 'Oh no, that was stupid, a leetle misunderstandeeng that I had with Meeses Hanbury, eet is forgotten long ago. What I ask you now is much more seerious. If you are not here, Sir Morton cannot be here alone. He too must go, eesn't it so?'

'Didn't Teresa tell you? I'm hoping to make arrangements so that he can stay.'

He waved this aside. 'Senhora, I make you a good offer to buy the queenta.'

She was astonished. If he could afford to buy it, whatever he did in South Africa must have been very profitable.

'It belongs to Mrs Hanbury's children,' she explained. 'I shall probably let it. Then they can decide what to do with it when they come of age.'

'No, that is not wise. The tenants, they complain because the plumbing is blocked, they neglect the garden, if you leave the furneeture they break it, they do not pay the rent. You sell me the queenta, I surprise you with the price I pay. You invest the money and you get a veree good return and no bother with the tenants.'

She was still bewildered. Did he really intend to abandon his hovel in the banana patch and install himself in the Quinta Coulson? 'If you don't mind my asking, Mr Freitas, what would you do with the place if you bought it?'

'Aha, I tell you. I turn eet into very small, very swish hotel. You see, the beeg hotels down by the sea, the palaces with the creestal chandeliers and the marble stairs, they are for the leetle people who come to them on cheap package tours and think they have the luxury and the elegance. The travellers with the taste and money, they say that is not for us, we want something better. For them one must provide the seelect atmosphere, the surroundings of true eleegance, the sophisticated cooking. At the queenta, I give them those things. You see, I was hotel manager in Cape Town.'

Despite herself, Celia was impressed. 'It sounds a very good idea, but I don't intend selling.'

'Perhaps later you change your mind. And please, do not speak to anyone about it, there are neebours who would make diffeeculties for me if they knew. Let it be a secret between us, yes?'

Suddenly he was sitting forward in his chair urgently with his eyes boring into her face. As he reached out a hand towards her, she realised with a shock that he was trying to turn what had been a business conversation into a sexual encounter. It was a ridiculous situation. She pulled back hastily in disgust, but he was not easily discouraged. In seconds he was on the settee beside her with his hand on her knee.

She let it stay there for a long moment: not because she was tempted, but because she was staring at something she had not noticed till now: the flashy gold-plated watch and armband on his wrist. It had a sweep second hand, and the hours were marked with blobs of something black and cheap-looking. Was it the one? It looked very like it.

Convinced that he was about to make a conquest, he moved the hand gently upwards. She brushed it off and stood up in horror.

'Don't be afraid,' he murmured. 'I will be veree gentle and no one will ever know.'

'I'm not afraid, only disgusted, Mr Freitas.'

He looked as if he knew better. 'You are not disgusted, senhora. You are perhaps afraid, but there is no reason.'

'Your itchy fingers won't persuade me to sell you the house, so please stop this nonsense and go.'

'I go, but we think about each other, yes?'

'No. As far as you're concerned, my mind is a total blank. I don't go in for casual sex, and if I did, I wouldn't want it with you.'

She hustled him out of the house, then ran up to Antonia's room. She was right, the watch at the bottom of the bed had gone.

SIX

Amid the conflicting emotions in Celia's mind, embarrassment was uppermost. Fascinated by the sight of the incriminating wrist-watch, she had let Freitas' hand wander about her person for far too long, then dismissed him in a flurry of agitation which had probably convinced him that she would flop into his arms without a struggle if he laid siege to her again. Somehow he must be disabused, and meanwhile there was another problem. How had the watch got out of Antonia's bed and back on his wrist?

Had he crept into the house and up to Antonia's bedroom to retrieve it? Unlikely, even if he had a key. After the burglary yesterday she had checked that the watch was there, and since then the house had never been empty. Even if he had sneaked in while they were all asleep he would have been lucky to avoid the time when the whole household was awake and in an uproar about Sir Adrian's stomach upset.

Did he have a key? If so, was he Antonia's murderer? He had the opportunity, but what was his motive? He wanted the quinta badly, but would killing its owner help? He might have thought so, if he knew enough about the family to calculate that Antonia's death would leave the place open to an offer. But what were the chances of the offer being taken up? He would have to be wildly optimistic to think it worth risking murder. Sleeping with her was another matter. It was to his advantage, because it would seal their bargain. He would supply the money, she would supply the house.

Suddenly Antonia's strange-seeming financial transactions made sense. This was why she had expelled her father to the bottom of the garden at considerable cost, and persuaded him to make the house over to her. She had intended either to sell it to Freitas, or to go into hotel-keeping partnership with him. Either way she would get what she lacked and clearly longed for: a settled source of income.

But how had the watch got back on to Freitas' wrist? Teresa was the obvious suspect. She and Agostinho were friends of his, perhaps allies in his plans for the hotel. Had he asked Teresa to retrieve the watch for him? If so, why had she not done so much earlier, before Celia and the children arrived on the scene? She went to the top of the stairs and summoned Teresa, then stood at the foot of Antonia's bed in accusing silence.

'Senhora?'

'There is something missing from here, Teresa.'

Teresa bridled, and proclaimed at great length that in her long years of service at the quinta, she had never been accused of theft.

Celia interrupted her protests. 'I'm not accusing you of theft, Teresa. What you did was to return the thing that's missing to its owner.'

Shocked, Teresa put a hand to her mouth, but said nothing.

'I'm not angry, you did it to protect Mrs Hanbury's reputation, is that right?'

She relaxed, and nodded vigorously. 'Lúcio, he told me, I am ashamed. I amuse myself with her and now she is dead. If her family find it there, they think bad things about her, and it make me even more ashamed. Please, Teresa, he say. Look for it and give me it back.'

'When did he ask you to look for it?'

'On the day when Mrs Hanbury, she died. In the evening.'

'But it was still there when I got here, two days later.'

'Because I could not find. I look everywhere. I tell him he makes a mistake, it is in some other place. He says no, it is there, look again. And I think today to look in the end of the bed, and I find it.'

'And how long had Mr Freitas been "amusing himself" with Mrs Hanbury?'

Teresa shrugged. 'Two months, perhaps longer. It is not easy for me to know.' After a pause, she asked timidly: 'Will the senhora sell the quinta to Lúcio?'

'No. I told you. It will be let till the children come of age.'

95

Teresa's face was wooden, showing neither pleasure nor displeasure. She made no comment.

It was time for the bombshell question. She put it as casually as she could. 'Did Mr Freitas have a key to the house?'

A glint of terror appeared in Teresa's eyes. She had grasped the import of the question at once. 'No, *minha senhora*. I swear it. He had no key.'

Celia dismissed her, and was about to return to Antonia's bank statements when a startling new insight hit her like a shock wave: she had been brutally unfair to Gerald, largely because he had no wrist-watch. Convinced that the explanation was sinister, she had been assuming that he was dishonest to the core and had been lying to her like a trooper. But as the watch belonged to Freitas, Gerald's claim to have sold an Omega to buy his air ticket must be true, and her estimate of him needed revision. She felt very guilty about some of the things she had thought about him.

As she settled down again to investigate Antonia's confused financial arrangements, the doorbell rang. Presently Teresa appeared, escorting a shrivelled old man with glasses and a pinched mouth, and a thin woman in the same age group, dressed in a dark vicarage-style print dress with a white collar. The astonishment on Teresa's face was explained when the pair introduced themselves as George Whiting, whose clan was in feud with the adherents of Sir Adrian, and his wife Ellen.

'I haven't been in this house for – what, Ellen? Seven, eight years?' he announced, looking round.

'Nine,' said his wife primly.

'And I wouldn't have come if I didn't have to, but it's urgent. You're Mrs Hanbury's executor, Mrs Grant, am I right? And I believe you had a visit this evening from a nasty little neighbour of ours called Freitas.'

'Yes, how did you know?' said Celia.

'I have my spies out. You need them on this island, especially in this neighbourhood. Did the little runt offer to buy the quinta? Ah, I see that he did. How much?'

'He didn't mention a figure, because I told him it wasn't for sale.'

'Oh, good show,' said Whiting.

'Quite right,' echoed his wife.

96

Celia asked why they wanted to know.

'Freitas is up to no good,' said Ellen Whiting, opening and shutting her mouth with a snap.

'Oh? In what way?'

'He's been buying up land all round us,' Whiting explained. 'Not under his own name, he's too clever for that. But three banana groves with little peasant houses on them have fallen in over the past year, old people dying and so on, and if you go to the *Conservatório de Registo* you find that one of them's registered in the name of an uncle of his, and the other two by cousins. The other day an old couple died in a tumbledown little cottage alongside my place, and guess who owns it now, according to the *registo*. The gardener here, Agostinho.'

Celia was surprised, but also puzzled. 'If Freitas is the real owner, why does he need to use friends and relatives as nominees?'

'You can't use firms as nominees here, you have to put things in the names of relatives if you don't want people to know what you're up to.'

'But can't they do the dirty on you and sell?'

'Of course. You have to offer them a cut.'

'But . . . a cut in what, Mr Whiting?'

'Ah. We thought at first that he was in partnership with a builder to put up little villas. But it isn't that, he's assembled a parcel of land big enough to erect a biggish hotel, which would block out the view for all of us behind it.'

'In that case, why does he want to buy this house?'

'Access. The only entry to the land is through an alley between properties he can't buy. It's barely wide enough for one car. The quinta gives him a way out into a quiet road, and there's another advantage for him. If he says he's preserving a beautiful old house by building bedrooms on at the back and turning it into a hotel, the planning authorities will find it quite difficult to say no.'

'But in fact none of this arises,' said Celia, 'because we're going to let the house till the children are of age. Then they can decide what to do with it.'

'Good. Splendid,' said Whiting. 'You've taken a weight off our minds, eh Ellen?'

'Yes, but she needs to watch Freitas. He may have some nasty tricks up his sleeve.'

'Such as what?' Celia asked her.

'He could burn the place down and buy the site,' Ellen suggested primly.

'Yes, I should insure it very heavily if I were you,' said Whiting, and rose to go. 'How is Sir Adrian? Very distressed, I suppose, by the loss of his daughter. I'd ask you to give him my regards and condolences, but he wouldn't thank me for them.'

'He and George are not on speaking terms,' Ellen explained. 'There was an unfortunate misunderstanding.'

'But I'm looking forward to reading his memoirs,' said Whiting eagerly. 'D'you know when they're coming out?'

'No. There's no mention of them in the papers I've been going through.'

'Really? I wonder why not.' He looked strangely disconcerted, as if her failure to announce a publication date was a piece of culpable incompetence. Then he pulled himself together with an effort. 'Well, goodbye, Mrs Grant, and thank you for taking a great weight off our minds.'

Next morning the wind had dropped and the airport was open, to the relief of the stranded package tourists. Barton and Fernandes were also relieved. Much-needed reinforcements from head office, held up for twenty-four hours in Lisbon, would soon be on the way.

'We're bored, Aunt Celia,' said Sarah soon after breakfast. 'What can we do?'

What indeed? Celia thought. Having been asked the same question at intervals since they arrived from England she was beginning to run out of answers. Her eye, ranging round the drawing-room in search of inspiration, was caught by a Georgian mahogany wine-cooler which was being used as a jardinière for pot-plants. It contained a mass of bright pink *Begonia ingramii* surrounded by ferns. They looked very dry. The last person to water them must have been Antonia. An occupation for the children suggested itself. The wind had fallen, it was a beautiful day. They could take these poor parched pot-plants out on to the terrace for an airing and water them.

As Peter and Sarah carried the plants out through the French windows, Celia realised that something about the wine-cooler was odd, though this had not been obvious when it was full of flowers and foliage. The zinc lining stuck up slightly above the edge of the mahogany case. Why? Normally, the rim of the metal lining would not even be flush with the wooden outer rim, but well below it. She investigated. On lifting out the lining she saw at once why it had not settled down properly. Something wrapped in a black plastic bag had been stashed away underneath it.

As she made this discovery Sarah, abandoning the watering-can to Peter, came back in through the French windows. 'What's that, Aunt Celia?'

'I don't know. Let's look.'

In the plastic bag was a manila envelope, which she opened. It contained a wad of typescript, with a title page which read: *Counterspy: The memoirs of Sir Adrian Morton, former Deputy Head of MI5*.

'It's a book by your grandfather.'

'Oh, goody, is it all about spies and how clever he was at catching them? That was his job, but we weren't supposed to say so. Is it going to be published?'

'I don't know. But wait. Here's a letter.'

It was from an august firm of London publishers, and dated two years back, before Adrian had his stroke:

Dear Sir Adrian,

Thank you for letting us see the typescript of your memoirs.

Our reader reports that although some of the incidents you relate are interesting and amusingly told, there is little or no fresh material about the various causes célèbres which occurred during your period of office. The references to George Blake have of course been outdated by recent revelations, and the mass of administrative detail about the organisation of the service, though probably useful to historians of MI5, would not interest the general public.

In short, we have had to conclude that the book would not command a wide sale, and it is with great regret that we return your typescript herewith.

Celia conveyed the sense of this to Sarah, who asked where she had found the typescript.

'Under the plants in the plant stand.'

'Why was it hidden there?'

'I've no idea.'

'Who hid it there, Mum?'

'I suppose so, if she wanted it to be safe. Her desk doesn't lock.'

'Why wouldn't she want anyone to see it?'

'I can't imagine, but Freda Bettencourt says it's "very hot stuff", and someone seems to have broken into the house to look for it.'

'The publishers don't think it's hot stuff,' Sarah objected.

'Well, there's only one way to find out who's right.'

'I know,' said Sarah. 'Come on, let's read it and see.'

'Very well, but where's Peter?'

'Back upstairs, drooling over his trains. It's very morbid, but I've given up the struggle.'

They settled down to read, with Celia passing the pages to Sarah as she finished them. She soon saw why the publishers had shied away from them. The backbone of the book was a painstaking account of the administration of MI5 and the way the organisation had developed during Adrian's period of office. He had enlivened it with character sketches of colleagues, none of them very unkind, and amusing anecdotes, including several about occasions when the counter-spying effort had gone amusingly wrong. As far as she could see there was nothing that officials concerned with national security would want to suppress, and no reason why anyone else should be interested. Why on earth had some unknown person ransacked the house in search of this mass of far from deathless prose? Or was it something else they were looking for?

Halfway through the typescript Sarah groaned. 'I give up. This is dead boring, worse than the Hundred Years War with Miss Murgatroyd. I think I'll go upstairs and get out all my dolls and burn them in the garden.'

'Really? You're sure you don't want them any more?'

'I outgrew them ages ago, but it's not just that. Mum had funny names for them all, and I don't want to be reminded.' After a moment of sadness, she broke into an impish grin. 'Peter can

100

help, he needs taking out of himself. We can fantasise about the Spanish Inquisition.'

Celia remembered suddenly that she had a guilty secret to confess. 'I meant to tell you. Your father's coming to lunch.'

Sarah was horrified. 'Again? Oh no!'

'I'm sorry, but how can I keep him away? He's entitled to see you, and if he didn't come here I'd have to let him take you off on his own.'

But Sarah would not listen. 'It's not fair! You shouldn't have done it! Peter will have a fit.'

'Do calm down, there's no need for anyone to have a fit. Don't you think you're being a bit unkind to your father? He's unhappy, he's been in prison, you're all he's got by way of family. You don't have to live with him if you don't want to, but do you really have to have hysterics because he wants to wield his knife and fork in your presence?'

'OK, but tell Teresa to lay great big ladles from the kitchen for Peter and me.'

Celia saw what was coming, but decided not to spoil what was intended to be a triumphant exit line.

When you lunch with the devil,' said Sarah with dignity, 'you need a very long spoon.'

Gerald arrived in due course and seemed very unsure of himself. 'Yesterday was a bit of a disaster. I hope it goes better today.'

'The signs aren't good, I'm afraid. Try not to pressurise them.'

'I'm not sure what you mean.'

'In your place, I'd take as little direct notice of them as possible. You're lunching with me. They're just a couple of children who happen to be there.'

He nodded, but looked unconvinced.

Teresa, sent to tell Peter and Sarah that lunch was ready, came back with a long face. 'The children, they say they not hungry, they are not wanting to come and eat.'

'Oh nonsense,' said Celia. 'Where are they?'

'In the little room where they have the trains.'

'I'll go and talk to them.'

'They lock the door,' said Teresa, and looked daggers at Gerald before retreating to the kitchen.

Outside the locked door, Celia fared no better. Her pleas were

101

met at first by silence, then by cries in chorus of 'No! No! No! We won't come down!'

Admitting defeat, she went back to Gerald, who was furious. 'This is your fault, damn you.'

'Oh really, what d'you expect me to do, break down the door?'

'I expect you not to poison their minds against me. No, don't interrupt, it's no use you denying it. Bettencourt says you're applying for custody, to get them away from me. I'll see you in hell first.'

Celia rose.

'Where are you going?' he growled.

'To wash. Lunch is ready.'

'It would choke me.'

'In your present state, you're not going to get any. Either go, or walk round the garden and calm down till you're in a fit state to eat. We will then attempt to discuss the problem of the children's future sensibly and without shouting.'

In the dining room Teresa was removing the children's place settings with a look of suppressed relish at high drama. 'And this one?' she queried with her hand hovering over Gerald's place.

'No, leave it. But if he hasn't appeared in five minutes, you can take it away and serve the soup.'

Gerald beat the soup to it by thirty seconds. 'Celia, I'm sorry. I don't know what came over me.'

'That's all right, I don't blame you for being a bit tense. But let's get one thing clear. I'm neutral, I'm not trying to come between you and the children. I'll cope with them if that's the only tolerable solution, but my cottage is too small for three and I'd have to move, which would be a hellish nuisance. I'm applying for guardianship because they're terrified of you and in the short term there's no alternative. If you can stop them disliking you, you're very welcome to them. But as I've told you before, you're going quite the wrong way about it.'

'You think I should lay off them for a bit? Is that it?'

'Yes. Their mother's been dead for less than a week. Don't rush them.'

'I suppose you're right in theory. But they were the one thing that kept me sane in prison, it's a gut thing, I can't help it.'

'Gut things aren't always the best guide when it comes to dealing with children. Why don't you go home and be sensible, and ring me at Archerscroft early next month?'

Their discussion of this suggestion went on right through lunch, with Gerald ignoring the food, then gulping it in sudden bursts of agitation. There were calm moments when he seemed willing to take her advice, but also fits of angry defiance, when he cursed Antonia for turning the children against him and said he would never rest till her handiwork was undone. It was as if the power drive that had made him a maverick financier had been redirected into his affection for his children. Both impulses struck Celia as slightly insane.

'Well, what have you decided to do?' she asked when he rose to go.

'I don't know, Celia. I really don't know.'

When he had gone, the children came out of hiding. 'Can we have our lunch now?' said Peter.

'You don't deserve any after being so silly.'

'But we're emotionally upset and starving,' Sarah protested.

'I dare say you are, but Teresa's gone home to cook lunch for herself and Agostinho. I'll see what I can find.'

'The ideal remedy for emotional disturbance,' said Sarah, 'is ice-cream.'

Having inflicted Gerald on them twice, Celia was feeling guilty and allowed herself to be blackmailed. 'Oh very well,' she said gruffly. 'Come along.'

Their route to the ice-cream parlour took them along the footpath which skirted the lower boundary of the quinta's garden. Rounding a corner, they came suddenly on Jonathan from the time share sales team and his red-haired colleague. They seemed to be making a minute examination of the quinta's wire fence, but sprang away from it guiltily when they caught sight of Celia. She was puzzled. They were living on a shoestring, were they perhaps looking for some way of breaking in? And what did they hope to steal from Adrian's cottage if they succeeded? Suddenly she felt threatened, but could not imagine why. Before she could question them, they brushed roughly past her and were gone.

Having performed prodigies of consumption in the ice-cream parlour, the children involved Celia in a game of leap-frog on the lawn of the quinta to work off their surplus energy. She was presenting her backside to them when Teresa came hurrying out of the house to announce that the Senhora Fuller had come to call. Her shocked expression underlined the fact that leap-frog was the last thing one should be found doing when a lady who belonged at the very top of Madeira's pecking-order came to call.

Winifred Fuller was sitting in the drawing-room, as impeccably turned out as she had been at the funeral.

'Hello, my dear,' she began, ignoring Celia's heated and dishevelled state. 'Who's going to be those children's guardian, not that shocker of a husband, I hope?'

'It's not been settled yet. There's nothing about it in Antonia's will.'

'Typical of her, she was such a scatterbrain. Don't let him get them will you?'

'I'll do my best. The children can't stand him, but he's being very insistent.'

'You told me you wanted someone to give Maria a hand and back her up. I've a suggestion, a very nice woman who's had awful bad luck with husbands, they kept dying on her like flies and leaving her very little money. There's no replacement husband in sight, and she needs work. Here's her address and phone number, do ring her. I've sounded her out and I'm sure you'll like her.'

After supplying a few biographical details of the much-widowed lady, she turned to wider questions. 'You've decided definitely not to sell this house?'

'Not if I can let it till the children come of age.'

'Bravo. If you did some shark of a speculator would buy it and pull it down and build horrible little bungalows on the site for retired pork butchers from Blackpool to make pigs of themselves in.'

Celia explained that she had already been approached by one speculator who had bought up a lot of land round the quinta, and wanted to build a hotel.

'Oh, who? I know most of the caddish developers on the island.'

'A man called Lúcio Freitas. He owns a peasant holding next door.'

'Never heard of him. Was he really naïve enough to blurt out his obscene intentions, instead of springing a nasty surprise at the last moment like they all do?'

'No, someone else told me what he was up to. A man called Whiting, who lives just up the hill.'

Mrs Fuller's eyes opened wide in amazement. 'George Whiting broke the taboo? What was he doing, consorting with the enemy?'

'He called here to beg me not to sell to Freitas.'

'That explains it. You know he and Adrian didn't get on.'

'Yes, but no one can tell me what started it.'

'I can, and I love gossip. Shall I brief you?'

'Yes please.'

'You see, Whiting came here to retire a few years before Adrian did. He had one or two introductions, and he and his wife were wined and dined a bit. You know how it is in a small expatriate community, after the umpteenth drinks party with the same people you say hooray, a new face. The wife turned out to be a common little thing, but he was good value to talk to because it appeared that he'd been a big shot in the anti-spy set up, what's it called?'

'MI5, I think.'

'That's right, and he had a whole raft of stories about successful cases he'd been in charge of and disasters that had happened because someone else was in charge, like that Spycatcher man who made out that everyone except himself was pretty incompetent. At the time when he bought the bungalow up behind you, Adrian and Julia weren't here. They'd put tenants in to keep the place occupied while he was still working in London. So Whiting didn't realise that he'd elected to spend the evening of his days in the back yard of a man who really was a big shot in MI5.

'When it was Adrian's turn to retire, he and Julia turned the tenants out and settled down here. In a closed community like this anything you say is repeated to everyone else in a flash, so it didn't take Adrian long to realise that Whiting was not only talking about things he shouldn't, but telling a lot of lies which were bringing his precious service into disrepute. This shocked Adrian dreadfully, he's always been as silent as the grave about what he did for a living. I don't think even Julia knew the details, though we all realised that he hadn't got his K for sticking stamps on to envelopes. Anyway, the whole thing blew up into an ugly scene at a party, New Year's Eve I think it was. Whiting started to reminisce to Adrian in front of a lot of people about their days with what he called "the old firm", trying to imply that he and Adrian were buddies and not far apart in seniority. Adrian erupted like a volcano, and told him in no uncertain terms to shut up, because he was talking out of turn.

'That left Whiting looking pretty silly, and he made himself look even sillier by spreading it around that Adrian had been a disaster as Deputy Head or whatever it was; that he'd blocked every sensible suggestion that came up from below, and was personally responsible for various fiascos that had occurred during his jumped-up period of office. Naturally this got round to Adrian, who went to see the wretched man and told him that if he didn't shut up, he, Adrian, would make public one story about Whiting's MI5 career which was so discreditable that he'd probably have to leave the island.'

'Did Adrian tell you the details?' Celia asked.

'No, he was his usual discreet self. But the story must have been pretty horrific, because Whiting shut up about his MI5 career like a clam. By that time everyone that mattered had dropped him, but he collected various rather common newcomers from England, mostly neighbours of his whom nobody wanted to know, and persuaded them that they were all being excluded from Madeiran high society through the baleful influence of that arrant snob Sir Adrian Morton.'

Celia thought for a moment. 'There's one thing that rather surprises me. You described Mrs Whiting as "a common little thing". She struck me as very prim and churchy, but not necessarily common.'

'She was at the start. When she arrived she was a peroxide blonde with a little-girl giggle and a cockney accent and her clothes were all wrong, bright red dinner dresses with sequins on, that sort of thing. Over the years she's toned herself down and got rid of the accent and as you say, she's become a pillar of the Anglican Church here, probably for social rather than religious reasons.'

'And when did all this happen?' Celia asked.

'Ten years ago at least. The feud still carries on, but most of the people involved don't know what started it, or if they did they've forgotten. And now, if you don't mind giving me an arm down all those hellish steps, I'll look in on poor old Adrian.'

Celia helped her down the terraces and the two old friends settled down for a one-sided chat, in which the old lady brought him up to date with local news. Seeing no reason to make a third, Celia went back up the slope and found herself facing a new riddle: what was the discreditable story of Sir Adrian's that made George Whiting shut up? Was it in the memoirs? They were discreet to the point of boredom. The name of an individual was always withheld if the story about him was embarrassing. Yet Antonia had thought it necessary to hide the typescript where it would be safe from the burglary that she seemed to expect, and which had in fact occurred. If the burglar's aim was indeed to steal the memoirs, then George Whiting was the obvious candidate. He had the opportunity, the break-in had happened during the funeral, from which he had been conspicuously absent. In view of his strained relations with Sir Adrian, he might well have feared that the typescript would contain revelations to his discredit.

It was locked up in her suitcase for safety. She went back indoors, retrieved it, and settled down with it in a long chair under the jacaranda tree to reread it in the light of Mrs Fuller's revelations. But the second reading brought no new insights, and presently Mrs Fuller appeared from below on Maria's arm.

Celia escorted her to the door in the wall. Her chauffeur-driven car was waiting outside. About to climb into it, she paused. 'I'm so glad you're not selling. The barbarian hordes are ruining Madeira, it's up to people like us to keep the flag flying and fight back. They should never have built that airport. The people who came by ship used to dress for dinner and knew how to behave.'

As they talked, a young woman standing a little way up the lane started photographing a *Bignonia unguis-cati* which was spilling its yellow flowers over the wall of the quinta into the lane.

'Oh dear,' said Mrs Fuller. 'My ugly car and I are in the way. Hold your fire for a moment, we're just off.'

She climbed in and drove away.

'It's fantastic, a real dream,' said the girl, aiming the camera at the bignonia.'D'you know what it's called?'

'I think it's usually known as a cat's claw vine,' said Celia, deciding not to weigh in heavily with Latin.

'Fantastic,' the girl repeated, snapping away.

Celia had seen the girl before, she was a member of the time share selling team. Something about the way she was aiming the camera worried her. Again, she felt threatened but did not know why.

Ignoring the children's demands for more horseplay, she went back to Adrian's memoirs and persevered till she reached a passage that had stuck in her mind. Deciding that one of the minor mysteries might as well be cleared up at once, she rang George Whiting.

'Last night you asked me what was happening about Sir Adrian's memoirs. I thought you'd be interested to know that the typescript has turned up.'

He sounded nervous. 'Where was it?'

'In a place where it hadn't occurred to me to look. There's one chapter that might interest you, would you like to come round and see?'

He was with her five minutes later, without his wife but in such a sweat of anxiety that his hands were trembling. She held the typescript out to him, open. 'This is the bit I thought you'd like to look at.'

He took it, and read avidly:

One night in 1972, just before Christmas, I was woken by the duty officer, who was in such fits of laughter that he had difficulty in making his report. When he was able to speak, he explained that two of our operatives had gone to a house in the East End of London to question an Irishman thought to have IRA connections who was known to be living there. The suspect did not correspond to the description of him they had been given, and was moreover in bed with a woman. Undeterred, they gave him and his bedmate a rough going-over in the hope of extracting a confession. Only when they had dislocated the suspect's arm and given him a black eye, and made the woman stand naked in front of them while they interrogated her, did they discover that they had gone to the wrong house and surprised a prostitute in bed with a client.

It fell to me to smooth matters over. Fortunately, the client was a respectable businessman from the North of England whose wife thought he was at a conference in Bournemouth. He was disinclined to make a fuss, but pacifying the lady was a different matter. There was talk of lawsuits. In the end we had to pay her an alarmingly large sum by way of compensation in order to prevent the story from becoming public knowledge.

After the settlement with her had been reached, we discovered that the operative responsible for bungling the operation was on intimate terms with the lady. In exchange for her favours, he had been using his inside knowledge of the negotiations to help her extract the largest possible sum from us. We were still far from convinced that she would refrain from causing us embarrassing publicity. But by then the operative in question, whose previous record was far from brilliant, was under notice of dismissal, and the question of his pension rights gave us some leverage. Moreover the lady seemed to have hankerings after a life of respectability. So we agreed to pay him his pension provided he married her, calculating that if they wished to figure as sober and worthy members of society, they would keep quiet about their misadventure. A bargain along these lines was sealed, and they departed to enjoy a prosperous retirement on his small pension and the much larger sum awarded to her as compensation.

'Your name isn't mentioned,' said Celia gently. 'I suppose Antonia told you it was, but Sir Adrian wasn't that sort of man. On the few occasions when he has to say something unpleasant, he doesn't tell who the person was.'

Whiting was red in the face and seemed to be working himself up for an indignant denial that the story was about him. Before he could commit himself to this line she added: 'Fifty thousand escudos a month, wasn't that it?'

'Yes!' he burst out. 'How did you know?'

'Antonia's bank statements made me suspect that she was a blackmailer.'

'Oh, damn and blast Mrs Hanbury.'

'She must have read the book and got your name out of her father. It started about a year ago, am I right?'

'What she told me was, there was a whole chapter about me and Ellen, mentioning our names, and he'd made it sound very funny. And she said having a full-time nurse for him was costing her a lot, so she was thinking of making both ends meet by accepting an offer she'd had from a publisher. But if I didn't want the book published I could help her with her expenses instead.' He looked at her anxiously. 'What's going to happen now?'

'Nothing. I shan't talk, and the book's not going to be published. Look at this.' She handed him the publishers' letter to calm him down.

'Where did you find the typescript?'

'In a rather clever hiding-place that you didn't find when you turned the house upside-down during the funeral.'

He reddened again, and said nothing.

'I don't blame you, Mr Whiting, and I shan't report you to the police or anything silly like that. You made rather a mess, but you didn't steal anything, and I quite realise that you were acting to protect your wife's reputation. But I'd like to know for my own peace of mind. It was you, wasn't it?'

'I was afraid you'd find the thing and try to get it published.'

'And you arranged with Freda Bettencourt to "forget" about arranging to have the house guarded? Why did she agree to make sure you had a clear field?'

'She's been on our side for some time.'

'In your quarrel with Adrian?'

'And with the whole Quinta Coulson clique. When you've worked in intelligence like me, you like to keep your hand in, and I try to have a few spies in the enemy camp. Ellen picked up a bit of gossip somewhere about the Bettencourts' marriage, and recruited her over coffee after morning service at the Anglican church.'

'The gossip being news of her husband's affair with Antonia?'

'That was what "turned" her, yes. I told her at once that Morton had written his memoirs before he had his stroke, and put in some very spiteful stories about me because I'd had the impertinence to quarrel with him; so would she please keep her ears open for any mention of plans to publish them. Then when Antonia died I put

110

it to her that if the manuscript was left lying about in the house, someone might send it to a publisher and make me look a fool.'

He sighed. 'I have been a fool too, paying all that money into a mare's nest. She knew I'd got more than my service pension because of what Morton says in the book about the compensation they paid to Ellen. And my God, she squeezed me hard.'

He went, and Celia crossed off one minor mystery as cleared up. But a major one remained. Whiting had an overpoweringly strong motive for killing Antonia.

She was on her way up to bed when the telephone rang. 'Celia? Gerald here. Sorry to bother you so late, but something awkward's happened. I'm being turned out of my grotty little flat.'

He explained that he had been lent it for a week, ample time to reach, or fail to reach, an agreement with Antonia. At the end of the week Antonia had died and as no one had arrived to claim the flat he had stayed on to meet Celia and try to arrange something about the children. But a rather disagreeable couple from Manchester had just arrived, deeply suspicious of him as a squatter, and had turned him out. 'I'm desperately sorry to be such a nuisance, but I haven't got the price of a hotel bed. You couldn't possibly give me a shakedown for the night at the quinta?'

'I'm sorry, Gerald, that's out of the question.'

'Why? The children are in bed and asleep, they won't know. I'll be gone before they get up in the morning. I promise.'

'I'm sorry, it's still no. I'd feel I was breaking faith with them, and if they did find out somehow they'd be furious and I'd be in a very uncomfortable dog-house.'

'Damn you, Celia, for letting them decide everything instead of taking a firm line. How are two children that age to know what's in their best interests?'

'They don't, and I'm not sure you do. It may all come right in the end, or rather it might if you'd pull yourself together and be sensible. I'm sorry about your predicament. If you like to come up here now, I'll give you the price of a hotel bed.'

'Hell, no. I'd rather sleep in the open than accept your charity. You realise what this means to me? Back to England on the first flight I can get, with nothing settled about the children and less than a thousand escudos in my pocket.'

'I'm sorry, but you were silly to come. Get yourself a respectable job and somewhere to live, then get in touch with me about them.'

Earlier in the evening she had solved the problem of keeping the children amused by promising to take them swimming next day.

'Yippee!' Peter shouted. 'Can we go to the Lido? They have chutes you can slide down and all sorts of things.'

'Right. Get your bathing things out before you go to bed, and we'll go first thing in the morning.'

But in the morning she was less keen on the idea. Antonia's beachwear was much too large for her, and the spare bikini of Sarah's that she had to settle for was very revealing and rather tight. And despite her brave words to Bettencourt, she was daunted by the thought of driving a strange left-hand drive car. But it was impossible to disappoint the children, so she went to the garage to fetch it.

The garage was separate from the house, and opened out on to what had once been the quinta's stable yard. The exit to the lane was through an arch in the high wall, closed by two heavy wooden doors which rolled aside on an overhead track. Having installed the children in the car, she drove out through the arch into the lane, then stopped, intending to shut the doors behind her.

'Oh no, look who's here,' moaned Peter. 'Him again.'

Gerald Hanbury was walking dejectedly up the lane towards them, holding a small suitcase.

'Pretend you haven't seen him and drive away,' urged Sarah.

'I can't, I must shut the doors,' Celia objected, and got out of the car.

Gerald came up to her. 'I'm on a flight out at noon. I've come to say goodbye.'

'Well, Peter and Sarah are in the car. I quite see why you want to milk the situation for pathos, but it won't get you very far.'

'I was right about you, Celia. You're a hard-hearted upper-class bitch, with a genius for hitting a chap when he's down.'

'Knocking some sense into you, I'd call it. I quite like you when you're not being your own worst enemy.'

'Then drive me to the airport, to show there's no ill feeling.'

112

'If I do, you'll be spoiling their treat and very unpopular. I've just promised to take them swimming.'

'Then drop me downtown where I can catch a bus.'

She agreed. He installed himself in the front seat and addressed himself earnestly to the children. Celia turned away to shut the heavy wooden doors. This had to be done from inside, after which one let oneself out through a personal door cut in the main one.

She was pulling the second door shut when the children started to yell in terror. The car engine roared and it shot away down the road with a screech of tyres. She rushed out into the lane, and was just in time to see Peter, Sarah and their half-mad father disappear at speed round the bend in the lane.

SEVEN

Celia was dumbfounded. She had more or less decided to give Gerald the benefit of the doubt. It had never occurred to her that he might abduct the children.

Fortunately, Bettencourt was in his office. 'I'll get the right people on to this at once,' he said. 'Can you manage to take Antonia's car and –'

'No,' Celia snapped. 'Gerald's commandeered it to kidnap the children in.'

'Sorry, I forgot. D'you remember its registration number?'

'Of course not, don't be silly.'

'Wait. I've got it here. It's the first thing the police will·want to know. I'll get them to give it to the traffic police and alert the post at the airport in case he tries to take them out of the country. We'd better get the harbour watched too. He may plan to get them away by sea.'

Celia thought rapidly. 'One moment, Mr Bettencourt. We mustn't be hasty, let's think this out first. Can he really be planning to take the children out of the country? He's broke, and he hasn't got their passports.'

'He could have got them fake passports under a false name. You can, if you've got the right contacts.'

'When?'

'In London, before he came.'

'Why would he? Presumably he didn't know then that Antonia would be dead and the children would be flown out to the funeral. If he's really trying to abduct them, how would he pay their fares?'

'He isn't broke. He lied.'

Had Gerald lied about that, as part of a bid for sympathy? If so, what else had he lied about? Was the real Gerald the big-shot criminal in the business suit, and not the down at heel would-be maths teacher? Suddenly light broke through, banishing these manic suspicions. 'It can't have been planned in advance,' she burst out. 'He wasn't to know that the car would be standing there in the road with the engine running and the children in it, ready for him to drive away.'

'That just made it easier for him to do what he'd intended to do anyway.'

'No. I've seen quite a lot of him in the past two days and I know a bit about his mentality. He's not a devious tycoon, he's a very insecure ex-convict who's fond of his children, and what happened was, he had a brainstorm. He's always suspected quite wrongly that I was carrying on Antonia's hate campaign and poisoning their minds against him. There they are sitting in the car with him, and he suddenly thinks: why don't I have them to myself for the day and see what I can do? So he drives off.'

'You mean, he doesn't intend to smuggle them off the island?'

'How can he? He'll give them a good time, and hope to bring them back perfectly happy to go and live with him.'

'I don't follow your reasoning, Mrs Grant. How does he give them a good time if he's down to his last penny?'

Celia thought about this. 'My handbag's in the car. I had about thirty thousand escudos in it.'

'Could he have reckoned on finding money in it when he had this alleged brainstorm? I don't say you're wrong, Mrs Grant, you may well be right. But there is also the possibility that he's lied to us all along, and has some devious plan to kidnap Peter and Sarah. In any case, we're under a legal obligation to tell the judiciary what's happened. Until a *tutor* has been appointed what happens to the children is very much their concern.'

'Oh dear, I suppose you're right. What ought we to do?'

'You'll have to come down to the justice building and make a formal deposition. Can I meet you there in half an hour?'

Celia agreed, then remembered that Gerald had kidnapped her handbag as well as the children, and had to borrow her taxi fare into town from Teresa. As promised, Bettencourt was waiting in the entrance hall. 'I've spoken to the judge. We'll go in and see him now.'

'Why? Surely this is a matter for the police?'

'The judiciary controls the *Polícia judiciária* who deal with crime. You have to tell the judge that a crime has been committed, and he sets them to work.'

'What a silly waste of time.'

'Actually no, they've got to work already. The post at the airport has been alerted, and the traffic police on the coast road have been told to look out for the car.'

Under Bettencourt's guidance, she made a formal complaint to a judge, to the effect that an attempt was being made to remove two minors, Sarah and Peter Hanbury, from the jurisdiction of the court. She tried to explain that he had probably borrowed them for the day on an impulse, and that there was no need for a full-scale hue and cry, but was told that this was only the least sinister of various possibilities. Moreover, even a temporary abduction was an offence, and must be dealt with seriously.

Filled with disquiet, she was led out of the building by Bettencourt and round to a separate entrance at the back where the judicial police had its headquarters. There she was asked to provide a detailed description of Hanbury, and explain exactly how he had managed the kidnapping. No, she did not know whether he had succeeded in having the children put on his passport, though she thought it unlikely. No, he was not staying at the Quinta Coulson. Where, then?

'In a time share flat he'd borrowed, according to him. I don't know where it was.'

The police at Santa Cruz airport rang to say they had found a booking for a Gerald Hanbury on a T.A.P. flight to London, but no trace of any for the two children. The car had not arrived at the airport.

Bettencourt looked at his watch. 'Even if the traffic on the coast road's very bad, it would be there by now.'

More reports came in. Despite a careful look-out, the traffic police had seen no sign of Antonia's car. The T.A.P. flight was closing. Mr Hanbury had been called on the tannoy, but there was no sign of him. The police thought it likely that his booking was a blind. They would have yachts and cruise ships in the harbour watched, also the ferries to Porto Santo, the other inhabited island in the Madeira archipelago. There was no point in Celia remaining

116

at police headquarters, they would phone Bettencourt's office as soon as there was any news.

All this hue and cry made Celia very miserable. By now Gerald was probably regretting his mad impulse, which must have made his relations with the children even worse. He would probably be arrested in some café along the coast where he was trying to bribe them out of their sulks with ice-cream. He would blame his arrest on Celia, from now on they would be at daggers drawn. She cursed herself for having told Bettencourt about Gerald's escapade. If she had kept quiet, none of this would have happened.

She changed a traveller's cheque and took a cab back to the quinta. Teresa and Agostinho were loud in their condemnation of Gerald Hanbury when they heard what he had done, and pursued her around the house with their lamentations and cries of sympathy. Partly to escape from their noise, she decided to go and break the sad news to Adrian.

But down at the cottage the second blow of the morning awaited her. She was totally unprepared for it, and at first was too numb with the shock of the children's kidnapping to take it in.

The entrance door of the cottage had been bashed in with enormous force, it looked as if someone had used a sledgehammer. The living-room had been wrecked. In the bedroom Adrian, still in his pyjamas, lay unconscious on the floor in a pool of blood. His pulse was weak, and her first thought was to give him oxygen. But she had to clean him up a little before she could apply the mask, and soon realised that the blood was coming from his nose, which had been hit hard with some heavy object, and also from a deep cut on his forehead. But he was not responding to the oxygen, and she suspected that he had swallowed a lot of blood.

Agostinho was working on one of the upper terraces. She called to him to telephone for an ambulance, and went back to Adrian to try mouth-to-mouth resuscitation. After a lot of effort she got him breathing again and gave him oxygen. But he was still bleeding heavily from the cut on his forehead, and she was very relieved when two ambulance men arrived to take the responsibility off her.

They suggested that she should go with them to the hospital, but she refused; not because she was exhausted and covered with Adrian's blood, but because she had to stay where she was in case

117

the police telephoned with news of Gerald and the children. The double blow had stunned her. She could not think clearly, but sat in a daze in the shade of the vine outside the cottage. Who had attacked Adrian and why? Rousing herself, she went inside to look for clues. There were none. Adrian's bedclothes were on the floor. It looked as if he had been dragged out of bed to be beaten up.

The door of Maria's room was open and she peered in. There, perfect order prevailed, except that the drawers in the chest had been left open. But they were empty. Maria's clothes and toilet things had gone. What had happened? Someone had broken in, what then? Had Maria packed her case calmly and at leisure and gone off with the burglar? Unlikely. But what other explanation was there?

She changed out of her bloodstained clothes, then wondered feverishly what to do next. Baffled and condemned to inactivity by the need to stay within reach of the phone, she craved some occupation to keep her sane. If Adrian survived and came out of hospital he would be annoyed if he found that his wretched orchids had died of neglect. She would attend to them. Filling the watering-can she began carrying out what she remembered of his instructions.

Working her way along the benches, she came to the little plant labelled *Oncidium varicosum* which Adrian had denounced as an impostor. He had also exclaimed against several other errors of labelling, having apparently spotted them for the first time. The plants must have been there, developing characteristics which contradicted their labels, for months. Why had he not noticed the mistakes earlier?

Near the end of the bench, a real shock awaited her. The three *Miltonias* which had been Adrian's pride and joy had gone, the purplish *spectabilis*, the reddish-brown *clowesii* and the hybrid resulting from a cross between them. Three plants with larger flowers in much the same colour range had been substituted in their place, presumably in the hope that the swap would not be noticed. Further along, there was a gap, which had been occupied by . . . what? A plant she had admired with Adrian, with a spectacular two-foot flower spike. The individual flowers were large and creamy white, with a crimson-purple lip and a yellow throat tinged with magenta. What was it? More important, where was it? She looked along the benches in case it had been moved. It had not. It had disappeared.

There was no doubt about it. A thief was at work, someone who took away choice specimens and substituted others, perhaps less rare or valuable, in the mistaken hope that Adrian, crippled by his disability, would not notice. It looked like a crazy throwback to the Victorian heyday of orchid-mania, when millionaire dukes paid vast sums for novelties and collectors in the field double-crossed each other ruthlessly in the race to bag rarities.

How much had been stolen? She went to the cottage in search of reference books, and came back to the orchid house with three magnificent works with illustrations in colour. The problem of the *Miltonias* was easily solved. The substitutes were what were known as pansy orchids. They had once been classed as *Miltonias*, but had since been expelled by the pundits into a species of their own called *Miltoniopsis*. One of the reference books was rather sniffy about them.

Further along the bench a plant in full flower looked different from what she remembered. It was labelled *Oncidium gardneri* but proved to be nothing of the kind. Unlike *gardneri* it had no scent and no pseudobulbs. Its five-foot flower spike was longer than anything *gardneri* could produce and the blooms, which should have been yellow spotted with brown, were maroon and buff with a white column and yellow lip. It was obviously an *Oncidium*, but here were dozens of them, not just species plants but hybrids. After much searching in the books, she decided that it must be a specimen of *Oncidium luridum*.

The alleged *Leptotes bicolor* had also been denounced as an impostor by Adrian. He was right, its pseudobulbs were not cylindrical and there was no 'fleshy, subcylindrical pointed leaf' growing out of their apices. It was not in flower, and she made no attempt to discover what it was.

But why steal one orchid and put another in its place? There seemed to be no rhyme or reason in it, unless perhaps there was some pattern in the substitutions. She went back to the reference books, trying to find links between plants stolen and their substitutes. On turning to the *Miltonia* family, she found that the proper *Miltonias* hailed from the hot and humid Brazil

119

lowlands, whereas the *Miltoniopsis* strain of pansy orchids came from high up in the Andes and therefore required different growing conditions; what they enjoyed was being rather cold and perpetually wet. The *Oncidium gardneri* also hailed from Brazil. Its substitute, *Oncidium luridum*, was listed as native to 'Central America, the West Indies and Florida'. Interestingly, the impostor labelled *Leptotes bicolor* would also have come from Brazil if it had been what it purported to be. Then, leafing through one of the books, she came on an illustration of the creamy-white orchid with the crimson-purple lip which was missing from the bench. That clinched it. It was *Laelia purpurata*, the national flower of Brazil.

All the missing orchids were Brazilian. So was Maria. Coincidence? Or was she the thief? Over the past few days she had done her best to keep Adrian away from his orchids. Because she did not want him to spot the substitutions?

Brazil had kept cropping up in minor ways too. There were bills from a firm in Rio de Janeiro among the papers in Antonia's desk. And the other day she had noticed that one of the drawers in her bedroom was lined with an English-language newspaper whose typeface looked unfamiliar. Curiosity had made her take it out to identify it. It was the *Latin American Daily Post*, published in Rio de Janeiro.

What else could she do to kill time while she waited for news of the children? For one thing, Mrs Fuller ought to be told that everything was in the melting pot; with no Maria, the impoverished widow she had recommended would no longer be needed to provide moral support. Celia rang Mrs Fuller and broke the news.

Mrs Fuller expressed deep concern for Adrian, and promised to visit him in hospital. 'Knowing Maria,' she added, 'I'm not surprised at her getting involved in this sort of thing. I saw quite a lot of her, you know, when I came to visit poor Adrian.'

'She certainly struck me as very tense and odd.'

'Yes. She was in hiding, wasn't she? Afraid of being found and put on trial or whatever.'

'You mean she was some kind of revolutionary on the run?'

Mrs Fuller thought for a moment. 'No. Not a revolutionary.'

'Why d'you say that?'

'To begin with, she was a Catholic.'

'But she was also Brazilian,' Celia argued. 'What with all this liberation theology a lot of Latin American Catholics are very left-wing.'

'I don't think that was her style. According to Antonia, her Catholicism consisted largely of rushing up to the church to confess her sins. Besides, real revolutionaries can't help giving the impression that they know better about everything, that they're your intellectual superiors. She didn't. I'm not brainy, but I never felt that she despised me. Or Adrian, for that matter. The person she despised was Antonia.'

'Goodness me, I wonder why.'

'I think she felt she was a cut above Antonia socially. She was right, of course. If there hadn't been a vulgar streak in Antonia, she wouldn't have married that awful man, and her attitude to money was rather common.'

'You mean, Maria came from a rather superior background?'

'It's difficult to tell when people aren't English, but . . . yes. One got the impression that nursing an elderly stroke victim was a bit of a come-down. Anyway, she's gone. What d'you propose to do with Adrian now?'

'Unless I can find a replacement for her, he'll have to go into a home. But he'd hate that, I'm afraid.'

'D'you know, I don't think he would,' said Mrs Fuller, sounding surprised by the thought.

'Surely he'd hate being separated from the orchids?'

'Not necessarily. He was getting rather bored with them before he had his stroke. Then Antonia used them as an excuse for moving him down to the cottage so that she could have the house to herself, and he grumbled a lot about that. After a bit he got interested in them again, poor man. I suppose he had nothing else to think about. How deep it goes, I don't know.'

'I'll sound him out about it in a day or two, when he's got over his battering.'

'Do, and let me know if you want any advice. I know most of the bins for the elderly, my friends keep collapsing into them. Old age is dreadful, I hate it.'

Struck by an afterthought, Celia asked her if she knew anyone who bred or collected Brazilian species orchids.

'It's no use asking me, my dear, I barely know an aster from a zinnia. Ring Betty Garton at Boa Vista and say you're a friend of mine. She's the uncrowned queen of the orchid world, she's bound to know.'

Greatly daring, Celia rang Mrs Garton, explained who she was and put her question.

'There's only one person I know of who specialises in them,' was the reply. 'Her name's Isabel Nielsen. You're at the Quinta Coulson, is that right? Then she's quite near you, a little way down the hill. I'll give you the address.'

Celia noted it down. 'Is she herself Brazilian?'

'Yes, married to a Dane. When I say she only grows the Brazilian species, she did. But lately she's been branching out a bit. The other day she came here and bought various things from me.'

To use as substitutes for what she intended to take away, Celia thought as she put down the phone. She would call on Mrs Nielsen as soon as possible.

There was still no news of Gerald and the children, so she rang the hospital and asked after Adrian: he was out of danger but would need to stay for several days. Could she bring clean pyjamas and his toilet things? Torn between her duty to him and her worry about the children, she told Teresa where she was going and made her swear to stay near the phone to take messages, then summoned a taxi to take her to the hospital.

She arrived in Adrian's room as Dr Mendes was leaving after examining him. He reported that Adrian had suffered a slight heart attack in addition to his cuts and bruises, which had probably occurred as the result of a fall which the heart attack had caused. He would have to remain in the hospital under observation for a few more days after which, if no alarming symptoms manifested themselves, it would be safe for him to go home.

Wondering who was to look after him there in Maria's absence, Celia went in to see him. She found him fully alert, and making the urgent noises which meant that he had something important to communicate.

'You want to tell me what happened?' she asked. 'Is that it?'

He nodded emphatically.

'Did you fall and cut yourself?'

An equally emphatic no. After a pause for thought, he made a pretence of hitting his face with his good hand.

'Someone hit you. Who? Not Maria?'

Evidently not.

'Was she there when it happened?'

No.

'She's gone. D'you know when?'

He mimed going to sleep.

'After you'd settled down for the night.'

He agreed, but had something else to convey. Having thought about it, he shut his eyes, then opened them wide and kissed his own hand.

'She woke you and kissed you to say goodbye? Did she say why she was going?'

Evidently not, but to judge from his agitated trembling motions she had been terrified.

'She didn't say why she was afraid?'

No.

'And it was after she'd gone that the person who hit you came?'

Yes, but followed by qualifying noises. She discovered by trial and error what they meant: there had been more than one attacker.

'How many of them were there? Two? Three? Four?'

He held up three fingers.

'Who were they? Teenage burglars wanting money for drugs?'

No.

'Did they steal anything?'

He seemed to think not.

But why had they hit him? She tried to work out possible explanations, and ways of putting them into yes-or-no questions that he could answer.

'Did they hit you because you got up and tried to stop them coming in?'

No, followed by urgent noises. He knew why he had been hit, and was in anguish because he could not tell her. After several repeats of the noises she grasped what he was trying to say: 'Asked . . . where . . Maria . . . gone.'

123

This began to make a sort of sense. Some time during the night Maria had packed her things, said goodbye to Adrian and left. Why? Because she sensed danger. After she had gone, the danger materialised. Three men broke into the cottage looking for her. Furious at not finding her, they had hit Adrian to try to make him tell them where she had gone.

When she put this to him, he agreed eagerly, then began to weep a little. She was filled with pity, and very angry. They had battered a defenceless old man because they were too brutalised by violent crime to grasp that he was physically incapable of telling them where Maria was, even if he knew. No wonder Maria had been terrified. Warned in time, she had fled. But who had warned her? And who were the bloodthirsty savages she had been frightened of?

Back at the house, she found that the telephone had been silent, there was no news of Gerald and the children. She rang Bettencourt at his office, but like her, he had no fresh news about their whereabouts. When she told him about Maria's flight and the attack on Adrian, he did not comment.

'Well?' she prompted. 'What d'you think we should do about it?'

'I don't know, Mrs Grant. What had you in mind?'

'The police would be interested, I imagine.'

'Would they?' he paused. 'We've already got them watching the port and airport for two allegedly abducted children who you now expect to be returned safe and sound this evening. Don't you think that's enough for one day?'

'You insisted on alerting them. I was against it.'

'We had to for legal reasons.'

'Is there no legal reason for reporting this? That unfortunate girl has run away in terror, and three thugs have battered Adrian about.'

'Who says so?'

'Adrian. He told me.'

'But Mrs Grant, Adrian can't tell anyone anything. He can only answer leading questions that are put to him. If you summon a member of the judicial police to his bedside and put questions to Adrian for the man to take note of, you will seem to be putting words into the mouth of a stroke victim, who is probably very confused after falling over and cutting himself badly. On your admission, Maria left of her own free will, the police can't do anything about that. By this evening, your formal complaint that Gerald Hanbury has abducted his children will probably prove to be unfounded. They'll judge what you say about Sir Adrian's misadventure in the light of that.'

His remark hit her like a blow in the face. 'Then you propose to do nothing?'

'If you want to unburden yourself to the judicial police I won't stand in your way. But I'd rather not be associated with it.'

She was furious, but had to face the awkward fact that his advice was probably sound. It had touched a raw nerve. Once bitten, she was twice shy. To go to the police with a story they did not take seriously had always been one of her nightmares.

Emerging from her black thoughts, she realised that Teresa was standing beside her, agog with curiosity.

'So Maria, she has gone,' she said, with an intonation which turned the remark into a question.

'Yes.' Celia summarised what Adrian had told her about the night's events. 'It's all very mysterious. How well did you know Maria?'

'Not well. That one, she was not easy to know.'

'Did it ever strike you that she might have enemies she was afraid of?'

'Enemies, *minha senhora*?'

'She went out so little, didn't want days off or a holiday. She might almost have been in hiding.'

'I think more, Maria she was a little mad. It was her way, to stay alone with the senhor and see nobody, and sometimes she was very hard with him, to make him do what she wanted.'

In a sudden gut reaction, Celia decided that she did not trust Teresa. She and her husband were hand in glove with the unspeakable Lúcio Freitas who had made a cold-blooded attempt to seduce her in furtherance of a sordid commercial deal. They knew about his affair with Antonia, and they were involved in his secret purchases of land. Suddenly she felt herself surrounded by people, Carlos Bettencourt, Gerald Hanbury, Lúcio Freitas, Teresa and Agostinho, who were all hiding unpleasant motives behind a mask of deceit.

125

Teresa's inquiry whether she wanted espada for lunch brought her back to her senses and made her struggle to get her persecution complex under control. But her mind gave her no peace. Why had Gerald not phoned? Surely he must realise that unless he rang to reassure her, she would put the police on his track? Suddenly it hit her that he was not just snatching a day out with his children. Something was horribly wrong, or he would have rung her. His extraordinary behaviour, her worry about the children, the attack on Adrian, Maria's disappearance, all these events and more went round and round in her head, and she no longer trusted herself to make sense of them.

The problem of the orchids nagged at her. Compared with everything else that was happening it seemed a side issue, but she had to start unravelling the knot somewhere. Dare she leave the telephone and go to confront Mrs Nielsen? Yes. If Gerald was going to ring he would have done it already. She left the Nielsen phone number with Teresa, so that any calls could be re-routed to her there, and set out.

The address that Mrs Garton had given her was in the Caminho São Luis. It ran across the slope of the hill a hundred yards below the Quinta Coulson, between smallish houses and bungalows in a variety of modern styles. Isabel Nielsen's was on the uphill side of the road. Her cluttered front garden sloped steeply up to the house. Elaborate flights of steps zigzagged uphill under wire arches smothered in hectically coloured climbers, with beds of garish bedding plants on either side. Wondering how anyone who liked rare Brazilian orchids could also like French marigolds, she rang the bell.

The woman who came to the door was in her sixties, with iron-grey hair cut short like a man's and a no-nonsense trouser suit. Celia explained not quite truthfully that she was a horticulturist from England with a special interest in Brazilian orchids, and had been given Mrs Nielsen's name by Mrs Garton of Boa Vista.

'I'm told that your collection's very fine. It would be a great favour if you'd be kind enough to let me see it.'

'But certainly, please come in,' said Mrs Nielsen as her severe face broke into a warm smile. 'You also grow the Brazilian orchids?'

If she was hoping to exchange notes with a fellow expert she was in for a disappointment. Celia began to backtrack hastily before her ignorance was exposed, and explained that she was just starting her collection.

'And why, please, do you choose the Brazilian varieties?'

Celia alleged that she saw no point in growing a miscellaneous hotch-potch of paphiopedilums and cymbidiums and cattleyas. There was much more interest and enjoyment to be had from a specialist collection, and she was attracted by the richness and variety of the Brazilian species.

At the word 'richness' Mrs Nielsen nodded in vigorous agreement. 'Come, please,' she said with the complacent air of one offering an unheard-of treat, and led the way through a living room chock-a-block with oriental furniture and knick-knacks. French windows opened from it on to the back garden. Like the front garden it sloped steeply upwards, and here too bedding plants prevailed. A man, presumably Mr Nielsen, was working energetically in it. Celia decided that he must be the lover of French marigolds, and marvelled at the survival of a marriage between people of incompatible horticultural tastes.

The orchid house was on a terrace not far from the house. Mrs Nielsen opened the door and stood proudly aside for Celia to go in. She had reason to be proud. The collection was stunning, far richer than Adrian's, and it had been arranged for effect, with specimens not in flower stowed away out of sight. A long perspective of flower spikes stretched away to the end of the house. Celia was tempted to stride along it like a dignitary reviewing a guard of honour, looking for the plants stolen from Adrian. But Mrs Nielsen lingered lovingly over each of her treasures, explaining their requirements by way of osmunda fibre, sphagnum moss, water and the withholding of water when the plant was resting. *Dryadella zebrina*, for instance, detested being too hot and dry. If it was not sprayed frequently during warm weather it would not produce its odd rather than beautiful flowers, with their long trailing green sepals covered with maroon spots.

Celia was agog with impatience. Ahead she could see a group of *Laelias*, with a *purpurata* among them. But there was no proof that it was the identical plant stolen from Adrian. When at last the moment came to take notice of it, she held her fire, apart

127

from making a tiny display of knowledge and asking whether this beautiful orchid was not the national flower of Brazil.

Further along the row the *Oncidium gardneri* complete with scent, pseudobulbs and flowers the right colour, presented the same difficulty. There were three plants. How could she claim that one of them had been stolen from Adrian and something else substituted? Only the *Miltonia* hybrid, crossed between *spectabilis* and *clowesii*, would provide convincing proof. It was unique, but where was it?

Presently she spotted all three *Miltonias*, a little further along the bench. With Mrs Nielsen trailing after her, she stationed herself in front of them. 'Tell me about these.'

'Ah yes, this is very interesting. Here is *Miltonia spectabilis*. Not the ordinary one which is quite pale, with a purple lip. This is a darker variety called *moreliana*. Here beside it is *Miltonia clowesii* and also a hybrid plant crossed between them.'

'Yes,' said Celia. 'And all three were taken in the past forty-eight hours from the collection of your neighbour Sir Adrian Morton. And so was much else besides.'

There was an ominous, shocked silence.

'How can you dare to say such a thing?' cried Mrs Nielsen, red with anger. 'I invite you in my house, and you insult me.'

'I'm sorry if you find it insulting, but I'm simply stating a fact. Those *Miltonias* were in Sir Adrian's orchid house the day before yesterday, and now they are here. This is something that calls for an explanation.'

'I . . . do not wish to talk about this.'

'Perhaps, but I'm afraid you'll have to. Maria Silva disappeared some time during the night, and Sir Adrian Morton is in hospital after being beaten up by thugs. Something very mysterious is happening. I'm determined to get to the bottom of it, and this business with the orchids is part of the mystery.'

Mrs Nielsen looked terrified. 'Maria has disappeared?'

'Yes. You know her well?'

'We are related. Not closely.'

'Was it you who recommended her to Mrs Hanbury as a nurse-companion for her father?'

'Yes. But tell me, please. What has happened?'

'Some time during the night she packed her things and left.

Shortly afterwards three thugs broke into the cottage and asked Sir Adrian where she had gone. He couldn't tell them, so they beat him up. If you know her, perhaps you can tell me what's behind all this carry-on.'

Mrs Nielsen's eyes opened very wide, in an unconvincing display of ignorance. 'I cannot tell. It is beyond imagination.'

'I don't believe that. I'm sure you know who she's been hiding from all this time, and who these people are who were after her.'

'No!' she cried. 'I know nothing.'

This was clearly untrue, but Celia decided to leave it for the moment. 'And how do the orchids come into it?'

'They are mine. I took back only what belong to me. I left others to take their place.'

'Fine, but how did orchids belonging to you get into Sir Adrian's collection?'

'I was lending them to him. Now I take them back.'

'I see. Why were you lending them to him?'

'He was becoming bored with his collection. I lent him some plants to make him interested again.'

Mrs Fuller had said something similar: that Adrian, banished to the cottage on the pretext of being near his orchid collection, had shown little interest in it at first. Later, he had become more interested. Why? Because new blood had been introduced into the collection. Who had organised that? Antonia, obviously, to make him take an interest in it again and stop him grumbling about being banished down to the cottage. But if the 'loan' arrangement was open and above board, why did the plants have to be removed furtively? And why were they taken away the moment Antonia was dead?

Suddenly the answer to these questions was obvious. 'Mrs Hanbury had a hold over you, didn't she? That's why you had to hand over the plants. No, don't deny it, it's the only logical explanation. You aren't the only person she blackmailed. I won't tell anyone, but I want to know what she was blackmailing you about.'

'Please go. I am not speaking to you any more.'

'No. I'm sorry, but I insist on knowing.'

'It is not connected with the affair of Maria and the men who attacked Sir Morton.'

129

'Then what is it connected with?'

'I . . . was stealing something from her shop,' Mrs Nielsen stammered, in what sounded like the result of hasty improvisation. 'She catched me, and promised to be silent if I gave her interesting orchids from my collection.'

'What did you steal from her shop?'

'Something . . . what business is it of yours?'

'What sort of shop was it that you stole from?'

'Please, I cannot speak of this, my husband does not know of it.'

'You're lying. You don't even know what sort of shop Mrs Hanbury owned. It wasn't shoplifting she was blackmailing you for, it was something to do with Maria. Come on, tell me the truth.'

'I do not lie,' she shouted. 'I know nothing of this affair of Maria and the men who attacked Sir Morton, and I am not wanting to speak any more to you. So go!'

Mr Nielsen, attracted by her shouts, had appeared in the doorway of the orchid house, and was advancing down it towards them. 'What's going on here?' he demanded.

'She asks me strange questions about Maria Silva. And when I answer them she calls me a liar.'

Mr Nielsen rounded on Celia. 'I think you'd better go.'

He was in his sixties, but large and determined-looking. Celia saw no point in arguing. He led her through the house in silence, and shut the front door behind her.

Expelled with her tail between her legs, Celia was discouraged. All she had learnt was that Antonia was blackmailing the Nielsens because of something connected with Maria. They were both involved, Mrs Nielsen could not have carried on the traffic between her orchid house and Adrian's without him noticing. He had probably helped.

But it was all still up in the air, if challenged they would stick to their denial. She was still stumbling about in a fog of uncertainties which must have some sinister pattern of wickedness hidden behind them.

The way back to the Quinta Coulson passed the entrance of the public footpath which ran along the bottom of its garden. Seeing it, she halted, then started along it.

I am an idiot, she told herself. Why had she not grasped at once that the footpath ran parallel to the Caminho São Luis, and along the top end of their back gardens? Some of them even had back gates opening on to the footpath. She hurried along, peering through fences and hedges, till she caught a glimpse of Mr Nielsen's deplorable display of carpet bedding.

The discovery that the Nielsens had a gate opening on to the footpath brought back disquieting memories. On the way to the ice-cream parlour, she and the children had come across the two time share boys. They had looked guilty too. She hurried round the corner to the place where they had been examining the fence so closely.

She had wondered at the time whether they were looking for a weak place to break in through, and she was right. A whole section of the wire mesh had been torn away from the upright, leaving a gaping hole. As the memory rose to her mind of Adrian lying covered with blood on the floor, fury seized her. Well, she would give those young men a piece of her mind.

131

EIGHT

Striding up the hill in a fury, Celia made one more discovery. The quinta's garden was not the only enclosure that had been broken into. Something odd had happened to the gates of the banana grove opposite the entrance to the Quinta Coulson. They were padlocked, but one of them had been lifted off its hinges and was standing askew. Puzzled, she slipped into the banana grove through the gap between the hinge end of the gate and the gatepost to investigate.

Inside, a trodden path led along the boundary to a point where an empty oil drum had been stood on end and used, to judge from earthy footprints left on it, as an observation post from which to look over the wall. Beside it there were banana fronds lying about which could have been cut off to provide a watcher with camouflage, and he had left behind two empty beer cans and the remains of what looked like a rather disgusting picnic. She climbed on the drum, and found that she was too short to see over the wall. But she worked it out that the observation post must be directly opposite the entrance to the quinta. A fresh wave of fury swept over her, but she controlled it. After so many far more serious outrages, it was absurd to lash oneself into a frenzy over the mere trifle of having the house spied on.

Experience had taught her that she was too small to lose her temper impressively. When she did she looked ridiculous, like the Queen of the Fairies in a tantrum. Before marching on up the hill to the square to confront the time share boys with their misdeeds, she stood breathing deeply for a time to steady herself. She would be very calm, she resolved, but very frightening.

It was midday. The flow of tourists had thinned out and the time share boys were having a break from their labours. They were sitting in the bar, making tiny cups of espresso coffee last a long time. The girl who had behaved oddly when pretending to photograph the cat's claw vine was with them. Celia marched up to their table. 'D'you mind if I join you?'

'Oh, it's you again,' said Jonathan with a charming smile. 'Of course, we'd be delighted.'

'Don't be delighted too soon, because I'm going to ask you some awkward questions, and I want straight answers. But first let's introduce ourselves. I'm Celia Grant. You're Jonathan, right?' She turned to the plump girl. 'And you're—?'

'Sue,' she said, trying to look amused rather than alarmed.

'And I'm Denis the menace,' said the red-haired youth, grinning.

'Fine. I want to know what you think you're doing. If you won't tell me, the information will have to be battered out of you by the police.'

Jonathan consulted the others mutely and mimed being at a loss. 'What does this doll-like little lady think we've done that would interest the police?'

Celia ignored this. 'Let's start with you, Sue. Yesterday you took two photographs of an old lady who came to call on me. Why? What did you think you were doing?'

Sue put on a look of puzzled innocence. 'I was photographing a lovely creeper that overflowed into the lane. The old lady and her car were rather in the way, so I took two more after she'd gone.'

'Nonsense. You took two close-ups of her, and didn't bother to refocus before you switched to the creeper.'

'Perhaps I'm not a very competent photographer,' Sue replied on a note of mockery.

Celia switched her fire sharply to Jonathan. 'Yesterday you and Denis here were loitering by the fence at the bottom of our garden. Why?'

He pretended to be thinking. 'I remember us walking past there, but did we loiter?'

'Yes. You looked very guilty when you saw me, and I know why. You were looking for a place to break in.'

Jonathan looked round at the others. 'Oh dear, what an embarrassing situation. You were sweet yesterday, hijacking that

133

very cross man and making him look at those awful flats so that we could earn the price of our lunch. You're much too old to be so pretty, and we don't want to be unkind. But you're suffering from delusions, dear. Why don't you go home and lie down?'

'If this is what comes of taking an innocent stroll,' said Denis, 'we must avoid that footpath in future.'

Celia moved in to the kill. 'When the police question you they'll want to know why there's a huge gap in our fence, and why an elderly invalid who lives just inside it is now in hospital after being beaten up during the night by three people. They will of course be interested in the fact that there are three of you. As another result of your activities a terrified young woman has disappeared in the middle of the night. Moreover you left a disgusting mess in the banana grove after your picnic at the place where you spied on us before committing your crime.'

There was a shocked silence.

Jonathan rallied first. 'I don't remember going near that foot-path yesterday, do you Denis? It's her word against ours.'

'Yes,' Celia agreed. 'Mine against the word of three public nuisances who pester tourists and are paid so little that they'd do anything for money.'

Jonathan had begun to look less sure of himself. 'She's right about that,' he reasoned. 'Little Miss Muffet here with the will of steel is a solid citizeness. In the eyes of the police, we're scum.'

'But all we did was help get some cuckolded husband his divorce,' said Denis. 'So why is she trying to frighten us with horror stories?'

'She isn't, it's true, what she's saying,' Sue exclaimed. 'We saw the ambulance! We watched it arrive and turn down into the lane. It must have been for the old gentleman, the one that got beaten up.'

'The person in the ambulance,' said Celia, 'was a retired civil servant called Sir Adrian Morton. He's still in hospital. He says three people bashed him about mercilessly because he couldn't tell them something they wanted to find out. Even if he'd known, he couldn't have answered because he's had a stroke that affected his speech. I hope you're pleased with your handiwork.'

After another shocked silence, they all burst into speech at once.

'God, we've been conned,' exclaimed Jonathan.

'We didn't expect anything like that to happen,' Sue cried, near to tears.

'They told us a pack of lies,' said Denis.

'Who did?' Celia asked.

'Horrible people,' cried Sue. 'You could tell they were crooks by looking at them. We were idiots to fall for it.'

'They said they were working on a divorce case,' Jonathan explained.

'Yes,' Sue chimed in. 'We were supposed to find out if this girl, Maria-José her name was, had a living-in lover.'

'And we needed the money,' Denis confessed with feeling.

The fury that Celia had been keeping under control ebbed away. These were not young thugs but innocents abroad living dangerously out of their depth. 'I think you'd better tell me this whole story from the beginning,' she said. 'And when the time comes, I'll try to make it easy for you with the police. Who were these people who contacted you?'

'There were two of them,' said Jonathan. 'Real thugs, but you expect private detectives to look a bit thuggish. One of them was thin and dark and fierce, the sort that carries a knife. Denis says he's not Portuguese.'

'No, Latin America somewhere,' said Denis.

'Denis is in his third season here,' Jonathan explained. 'His diagnosis of nationality's infallible. How about the other one, Denis?'

'The States. Possibly Florida,' said Denis confidently.

'He was fat,' Jonathan continued, 'with popping eyes and a clotted, angry face and a funny haircut, I think he dyes it yellow. They didn't look like.y time share prospects but you never can tell, they could have been pimps looking for somewhere to put a prostitute in, so I waded in with the sales talk. When they realised that we were more or less fixtures in the square, they produced a photo of this girl and said had we seen her around. We said we had, and she lived somewhere down the hill from here, and that gave enormous pleasure, the thin one looked less hungry and the fat one a bit less cross. So they thought for a bit, and

135

then they took us over to their car and showed us a lot more photos.'

'Taken with a Polaroid camera,' Sue put in. 'All of people coming in or out of your gate.'

'Have you got these photos?' Celia asked.

'Yes,' said Denis. 'But it was only to remind us, we weren't to show them to anyone because that would give the game away. The idea was, if we saw any of the people about, we were to ask casually who they were without arousing suspicion. That was a piece of cake. We took Vicente here, he's the barman, into our confidence and he knows everybody for miles around.'

Vicente, wiping glasses behind his bar, nodded and smiled in agreement.

'Who were the photos of?' Celia asked.

'You and two children, a boy and a girl,' Denis recalled, 'and the man you dragooned into falling for the time share thing, Vicente says his name's Gerald Hanbury. Who else? Oh yes, a policeman and also a sickeningly pretty man with a fancy beard who Vicente says is a lawyer called Bettencourt and lives just down the hill. Apart from Agostinho and his wife, that was the lot.'

'So you innocently identified all these people,' said Celia, then added grimly: 'But there's also the less innocent little matter of that break in the fence.'

Jonathan gave Celia a stricken look. 'God, I feel embarrassed about this.'

'We'd have copped out if we'd known what would happen,' said Denis. 'But we didn't, honest. What they said was, they weren't sure they were keeping watch on the right girl, the one they said was cheating on her husband. The photograph of her that they'd shown us wasn't recent, so were we sure it was the same girl?'

'We said we were pretty sure,' said Sue. 'But they still seemed doubtful, and in the end they handed over the camera to us and showed me the place in the banana grove where they'd taken the pictures from. We were supposed to try to get a shot of Maria-José, and also of any man who went in or out and might be her boyfriend.'

'But Maria-José never showed,' Jonathan added. 'And later on we discovered that she had a secret way in and out, somewhere down at the bottom of the garden, so she could avoid the front entrance when she wanted to, and come and go without being seen.'

'How on earth did you find that out?' Celia asked.

'Vicente again. He got it from Agostinho, who's a regular here every evening after work.'

'So you went to look for it.'

'That's right,' Jonathan confessed. 'It was quite cleverly hidden, the wire was up against the post but it wasn't fastened to it, you only had to bend it back to get in.'

'And of course you passed on this interesting titbit to your paymasters?' Celia asked.

'Yes,' said Jonathan ruefully. 'We met them last night for a debriefing session at a café down on the waterfront.'

'But we didn't know they'd use it so viciously,' said Sue with a shiver. 'What they said was, if one sneaked through the fence, could one get near enough to the cottage without being seen to get a good clear photo of Maria-José?'

This was a new insight for Celia. So the breach in the fence had not been made by Adrian's attackers, it had existed long before that. Her memory threw up a vivid image. Maria, excusing herself from attending the funeral by pleading a stomach upset; and after they all got back from it, looking guilty as she crept away from the hidden break in the fence. Where had she been? To her friends the Nielsens? Helping Isabel Nielsen to remove her precious Brazilian orchids and bring back substitutes in their place?

Another thought: Agostinho had known all along about the break in the fence, and had said nothing, even after the burglary. No wonder she felt conspired against by everyone.

'What else happened at the debriefing session?' she asked.

'They were only interested in the men, they said. On account of the whole thing was supposed to be about a divorce.'

'No interest in me?'

'No. We told them you were only here for a few days to settle Mrs Hanbury's estate. But Gerald Hanbury was a big hit, they got very excited.'

'Really? What interested them particularly?'

'The fact that he'd been in prison for fraud. That was the big attraction, it was as if they'd struck gold.'

'How did you find out about the prison sentence?'

'Vicente again, he gets all the gossip about the Quinta Coulson from Agostinho.'

Vicente nodded enthusiastically. 'Everyone here, we all are interested into the affairs of the Quinta Coulson because of the fraud and the divorce, and also because of the great scandal when the Senhora Hanbury drove out of their house Teresa and Agostinho. She wanted to have for herself the big house, so she turn the poor senhor out into their cottage. That is not our idea of proper behaviour to the old people.'

'Tell her about how Mr and Mrs Hanbury used to meet here,' Jonathan prompted.

Vicente nodded. 'Three times they came. I was very much interested to see this husband who was a famous criminal. They sat at that table into the corner, whispering to each other very soft, very confidential.'

'Quarrelling?' Celia asked. 'Or were they conspiring?'

'I cannot tell,' said Vicente with an evasive gesture. 'They whisper in English.'

'How odd,' said Jonathan. 'Our thugs asked us exactly the same question: were they conspiring?'

'And what was the reaction when you couldn't give a clear answer?'

Jonathan pondered. 'Disappointment, I suppose. But when we told them we'd actually met Hanbury here in the bar face to face they were fascinated.'

'Yes,' Denis added. 'They made us describe everything we'd noticed about him. What was his nationality? What had he said to you, what seemed to be your relationship with each other? What sort of accent did he have? I said middle-class English but not older generation, and that puzzled them a bit.'

'But the thin one muttered something I couldn't quite catch,' Jonathan added, 'something about how easy it was to disguise one's voice. But it was the prison sentence that interested them most.'

'They asked us what he'd done,' said Sue, 'and whether it was his first offence and when he'd come out of prison. But we couldn't tell them anything except that it was fraud, because Vicente doesn't know.'

'Anyway they were pleased with us,' Jonathan summed up.

'We'd given them far more information than they'd expected, in fact we thought we'd overdone it, because the thin one was a bit suspicious and said were we sure we hadn't made it obvious we were spying on all of you. We said of course not, we had a lot of contacts and we'd just asked around, and that more or less satisfied him. Of course that wasn't strictly true, but Vicente's a good friend and when we offered to give him a cut of our immoral earnings he refused.'

'They need more the money than I do,' said Vicente with a wide grin.

'I hope your immoral earnings were substantial?' Celia asked.

'Not bad. They gave us twenty thousand escudos each. They were very firm about one thing, though: the operation was over. We were to stand down, and we'd be in trouble if we talked to anyone about it.'

'Which is exactly what you're doing now,' Celia pointed out. 'Goodness, I'd better go before you're seen consorting with the enemy.'

'It's OK, there's been no sign of them,' Jonathan told her. 'I've been keeping a look-out.'

'Before I go there's one other thing,' she said. 'Sue, what on earth did you think you were doing with that camera down in the lane?'

'It was a silly business really. I'd got very bored standing on that oil drum waiting to photograph Maria-José, who didn't appear. Nobody else had come to your gate except Mr Hanbury, who was in the bag already. So when that old trout arrived in her car, I thought I'd show them how conscientious I was and add her to the collection. But I couldn't get a decent shot because her car was in the way, so I hung about in the lane till she came out and pretended to be taking the climber on the wall. But I wasn't very clever about it, was I?'

'The trouble was, you looked like a small girl doing something she knew was naughty.' Celia thought for a moment. 'Did you go back into the banana plantation after that?'

'Yes. It was almost time to keep our date with the hoodlums at the café, but I had to clear up first, there were strict orders about that. I was supposed to put the oil drum back where it came from and make sure the gate was back on its hinges.'

'And did you?'

'Yes,' said Sue. 'That gate weighed a ton, getting it off and on again was quite a job, but I did. Incidentally, I didn't picnic and leave a disgusting mess in there. If you found a mess, someone must have picnicked in there after we left.'

This was a puzzling piece of news. As Celia digested it, Jonathan continued his look-out over the square, which was now filling up with tourists. 'You see those three men, standing by the fountain? They remind me of our two, real thuggish types.'

Three heavily built men with grim expressions were surveying the scene from the middle of the square. Denis turned and examined them casually. 'Hispanics. But from the States,' he diagnosed.

'Nonsense, you're showing off,' Sue mocked.

'No I'm not, it's obvious. Look at their haircuts. Look at their shoes.'

'Anyway, they're tourists,' said Jonathan as the three men turned to admire the view over the town.

A car drew up. Two men got out. One of them had a thatch of badly cut yellow hair.

'Oh-oh, it's our two,' said Jonathan. He turned to Celia. 'We're not supposed to talk to anyone, least of all to you. D'you mind if we get Vicente to hide you in the back premises?'

'Too late, they've seen her,' Denis shouted. 'Let's run.'

In a flash their footsteps were pounding down an alleyway beside the café and Celia was alone at the table. Barton and Fernandes had joined forces with the three Hispanics. They muttered ominously together, then advanced across the square in a huddle, glaring at her. She was very frightened. But there was nothing she could do, so she glared back.

For a scary moment she braced herself to meet an attack. Then they realised that there was nothing much they could do about her in a public place crowded with tourists. They hesitated and turned away. After a muttered consultation they climbed into two cars and drove off.

Unnerved, but filled with new thoughts to be followed up, Celia went back to the quinta. Her first act was to summon Agostinho and tell him to repair the gap in the wire fence. When told that this was where Adrian's attackers had broken in, he pretended to

140

be shocked and surprised, and asked her where the break was. She was tempted to retort that he knew perfectly well where it was, but refrained and dismissed him. What she needed to do now was to think.

In a haze of concentration she picked at the fillet of espada that Teresa had prepared for her lunch, only dimly aware that it was swimming in oil and had a fried banana balanced nauseatingly on top of it. Suddenly aware of this, she pushed it away in disgust.

'The espada with banana, it is special Madeira dish,' said Teresa reproachfully as she removed the plate. 'The senhora don't like it?'

'It's just that I'm not hungry.'

'You are sad for the children, because that bad man, he has taken them away. But you must eat, *minha senhora*, you must have the strength for when they return.'

Suddenly an awful fear came over her: the children might never return. That was the worst conclusion to come out of the insights of the past few hours. But her head was in turmoil, she could still discern no overall pattern. There must be one, she felt instinctively that she knew all the essential facts. Telling Teresa to bring her coffee into the library, she sat down at Antonia's desk to do some concentrated thinking.

When Teresa brought the coffee, she was staring blankly at the bookcase in front of her, deep in thought. She stayed there motionless for a long time, letting the coffee get cold. Then, in a sudden burst of activity, she searched through the welter of paper in the drawers of the desk till she found the document she wanted. It was a bill with a letterhead in Portuguese, and she searched the bookshelves for a Portuguese-English dictionary. Having consulted it, she sat down again at the desk, plunged once more in thought.

She was still trying to get her ideas in order when Bettencourt rang with news of a discovery by the police. They had found Antonia's car abandoned in a car park by the harbour.

'I see. That means Gerald hasn't just borrowed the children for the day.'

'Not necessarily. He must guess you've put the police on his track and given them its number. He'd have to ditch it.'

'But surely you agree, Mr Bettencourt, that this is a fairly

141

sinister development? Or am I still being stood in the corner as a hysterical female who wastes police time?'

After marking an offended silence, he said: 'You're not being quite fair, Mrs Grant. If you're alluding to the alleged attack on Sir Adrian, I dissuaded you from reporting it because I foresaw what attitude the police here would take. One doesn't want to exhaust their goodwill, and they're very reluctant to move unless there's cast-iron evidence that a crime has been committed.'

To convince him that a crime had indeed been committed, she told him about her encounter with the time share youngsters and the sinister parade of thugs in the square.

He considered. 'Oh. That alters things. I think we've got enough now to make a case to the police about the attack on Sir Adrian.'

'We don't need to "make a case". They're investigating it already.'

'I'm sorry, I don't understand.'

'They're supposed to be finding out what's happened to Gerald and the children.'

'But are the two things related?'

'They most certainly are. I don't believe Gerald's taken the children away for a paternal love-in, intending to bring them back when he's won them over. If it was that he'd have phoned me ages ago to tell me he'd only borrowed them, so that I didn't start a police hue and cry. And I still don't see why he'd want to dump Antonia's car in the middle of Funchal. If he's acting as a free agent, his behaviour just doesn't make sense.'

'Are you seriously suggesting that he isn't a free agent?'

'Yes. Don't you see? According to the youngsters up in the square, the two hoodlums started by being interested in everyone who came to the house. But the more they heard about Gerald, the more interested in him they became. And in the end they decided he was the one they needed to kidnap.'

'Oh really, Mrs Grant. Why would they want to do that?'

'I'm not sure. Perhaps the police can make sense of it.'

'You're seriously suggesting that Hanbury and the children were kidnapped by these mysterious people who attacked Sir Adrian?'

'And who frightened Maria Silva so much that she ran away in the middle of the night? Yes.'

'Mrs Grant, I'm sure everything you've told me is true, and I agree that criminals are at work. But it's very difficult to make sense of what you're suggesting. According to you, Hanbury decides on a sudden impulse to have the children to himself for the day. While you're shutting the garage doors he seizes his chance and drives away. At some point during this pleasure trip he and the children are kidnapped by persons unknown. Can you really believe that?'

'No. I'm suggesting something quite different. I told you I found the gate to the banana plantation off its hinges and went inside. The oil drum was up against the wall ready to be stood on and someone had left traces of a picnic lying about. But the time share girl who was in there yesterday on watch had been told to clear up when she'd finished and leave no trace. She says she put the oil drum away where it belonged before she left and put the gate back on its hinges. She also says there wasn't any litter left there. In other words, someone else was there in the plantation this morning, and left unexpectedly in too much of a hurry to clear up.'

'Very well, but what are you getting at?'

'You'll soon see. Let's go back now to the moment when I'm getting the car out of the garage to take the children for a swim. Gerald comes up the lane to say goodbye and asks me to drive him to the airport. I refuse, but say I'll drop him in town where he can catch a bus. He gets into the car. I leave the engine running and go back into the yard because the doors have to be shut from the inside. The people on watch among the bananas see the man they're interested in sitting in a car with the engine running, and the driver out of sight, shutting the doors. It's a heaven-sent opportunity. They jump in and drive off. The fact that there are two terrified children in the car is inconvenient. But they don't mind leaving the gate open and the remains of their breakfast inside. They've got their man, so what does it matter?'

Bettencourt received this in silence. It lasted a long time.

'Gerald didn't kidnap the children,' Celia insisted. 'He and the children were kidnapped.'

'Really?' His voice rose in a mystified cackle. 'Why would anyone want to do that?'

'I'm not quite sure. I have an idea, but it isn't quite worked out yet.'

A long silence followed.

'Well?' Celia queried.

'I'm wondering how the judicial police are going to react to a theory that isn't quite worked out yet.'

'Oh for goodness sake. If I don't put a theory to them they won't have to react to it. We tell them the facts and leave it to them to make sense of it all. That's their job, not ours, and good luck to them.'

Another long pause.

'Very well, Mrs Grant. I'll try to make an appointment for us with the judicial police and ring you back.'

Ten minutes later he called again, to say that he had made the appointment in an hour's time, and would meet her then at the judicial police headquarters behind the Courts of Justice. 'Don't bother with a taxi,' he added. 'Freda's coming downtown to shop, so I've asked her to pick you up.'

Sitting rigid at Antonia's desk, Celia suddenly gave way to panic. She was horrified by the prospect of having to confront the police with unorganised thoughts swirling round and round in her head, and forced herself to marshal them as best she could. Slowly and painfully she followed three separate chains of reasoning to their logical conclusion, but nothing she could do would bind the three together into a coherent pattern. In due course Freda Bettencourt arrived to drive her down to the police headquarters. The key to the puzzle still eluded her. She would have liked to be driven downtown in silence, so that she could go on thinking. But Freda was bursting with news of her own.

'Did Carlos tell you we were getting divorced?'

Celia forced herself to concentrate. 'Yes. I believe he did.'

'Well, we aren't. Antonia's dead. Anyway, his thing with her had been over for months, she'd shacked up with someone else. So we decided to make it up.'

Had it been over for months? Celia wondered. Or had Bettencourt lied to rescue his marriage? If Gerald was to be believed, Antonia was highly promiscuous, and quite capable of running two lovers at once.

'You'll never guess who the replacement was,' Freda said

144

with a scornful little laugh. 'It was that frightful little would-be heartthrob Lúcio Freitas, who's buying up all the land round the Whitings' place.'

Celia let out what Freda took as a cry of surprise at this revelation. It was not. It had escaped from her because Freda's last remark had caused the connecting link between her three chains of reasoning to fall suddenly into place. Freda burbled on happily about the repair job she had done on her marriage, and the sexual voracity which had prompted Antonia to admit an upstart peasant to her bed. Meanwhile, Celia embarked on a train of thought which lasted till they reached the Justice building.

'And thanks a million for putting poor George Whiting out of his misery,' Freda called as Celia got out.

With her thoughts elsewhere, Celia looked blank.

'Over Sir Adrian's memoirs, Mrs Grant. Fancy him being in a stew all those years over nothing.'

Had he been in enough of a stew to kill Antonia? That neglected corner of the problem area was still dark. Brooding over it, Celia went round to the back of the building to the entrance of the judicial police headquarters. Bettencourt was there to meet her, looking nervous. 'Would you like to brief me, so that I can marshal the facts and present them in a logical order?' he asked. 'Or would you prefer to tell the story in your own way?'

'I would prefer to present the facts in a logical order myself.'

Looking doubtful about her ability to do so, he escorted her to an office where a short, alert-looking plain-clothes policeman in his fifties with tidy grey hair was sitting behind a desk. 'Inspector Pinto is investigating the kidnapping of the two children by their father,' he explained by way of introduction, then plunged into explanations in Portuguese.

When these were over, Pinto turned to her. 'Our friend Mr Bettencourt tells me that you have some new information about this matter, which I should hear.'

Celia launched out into her narrative, beginning with the disappearance of Maria and the attack on Sir Adrian. When she told him what she had learnt from the time share youngsters, he made a note. 'They work for the development behind the church of São Lourenço, you say? We will certainly question these young people.'

'I doubt if you'll find them there. The so-called private detectives they were involved with arrived in force and behaved very threateningly because they were telling me the whole story. So they ran away.'

'The developers will know the addresses where they are living. Excuse me a moment.' He gave brief orders on the telephone in Portuguese.

'Do be gentle with them,' she pleaded. 'They thought they were helping with a harmless matrimonial inquiry.'

'Thank you, I will remember that. These men who appeared threateningly in the square, can you describe them?'

She did her best, and he complimented her on the result. 'What interests me most in what you tell me,' he added, 'is that according to the young people, the two men expressed a special interest in Mr Hanbury.'

'Yes. Mainly because they'd discovered that he had a criminal record.'

Pinto frowned. 'The facts we have at our disposal do not explain the behaviour of Mr Hanbury. Let me begin by asking if you have some understanding about his mentality?'

'Not really. There are two possible views. The first, very obvious one, is that he is passionately devoted to his children, and came to Madeira to reach some sort of understanding with his ex-wife about them. But that theory raises questions. Was it reasonable to make the journey so soon after he left prison? He had no job and very little money to meet his expenses here. Wouldn't it have been more sensible to leave the problem of the children till later, and concentrate on establishing himself first?'

'Yes. And the other possibility, Mrs Grant?'

'That the children are only an excuse to explain his presence here, that he came to Madeira with some other aim in mind; some money-raising scheme, perhaps, which involved his ex-wife's consent or co-operation.'

'A scheme in which the two criminals whom you mention are also interested?'

'Well, they have to be on opposite sides, don't they? To begin with they didn't know who he was. They had to identify him as the person involved by means of an elaborate spying operation at the Quinta Coulson.'

'Let us assume, then, that they are on opposite sides. Are the two criminals responsible for the disappearance of Mr Hanbury and the children?'

'Yes,' said Celia. Avoiding Bettencourt's eye, she expounded her theory of the way they had been kidnapped while she was shutting the garage doors.

Pinto nodded eagerly. 'It is a possibility. It is perhaps the only possibility.' He plunged into thought. 'But it assumes that your second thesis is correct; that Mr Hanbury came to Madeira for some undercover reason.'

'I'm sorry, no. I don't think that follows. The criminals are looking for some person connected with the Quinta Coulson who they believe is acting against their interests in some way. They learn that Gerald Hanbury has been in prison, but they don't know the details of his one offence and assume that he's a hardened criminal and the person they're after.'

'And they are wrong? Which of your two theories concerning his mentality do you prefer?'

Celia considered. 'Seeing him with his children, I think his devotion to them is genuine. He made awful mistakes, rushing them into a relationship they weren't ready for, and it was silly of him to come to Madeira so soon after his release. But that's understandable. I can imagine that a prisoner could get obsessed with something outside that they wanted to cling on to in the wreckage of their life. I think in Gerald's case it was his children.'

'So now we face this problem: who at the Quinta Coulson is acting against the interests of these criminals, and what is the nature of his action?'

'Her action,' she corrected. 'The person behind this whole thing is Antonia Hanbury.'

'But she is dead. Ah, but I see what you suggest. Someone else, an associate of hers, has continued her activity.'

'Of course. When the criminals are told that Gerald and Antonia met several times in the bar in the little square, their first question is, were they conspiring together? They assume that the answer is yes. It looks to them as if Gerald and Antonia were in this together, and he's carrying on the operation now that she's dead.'

147

'Mrs Grant, the theory you have constructed gives me great pleasure because of its neatness. I give you now a challenge. Construct me now a theory concerning the activity of Mrs Hanbury which causes such trouble.'

'It's a very simple one-word theory: blackmail.'

NINE

'Blackmail,' Pinto echoed. 'It is a splendid one-word theory. But are there not more words which follow?'

'Yes. I'm pretty sure it's blackmail because of something the youngsters told me. The men asked them what sort of accent Gerald had, and were puzzled when they said it was standard English. One of them muttered something about it being easy to disguise a voice, and that can mean only one thing. They heard the voice on the telephone. Someone rang them with a demand for money or action of some kind. In other words, blackmail.'

'Blackmail by Mrs Hanbury?'

'Yes. Ever since she came to Madeira after her divorce she's been scratching around for money, and blackmail is one of the ways she's been raising it. I've talked to two of her victims, I'll tell you about that later. What she got out of them was relatively minor. To judge from the scale and fury of the bully-boys' reaction, this is quite major.'

'But how does this lady, living quietly in Madeira and looking after her invalid father, find a matter for major blackmail?'

'I don't know, but here's a clue.' She produced it from her handbag. 'This is a bill from something calling itself an *Agéncia de Recortes de Impresa*, which I believe means a press-cutting agency.'

'Correct,' said Pinto.

'Why was Antonia subscribing to a press-cutting agency in Rio de Janeiro?'

'I have no idea, Mrs Grant. Please continue to construct your theory.'

'Brazil has been cropping up all over the place ever since I got here. Antonia had used a page from a paper published there to line a drawer, it's called the *Latin American Daily Post*. I even ran into a complication about some Brazilian species orchids. But the main point is, Maria Silva is Brazilian.'

'She is Sir Adrian Morton's nurse who has disappeared?'

'Yes, and a mystery woman. She goes out as little as possible, doesn't want days off or holidays and gives the impression that she's hiding from something. But Antonia has guessed that she's in hiding. She takes a Latin American paper in the hope of discovering why. In it she finds details of some crime story or whatever that looks as if it fits Maria's circumstances. So she subscribes to a press agency in Rio, asking for cuttings about that particular story. When she knows the full details and her suspicions are confirmed, she's all set for major blackmail.'

'But the person she should then blackmail is Maria Silva.'

'No. Maria's in hiding. She hasn't any money. If Antonia's blackmailing her, why are the bully-boys trying to find her? And why does she take alarm and run off in the middle of the night as soon as they appear on the scene?'

Pinto thought about this. 'Your criminals want this Maria Silva. Mrs Hanbury says, "You shall not have her unless you pay me money"?'

'Possible, but is it as simple as that? Maria isn't a prisoner. She's free to come and go, she can't be traded across the counter like a pound of sugar. What keeps her where she is is her fear of being found.'

'So?'

'Antonia has found out from the press agency in Rio what Maria did to land herself in this trouble. I don't know what it was, but it was something that will cause enormous embarrassment to the bully-boys and the organisation behind them if she surfaces in public. What Antonia says to them is, unless you come across with a lot of money, we shall produce Maria and ruin you.'

Pinto thought for a moment. 'But suppose your Maria will not co-operate?'

'She doesn't have to. She doesn't even know this is going on. The threat is enough. You send them a snapshot of her along with your letter, with a newspaper in the picture to show the date. Then they know the threat's genuine.'

'It is a possible theory.'

'But the blackmailing telephone calls have not been from Antonia. They were from a man who they think was disguising his voice. Antonia has died, but this man is still alive and will go on blackmailing them.'

Pinto nodded. 'And the criminals, learning that Mr Hanbury has a criminal record, assume that he is the man they want. They kidnap him, and try to make him reveal to them Maria's whereabouts.'

'Yes, and they give him an uncomfortable time trying to make him tell them something he doesn't know.'

'You are sure of that, Mrs Grant?'

'Almost. To all appearances the Hanburys were divorced and at daggers drawn. If they were partners in a blackmail racket, why should they bother to be so devious?'

'But who is the associate who continues the racket after Mrs Hanbury's death, if it is not her former husband?'

'There's one obvious candidate, a man called Lúcio Freitas. Mr Bettencourt can tell you more about his background than I can.'

'He has a little house and banana patch up behind the Quinta Coulson,' Bettencourt said uncomfortably. 'Made his pile in South Africa and came back here to settle.'

'The way he talks English is weird,' Celia added, 'a mixture of Portuguese and South African accents. No wonder the bully-boys thought he was disguising his voice.'

'But why is Mr Freitas an "obvious candidate"?' asked Pinto.

'Partly because he was Antonia's lover.'

Pinto's eyebrows rose in an expression of polite shock. 'But surely, Mrs Grant, there is a separation of social level which makes such a liaison unlikely.'

'I know, I was surprised when I found out. But I'm right, aren't I, Mr Bettencourt?'

Bettencourt's face was a study in embarrassed vexation. 'What happened was, Freitas approached Mrs Hanbury with an obviously trumped up claim about the share-out of the levada water, but that was just an excuse for making her acquaintance. I happen to know about it because she consulted me about the legal aspects. He dropped the claim almost at once but he went on seeing her, and yes, I understand that they did become lovers.'

'It's not really so surprising,' said Celia, as Bettencourt retreated

151

into an absorbed examination of his fingernails. 'Mr Freitas' love affairs are not wholly disinterested. He uses sex to further his commercial interests.'

Asked what these interests were, she explained about his purchases of land, his offer to buy the Quinta Coulson, and his hotel-building ambitions. 'I wondered at the time whether he'd really made enough money in South Africa to pay for all this, and if not who his backers were. But he doesn't need backers, the whole thing is going to be financed by the proceeds of blackmail.'

'But why did not your criminals kidnap this Freitas,' Pinto asked, 'and leave the unfortunate Mr Hanbury alone?'

'Because they don't know about Freitas. They photographed everyone who came to the Quinta Coulson, but only in daylight. He came after dark, and they couldn't use flash.'

There was a long pause while he digested all this. 'It is a very elegant theory that you have constructed.'

'Thank you. But the inelegant bit is that poor Gerald is probably being tortured in front of his terrified children to make him disgorge information he doesn't possess. Can't we tell these creatures somehow that Freitas is the man they want?'

He smiled. 'I am sorry, that would be contrary to correct police procedures.'

'Then what can you do to find Gerald and the children?'

'We can approach the agencies which let furnished houses to visitors, and ask if any of their clients correspond with the description of the two gunmen which we shall get from the young time share salesmen. It is the surest way to find criminals who come to the island from elsewhere, but unfortunately it takes time.'

'There isn't any time! Just think what may be happening!'

Faced with her dismay, he ceased to be an amused listener to a neat theory, and became a policeman on the job. 'We shall of course give the highest priority to this matter. And now if you will excuse me, I shall arrange the questioning of the time share youngsters, and immediately ask the colleagues in Rio de Janeiro to discover from this press-cutting agency what subject it was that interested Mrs Hanbury. When there is any development I shall inform you at once.'

It was dark when Celia and Bettencourt came out of the

building. Driving her back up the hill to the Quinta Coulson, he said: 'That was terrific, Mrs Grant. You handled him perfectly, I give you full marks.'

'He was easy to deal with, open to ideas and not at all stuffy and official. But how effective is he?'

'Very, once he's convinced that something nasty needs sorting out, and this is very nasty.'

'Yes.' Celia shuddered, thinking of Gerald and the children.

'I don't like the idea of you alone in that big house with all these strong-arm people about. Would you like to take up your quarters with us?'

'That's very kind of you, but I ought to be at the Quinta Coulson in case the children turn up suddenly, or there might be a phone call. I'll be all right.'

She had considered asking Agostinho and Teresa to sleep at the quinta, but decided against it. To be alone would be better than having the company of two people she did not trust.

Bettencourt dropped her at the gate of the quinta. 'I was in a panic when I went out to the airport to collect you,' he confessed, 'because I didn't know what sort of person to expect. Just think of the mess we'd be in if you'd turned out to be an adorable little goose.'

'Geese are noisy and messy and not at all adorable,' she replied.

He laughed and drove away.

As she fitted her key into the lock, Lúcio Freitas stepped out of the shadows lower down the lane and murmured a soft 'Good eevening, senhora.'

'Oh, it's you. What d'you want?'

'I wait here for you to come home. I must talk weeth you.'

'What about?' She was determined not to let him into the house.

'You have been theenking about me, yes? I think also of you. It's better we go inside and relax.'

'Oh no it isn't. If that was the idea, I think you should go home and cool your ardour under a cold shower.'

'I come with manee ideas. We must talk the beeziness again together.'

'What business? If it's about selling the house to you, the answer is still no.'

'You are beauteeful, but you must also be practeecal. Maria Silva, she is gone, weethout her Sir Morton cannot stay. Why you want to let eet, that ees not practeecal. Much better you sell eet to me.'

'Good night, Mr Freitas. I've told you, I'm not selling.'

Not to him, she thought, whatever happened. That would involve pocketing the proceeds of blackmail. She turned to go into the quinta. But he was standing very close behind her, ready to force his way in with her when she unlocked the door. He had not touched her yet, but she was very frightened.

'Go home now, please,' she said.

'But why? I do not make you any harm. Why may wee not eenjoy each other's companee?'

She turned to face him. 'Because I don't intend to open this door until you have removed yourself to a safe distance. And do stop looking at me like a tom cat on heat, it won't get you anywhere.'

Still exuding high-octane menace, he muttered something bad-tempered and strutted away up the lane.

Safely inside, she tried to relax. But the elegant house seemed menacing. For the first time, being alone in it frightened her. As she picked at the cold supper that Teresa had left for her, she suddenly realised that a whole area of the problem had been ignored in her exchanges with Pinto. Where was Maria Silva? Surely it was important to find her before the gunmen did?

There were various possibilities. Maria could have made straight for the airport and left the island. She could have taken refuge in a convent with the help of her friend the parish priest. Or she could have found a private bolthole with the help of her Brazilian relative Mrs Nielsen. As she was wondering which of these three was the most probable and how they could be investigated, a sudden insight struck her. She had omitted from her list a possibility with very dangerous overtones.

But she needed to check. Agostinho would have the answer. With any luck he would still be at the bar in the square, he went there after work. She rang it, and got him.

'Agostinho, did you know that some rather frightening men

154

have been making inquiries about people who come to this house?'

He seemed to be searching his memory. 'I think, yes, *minha senhora*. Vicente here tell me something of it.'

'But you didn't mention it to me.'

He answered on a cringing note of excuse. 'I did not wish to make anxious the senhora.'

'Did you mention it to anyone else?'

Agostinho mumbled something vague.

'Did you mention it to your friend Lúcio Freitas?' she insisted. Silence.

'Answer me, Agostinho,' she said sharply. 'This is important, you've got to tell me.'

'Lúcio, he knows of these men.'

Dismayed, she faced the new scenario that confronted her. Freitas learning from Agostinho of the looming threat to his scheme; knocking on the door of Adrian's cottage in the middle of the night, waking Maria, telling her that her pursuers are very near. She is too frightened to wonder how he knows about her plight, and when he offers to find her a fresh hiding-place, she accepts because she is ready to grasp at any straw. When she is safely installed with some relative, Freitas sighs with relief. Despite the arrival of high-powered opposition, he is still in business as a blackmailer.

Suddenly she knew that this was the right answer, she could prove it to herself. He had just been pressing his offer to buy the quinta. But unless he had spirited Maria away himself, he had no means of knowing that her pursuers had not done so when they broke into the cottage; in which case there would be no blackmail and he would be in no position to produce the purchase money.

She took her coffee into the drawing-room, defying its spacious grandeur to intimidate her, and was trying to concentrate on a book when the telephone rang. She went to the library and picked it up. Silence greeted her.

'Hullo? Who's there?' she demanded.

The silence continued. Someone could be heard breathing faintly at the other end. After waiting a few moments she put the phone down. It began to ring again almost at once. This time she let it ring.

155

It went on ringing for ten minutes, making it difficult for her to concentrate on the book about the British occupation of Madeira which she had picked from the shelves. Was the caller Lúcio Freitas? He was capable of it, but could he have resisted the temptation to breathe more heavily?

Twenty minutes passed before the phone rang again. Hoping that this time it might bring news of the children, she answered it. A man's voice said: 'Don't hang up on me this time.'

'Then say what you want to say, and be quick about it. I'm too busy to listen to you suffering from lockjaw.'

Another long silence followed. She put the phone down. It rang again almost at once. 'That was naughty,' said the voice. 'Don't do it again.'

'Very well,' said Celia, determined not to lose this battle of wills. 'I shall put the phone down on the desk and go on reading my book. When you've decided what you want to say, make a loud noise and I'll pick it up again.'

'Don't you try getting tough with me, lady, or you'll be sorry.'

'Then stop wasting my time.'

'Where's Maria-José Beleza?'

'I don't know anyone of that name. If you mean Maria Silva, I have no idea where she's got to.'

'I want an answer, lady.'

'Here you are again, then. She left on a flight to Lisbon this afternoon. She's taken refuge in a nunnery. She's jumped into the sea. She's gone to ground in the bridal suite at Reid's Hotel. Is that enough answers, or d'you want some more?'

'You tell me where she is, or we shoot you.'

'That won't do much good to either of us, because I don't know.'

She put down the phone, shaken by her own audacity and convinced that it would ring again. It did not, and after an unnerving wait she went back to her book. But she found it impossible to concentrate on the ins and outs of Madeira's love-hate relations with the British, and was wondering how else to occupy herself, when the bell from the front gate echoed through the house. She started up in terror, dropping her book, and cursed herself for not having made Teresa and Agostinho keep her company for the night.

The bell rang again. Pulling herself together she opened a shutter in the drawing-room and shouted: 'Who is it?'

'Luis Pinto from the *Polícia Judiciária*.'

Relief flooded over her. 'One moment, I'll come and let you in.'

Walking through the shadowy garden from the front door to the gate, she had a job controlling her nerves. But having a senior policeman in the house was comforting, and when she told him about the threatening phone call she even managed to make light of it. 'In a way it's good news. If they've started asking me where Maria is, it means Gerald's managed to convince them that he doesn't know.'

'They have also taken other measures to find her,' said Pinto. 'This will surprise you, Mrs Grant. I was in the neighbourhood, so I come to tell you in person. Your band of criminals has now seized upon Mr Bettencourt and carried him off.'

'Really? How astonishing. They decide that Gerald isn't the blackmailer, so they scoop up the only other man they know about and assume it must be him. When did this happen?'

'An hour ago. The method was almost the same as in the case of Mr Hanbury. They waited outside his house for him to return home from work. While he is opening the garage to put away his car, they push him back into the car and drive him away in it.'

After a moment's thought, Celia said: 'I suppose this isn't altogether surprising. He and Gerald are the only two men with contacts at the quinta that they know about. And they may even have got wind of something I couldn't very well mention in your office in front of Mr Bettencourt. He was Freitas' predecessor in Antonia's bed.'

'Mrs Grant, is there anything you do not know?'

'Plenty. I only know about this because Freda Bettencourt is rather talkative. Is she very distressed?'

'Distressed and very angry.'

'Oh dear, I'll ring her later and try to cheer her up.'

They were standing in the hall. She took him into the library and settled him down with a glass of Madeira.

'Is it possible,' he asked, 'that Mr Bettencourt and not Mr Freitas is the blackmailer?'

She considered. 'I don't think so. His affair with Antonia was over months ago. When she died, she and Freitas were as thick as thieves commercially as well as sexually. I suppose it's heartless to say so, but this is the best thing that could have happened.'

'Aha. You have understood. Bettencourt, having been present during our conversation in my office, will at once say to the gunmen, "You have taken captive the wrong man. You should address yourselves to Lúcio Freitas."' Pinto leaned forward eagerly. 'It is a great pleasure, Mrs Grant, to find that our minds communicate so quickly.'

'I'm enjoying it too. When they pull in Freitas you follow them to their headquarters, where all these people are holed up.'

'Exactly. Already I have put in place a large operation of surveillance in preparation for his kidnapping. It takes almost the whole of my resources, which are small. I hope only that all the other criminals of Madeira will keep quiet and attempt nothing until this matter has been resolved.'

'But it won't be resolved, will it, till you've found Maria Silva.'

'If she has gone abroad already, as I hope, that will not be my problem.'

'I don't think she has gone abroad. In fact I'm sure she hasn't.'

'Please, I don't understand.'

'This evening Lúcio Freitas came here to repeat his offer to buy the quinta. That must mean that he's still hoping to pay for it with the blackmail money.'

He took alarm at once. 'You are saying, he knows where Maria Silva is to be found?'

'More than that. He knew the bully-boys were watching the quinta for her, because Agostinho, the gardener here, told him. I think he warned her they were around and terrified her into letting him take her away and hide her from them somewhere. That's why he's still hoping to cash in.'

'Aha.' Pinto digested this grimly. 'What is your opinion of the courage of Lúcio Freitas?'

'You mean, would he tell them where Maria was if they tortured him? I've no idea, that's always a difficult question.'

'We cannot rely on his silence.'

'No. Maria must be in very serious danger, don't you think?'

'Yes. The danger is more serious than you can imagine.' He plunged into deep thought. 'To find her, we must first discover what associates Freitas has who could have hidden her. But it will take time, and we have no time.'

'I can offer you one short cut, Mr Pinto. Freitas has been using friends and relatives as nominees for the land purchases I mentioned. One of the neighbours here, a man called George Whiting, got alarmed about his activities and did some research at the land registry to find out who's involved.'

'Aha. He could give me some names?'

'Probably.'

'I shall have him questioned at once. You know where he lives?'

'Somewhere up behind here. Let's look him up in the phone book . . . Here you are: Whiting, George, Casa Kenilworth, Caminho Santa Maria.'

'Thank you, I shall send a man there now. May I please use your telephone?'

'Of course.'

While he was in the library phoning, she had a sudden attack of nerves. Never before had she worked in such close co-operation with a policeman. Everything she said was taken at its face value, none of her suggestions were challenged. What if there were flaws in her reasoning? What if she had set a huge police operation in motion only to be made to look a fool when the trail proved false? She had always had an ingrained fear of going to the police with allegations she could not prove, and being mocked at. Being taken seriously, and later proved wrong, would be even worse.

She was trying to master her dread of this dismal prospect when Pinto came back from the phone looking thoughtful. 'The priest at the church here will know the Freitas family, and what connections it has. I think I shall question him myself.'

'Do, but may I sound a note of caution? Don't tell him why you want to know, because he's Maria's confessor. I don't know how much she's told him under the seal of the confessional about her troubles, but he may not take kindly to inquiries from a policeman who is trying to locate her.'

He looked grave. 'Thank you for this warning, it is an extra complication. Our relations with the Church are delicate. When

159

we approach it for information, we have to give our reasons, and it is for it to judge whether the reasons are sufficient. As you yourself have pointed out, our inquiries concerning the whereabouts of this penitent may be badly received unless they are presented in the right light.' After a moment's thought he added: 'Mrs Grant, would you agree to come with me to the presbytery to see him?'

'Of course, if you think I'd be any use.'

'I think we present it to him like this. Maria has disappeared. You are her kindly employer, and you are concerned for her safety because you know that she has enemies who are pursuing her. I am present because you have spoken to me about your anxieties.'

'Will that persuade him?'

'Oh, I think so. He will tell us that he cannot break the seal of the confessional, and I shall say it will not be necessary, because we already have the information.'

'Do we?'

'I do. And I shall now inform you, so that you too are not intimidated by the confessional.'

He settled back in his chair and launched out into his recital. 'When Maria Silva, as she called herself, installed herself as nurse to Sir Adrian Morton, Mrs Hanbury quickly noticed that she behaved like a person in hiding, and thought how she might turn this to her advantage. You yourself have pointed out how she searched in the press for any mention of circumstances which might cause a young Brazilian woman to hide from the world. The cuttings from the agency were of course in Portuguese, but fortunately she had a confederate who could translate them for her.

'The police in Rio de Janeiro have been most prompt in helping us. Just now I received by fax their answer to our inquiry. The subject on which she ordered press cuttings was an air crash in Brazil two years ago. In the past few months the relatives of victims began seeking compensation from the airline, and as some of the circumstances are a little curious, the matter was reported in great detail in the papers.

'For various reasons the police became involved in this matter, and they have sent us a fax of their report. The plane, which was on a flight to Mexico City, broke up in the air soon after leaving

160

Rio. All on board were killed and there was no doubt that the cause of the explosion was a bomb. Examination of the wreckage showed that it had been placed in the forward baggage hold, and suspicion fell on one of the baggage porters, who was nowhere to be found afterwards.

'Among the passengers were a dozen officials and experts, on their way to a conference in Mexico City concerned with the preservation of rain forests and the prevention of their destruction for the purpose of large-scale cattle ranching. A small determined faction among the cattle ranchers had already proved unscrupulous in defence of their interests, and it was widely believed at the time that they had planted the bomb, in order to delay action against them by eliminating most of the Brazilian experts on the conservation issue.

'The plane belonged to a commercial company based in Miami, and its very shady finance came from Central America and Florida. For various reasons the relatives of the victims sought the right to have their claim heard in Rio, and this was granted six months ago. They based their case on a curious circumstance. According to the airline's records the plane carried three hundred and twenty-three people, including a cabin staff of six. But when the wreckage, scattered over a wide area, was collected, the remains of only three hundred and twenty-two people were found. According to the claimants, who had access to the official report on the investigation, the missing remains had to be those of Maria-José Beleza, one of the stewardesses.

'The claimants proposed to produce witnesses, some of whom would say that shortly before the plane took off members of the cabin staff were heard to complain that one of their number was missing. Others claim to have seen an air hostess in the uniform of the airline in conversation on the tarmac with the baggage handler who was suspected of planting the bomb. They also say that she went with him towards the administration building, and that she resembled a photograph of a stewardess called Maria-José Beleza which was published in the press among pictures of the cabin staff. The claimants maintained that this air hostess was indeed Miss Beleza, who had known about the bomb and had deserted her duty in order not to share the fate of the other passengers and crew.

161

'This was of course a matter of great importance to the claimants and also to the airline. If Maria-José had known of the bomb, and had not informed the captain immediately, she had failed in her duty as an employee of the airline. The airline itself had been negligent through the action of its employee. In such circumstances its liability would be unlimited and the sums likely to be awarded would mean ruin for any but the largest international airlines.

'The airline naturally dismissed these allegations, pointing out that with the wreckage scattered over a wide area it was quite possible that the remains of Miss Beleza had escaped notice, and alleging that the stories about her desertion at the last moment had undoubtedly been invented in order to support allegations of negligence against them. Why, they asked, should she have failed to give warning of the danger if she knew of it? And if she had not perished in the accident, why was she nowhere to be found?

'These are powerful arguments, which will certainly be accepted by the court if the claimants can produce no proof to the contrary. But a press cutting containing perhaps a photograph of the missing air hostess has proved to Mrs Hanbury's satisfaction that Maria Silva is Maria-José Beleza. Suddenly, a few weeks before the court hearings are due to begin, the airline receives a letter containing a photograph of Maria-José Beleza reading a newspaper as proof that she is alive, and demanding a large sum of money.

'The directors of this not very reputable airline are in despair, and take energetic action. One of the witnesses claiming to have seen Maria-José leave the plane is shot and seriously wounded; the others have to be given police protection. A worldwide search for her begins. As long as she is alive, the blackmailer can repeat his demands again and again. She must be found and killed.'

'And Maria Silva is Maria-José Beleza?' Celia asked. 'There's no doubt about that?'

For answer, Pinto produced a faxed photograph from his brief-case. It showed a younger, less careworn version of her. 'Taken two years ago, just before the accident to the plane.'

'If she knew there was a bomb, why on earth didn't she warn the captain?'

He gave a wide shrug of ignorance. 'The mysteries of human behaviour are infinite, Mrs Grant. Let us go now and confront this priest.'

The presbytery, a modest building behind the church, opened directly on to the street. The priest's elderly housekeeper admitted them. When Pinto explained their business, they were shown into a parlour whose austerity was relieved by what looked like a much-loved collection of saintpaulias and streptocarpus on a windowsill.

Father Rodrigues, who joined them after a short pause, proved to be stout, brisk and matter of fact. But he clearly had very little English. Pinto explained in Portuguese who Celia was, and said that her concern for Maria's safety had brought them there.

Father Rodrigues made a neat little bow in Celia's direction and spoke at some length. Pinto translated. 'Father Rodrigues asks me to say how grateful he is for the kindness you've shown to Maria, who is a lonely person and needs friends. He tells me that although she's only known you for a few days, she has become deeply attached to you.'

This was news to Celia. She could only assume that Antonia, by contrast, had failed to treat Maria as a human being. As the exchanges continued in Portuguese, she could gather only that they were amicable, and that Father Rodrigues belonged to the brisk and practical branch of the priesthood rather than the remote and saintly one.

'My parishioners bring me all sorts of horror stories,' he was telling Pinto, 'about kidnappings and spyings of one sort or another, but if you want to ask me what's happening or why, I'm afraid I can't help you.'

'Of course you can't, Father, and I understand why. But if I tell you that I know all about the bomb on the plane at Rio two years ago, and your penitent's connection with it, you'll see that knowing the secrets of the confessional wouldn't add much to my knowledge.'

'Splendid. That makes things simpler. But what d'you want from me?'

'As I'm sure you know, what's going on round here means that Maria is in danger of her life. Powerful interests, you can guess who they are, intend to kill her before the compensation proceedings come to court. We must find her and protect her.'

'Fine, but I haven't seen her since she came to Benediction two days ago. I'm told she's vanished, but I've no idea where she is.'

Pinto explained that Maria was believed to be under the dangerous protection of Lúcio Freitas, who for various reasons was not to be trusted.

'I should think not indeed, he's a shocker. Christenings once a year for the last five years, no self-control at all.'

'Tell us about these christenings, Father. What does the family consist of, who comes to them?'

'That's what you want to know?' Father Rodrigues hesitated. 'You think he's got her tucked away with a relative somewhere?'

'It's one of the possibilities we're investigating.'

'But look here, you're a policeman. I'm not sure if I ought to help you. If the law gets hold of Maria, she'll be tried for letting all those people be killed in the plane.'

'Yes. But don't tell me the Church is happy for her to be massacred by criminals instead of doing a stretch in prison.'

'Oh dear, you're right I suppose. Let me see now. Mrs Freitas has an uncle in Camara de Lobos, but he's gaga if I remember rightly, his flat would be no place to hide anyone, too cramped and right on the tourist circuit. There's a cousin with a bit of land over near Serra de Aqua, you could try there. At the last christening the godfather was from Canico, friend of the priest there, but I don't remember his name and I'm not sure if he was a relative . . .'

He rambled on for some time, with Pinto making notes on everything he said. When his information dried up, Pinto made a sign to Celia and rose to go. Father Rodrigues took her hand and said something in Portuguese.

'He thanks you again for your kindness to poor Maria,' Pinto explained.

Outside in the street, Pinto paused for a moment. 'There was one question which I longed to ask. He knows, but there is this obstacle of the confessional, he cannot tell us.'

'Yes. I'd love to know whether she's a terrorist or not.'

'The bomb was in the forward baggage hold. An air hostess would not have access to the passengers' baggage.'

'An accomplice, then?'

'Would an accomplice put herself into the situation of having to desert her duty at the last moment before departure?'

'But Mr Pinto, if she's not a terrorist or an accomplice, why on earth did she walk away from that plane without telling anyone there was a bomb on board? And why did she disappear and stay underground for two years?'

'Let us suppose that she had a perfectly good reason for leaving the plane at the last moment. The other members of the cabin staff are dead, and cannot give evidence about it. The coincidence creates a bad appearance against her. She is afraid that she will be accused of complicity in the plot, so she disappears.'

'Mr Pinto, can you believe that?'

'No. The varieties of human behaviour are infinite, but this is altogether too extraordinary. And now I shall escort you home. Please lock all doors and windows securely, and do not have bad dreams.'

TEN

After bidding Celia good night, Pinto drove back downtown to his office in the Courts of Justice, and began brooding on the probable course of events during the night ahead.

When the criminals accused Carlos Bettencourt of being a blackmailer he would tell them that the man they wanted was not him but Lúcio Freitas, that was the obvious and sensible thing to do. Knowing that Freitas was the next victim on the kidnap list gave the police a huge tactical advantage. Presumably Bettencourt could be relied on not to reveal that he had learnt about Freitas' iniquities at a conference about the case in the offices of the *Polícia Judiciária*.

Pinto reckoned that it would take about two hours for the gangsters to convince themselves that they had got the wrong man, and perhaps another hour to arrive in force at the Freitas establishment and pull him out of bed. The trap had been set, five unmarked cars linked by radio were standing by, ready to tail the criminals when they took him to wherever they were holding their prisoners.

Meanwhile he stuck pins into a map of Madeira. Each pin marked the home address of a friend or relative of Lúcio Freitas who had been mentioned by Father Rodrigues. One of his detectives had extracted a list of Freitas' land-purchase 'nominees' from George Whiting, in the teeth of fierce questioning by Whiting into why he wanted to know. When these too had been plotted on the map he looked at the result with satisfaction. Locating Maria-José Beleza would not be very difficult. All the likely locations were out in the country. Country people were intensely curious about each others' affairs, and the presence at a neighbouring farm of a stranger, apparently a foreigner, would become public knowledge in the end. For Pinto, finding her was less urgent than neutralising her would-be killers. If that was done she would be in no danger and could be sought at leisure.

Everything, therefore, depended on the trap he had set. If the gang kidnapped Lúcio Freitas and led the detectives to the hide-out where their captives were being held, all would be well. But time wore on, and still nothing happened. He wandered into the outer office and began looking at routine reports as they came in. There was nothing of any importance; a robbery at Ribeira Brava, where the receptionist at a hotel had been held up at gunpoint while an insignificant sum of money was taken from the cash register; a routine crop of car thefts, and a drunken-driving offence. There was only one item of interest: the patrol which looked after the yacht marina reported a suspicious hiring of a motor-cruiser.

On a hunch, he rang through to the police post which had reported it. 'What did you make of it? The usual? Drugs?'

'Possibly. We have notified the coastguard service.'

'Any descriptions?'

'Two men. Speaking Spanish. No special distinguishing features, but the charter people say they were heavies. They let them have the boat because they were too frightened to refuse.'

Was there any connection between this and the Maria-José affair? Probably not. Nevertheless, Pinto decided to have a word with the officer in charge of the coastguard cutters, who assured him that they had it under control.

It was one in the morning, and he had fallen into a light doze, when one of the plain-clothes patrols watching developments at the Freitas household reported in by radio-telephone. 'It's started. They've got him out among the banana trees and they're bashing him about.'

'And the family?'

'Being kept in the house at gunpoint, we think. Too terrified to make a noise.'

'Good. As soon as they move, let me know which way they go.'

In due course he was told that a car containing four heavies, with Freitas slumped between two of them in the back, was heading into one of the hillside suburbs north of the town. This surprised him.

It was a working-class quarter with no houses or flats available for rent by people claiming to be tourists. What surprised him even more was that the car climbed on out of the suburb and took a winding road leading into the mountains, a lonely area inhabited by foresters and workers on the levadas. There was no place there for the headquarters of a criminal conspiracy, its isolation would make it too conspicuous and the road communications were too bad. He had miscalculated. The kidnappers of the unfortunate Freitas were not leading him back to their hide-out. They were making Freitas take them to where he had hidden Maria-José.

A glance at the array of pins on the map confirmed this. One of them, high on the mountainside and just off the road ahead, represented the home of a forestry worker who according to Whiting was a cousin of Freitas and the nominal owner of one of his parcels of land. Pinto thought rapidly, and decided the risk of their going elsewhere was negligible. He would set an ambush there, to deal with the criminals when they arrived.

There was a police post over on the far side of the pass, beyond the forestry worker's house. He rang it and ordered two car-loads of policemen to go at once to the spot and set an ambush with a view to making arrests. If the inhabitants of the house asked them what they were doing, they were to say they were taking precautions for their safety, and send everyone back into the house to await developments. 'And among the people in the house there will be a young woman calling herself Maria Silva, who will be in a state of terror. Explain, please, that she is not under arrest, we have not been notified of any accusation against her.'

Privately he hoped to persuade her to leave the island quickly and without attracting a lot of publicity. If the Brazilians wanted to extradite her, they could do it from somewhere else. Without her there, her part in the bomb attack on the plane need not be mentioned and the trial of the men he was about to arrest could be toned down into something less likely to make banner headlines in the international press. It was official policy to avoid drawing attention to crimes of violence on the island, for fear of the effect on the tourist trade.

Having given his orders he went out to his car to drive to the scene of the action. Meanwhile, up at the forester's house, the ambush was already set. One of the police cars had gone up to the house and turned, so that it was facing down the track with its lights off. Armed police took up positions covering the approach to the house and the other car, stationed in a clearing just off the track, was in position to move in and block off any attempted retreat.

Minutes after everything was in place, a car could be heard, stopping at the junction of the track with the main road. Steps approached. When they were near enough the car lights were switched on, catching five men in their beam. Taken by surprise, three of them started firing at the lights, but were soon overpowered. The fourth shot Lúcio Freitas dead. There was no point in letting him survive, to tell the police who 'Maria Silva' really was, and why certain Latin American interests wanted to kill her.

Maria-José Beleza was having her standard nightmare. She was in Manuel's arms, they were thrashing about in the bed, the great moment was approaching, the moment that Manuel always managed so perfectly, it was going to be wonderful. Then suddenly fear set in. She knew suddenly that this was all wrong, it ought not to be happening, she was damned in the eyes of the Church, fingers were pointing at her from all sides. The moment was still approaching, but now it was a moment of terror. It came. The explosion shattered the sky, bodies and wreckage began to fall. Her sin had caused this disaster, she too was falling, straight down into a bottomless pit of guilt.

Awake and shivering, she faced the eternal question: why had it all happened? Each step in the sequence had been one step towards disaster, but that was not obvious till afterwards.

Not many invitations come the way of a student nurse who spends most of her free time quietly with her widowed mother. Was she wrong to have accepted a really glamorous one, to the Hawaiian Ball at the Yacht Club, which traditionally opened Rio's pre-Lent Carnival? Surely not. The carnival balls were raunchy affairs involving a lot of near-nudity, but Manuel, who had invited her to be his partner, was an officer in a smart regiment living on a generous allowance from his father, and a distant connection of the Beleza family. Mrs Beleza decided that he could be relied on to behave correctly, and so it proved.

In the weeks which followed he made a dead set at her. Should she have brushed him off? If he had wanted a casual affair, she would have told him there was nothing doing, but he was serious about her. Flowers, presents, invitations to the homes of the wealthy and powerful, all this swept her off her feet. Her mother approved. The offer of marriage came, was accepted. Only after that did they end up ecstatically in bed.

And then the shadows began to gather. Manuel resigned his commission in the regiment rather abruptly, pleading family commitments on the great cattle ranch at home. But a relative with Army connections came to Maria-José's mother with a story of a scandal which Manuel's father had used his political influence to suppress; something about an orderly committing some minor misdemeanour, and having his face beaten to a pulp by Manuel in an ungovernable fit of temper. Taxed with this story, Manuel alleged that he had been framed by jealous fellow officers. Maria-José believed him, but a tiny seed of doubt had been sown.

The doubts grew stronger when she went to spend the summer on the ranch with his family. She was shocked by their cynical arrogance, the way political discussion always centred round which politicians could be bought, and which had to be manipulated by intimidation. With the arrogance went an insatiable right-wing greed. They were already rich, but wanted to be richer even at the expense of the poor. Some squatters who had dared to occupy a small piece of waste land were turned off brutally. There was talk of adding to the family's holdings, already enormous, by opening up land at the expense of the forest.

Then came the final straw. An Indian stable-hand had ridden a horse which had cast a shoe, causing it to go lame. Manuel had half killed the man, causing a near-revolt among the other employees. The family had supported him, remarking simply that one had to be firm with these people, they must learn not to be so stupid. Maria-José, appalled, had said she could not marry him. He flew into a rage, and had to be restrained from hitting her by his father.

Back in Rio, she decided not to return to nursing. After the life she had been leading, it was too humdrum and not well enough paid. The job of an air hostess offered a prospect of travel, contacts with interesting and well-to-do people, and perhaps even marriage. As a presentable-looking applicant with languages and a nursing background she had little difficulty in getting hired, but the reality did not quite come up to her expectations. She had various casual affairs, none of which led to marriage, and was thinking of changing her job again when disaster struck.

This was the moment she would relive to the end of her days, going over all the things she should have done rather than take the split-second decision that had been her ruin. It was two in the morning, and very dark outside the pool of light round the plane. She was walking towards it across the tarmac when she encountered the sight that was etched for ever in her memory; Manuel, disguised in a baggage porter's uniform, staring at her as he trundled an empty baggage trolley away from the plane.

In a moment of appalled recognition she knew at once why he was there. Among the passengers were a minister and his staff of experts on their way to an important United Nations conference on the conservation of rain forests, to be held in Mexico City. She had read in the press about the family's violent opposition to controls on the burning of rain forest, it was all of a piece with their greed for money and land. Manuel was a half-mad brute, who lashed himself into a frenzy of hate when crossed and would think nothing of mass murder to gain his ends. Appalled, she started to run towards the plane. She must warn the captain, the plane must be evacuated while the police searched for the bomb.

Manuel followed her and caught her by the arm. 'Don't,' he said softly. 'I've got a remote control device. If you do, I shall blow it up here on the ground.'

Could he have? Probably not, she realised that now. The remote control device was a myth. At the time, all she knew was that he was greedy and violent and capable of all evil. She stood there, paralysed with fear.

'Steady now,' he said. 'I've got a knife, but I don't want to have to use it.'

The knife was real, not a myth. It was in his waistband under his shirt, and he had pulled his shirt up to show her. This was the moment when she should have run for it, she knew that now. There were people about, even if he half killed her with the knife he would have been stopped, the alarm would have

171

been raised. This was her basic sin: cowardice. She had let three hundred and twenty-two people be killed because she was afraid of being hurt.

He dragged her on to the baggage trolley and settled behind the controls. 'No!' she screamed over the noise of the plane's engines. 'I must warn them, you can't do this.'

The trolley started with a jerk. But it was not heading towards the passenger terminal.

'Where are you taking me?' she screamed.

For answer, he began to tell her, in brutal and revolting detail, all the things he would do to her if she betrayed him; disgusting forms of sexual abuse, torture and finally murder which no one but he would have thought of, but which he, being Manuel, was perfectly capable of carrying out. He would do the same to her mother, he shouted, and worse. And when they were both dead, he would tell the world she was a whore, and her mother a procuress.

His car was in the staff car park behind the administration block. 'Get in,' he roared.

'No.'

Pinning her against the car door, he drew the knife and held it against her crotch. 'You know what I said I'd do. Shall I begin?'

'No, Manuel. No!' she screamed.

'Then get into the car.'

As they drove out into the suburbs of Rio, she begged him again and again to stop and let her out. He took no notice, but drove on furiously, ignoring traffic lights and on-coming vehicles like a man with a death wish, till they came to a sordid apartment block in a sordid street. He half carried, half dragged her up a filthy staircase and into a one-room apartment containing dirty crockery and an unmade bed. When he started to undress her she was too frightened, demoralised and confused to resist, and let him have his way with her.

Later, when she read the newspaper reports of the crash, she worked it out that they must have been making love, if that was the right expression, at the moment when the bomb exploded.

As she struggled into her clothes, she knew what she must do; go to the authorities, denounce Manuel.

'Of course, you'll have to go underground, change your identity,' he said in a matter-of-fact tone.

'No. Why?'

'Everyone thinks you're dead, like the rest of the people on that plane. Everyone but me, that is.'

'I can say I wanted to warn them, but you held me at knife point.'

'Who's going to believe that? There were people about, you could have run away if you'd wanted to. If you don't sham dead, you soon will be for real. They'll put out a contract on you quick as they can.'

'Who will?'

'Those hoodlums who run the airline. You knew there was a bomb on board, and didn't tell them. You're their employee. That makes them as a company guilty of negligence and the compensation claims will be enormous. They'll want you dead.'

It had the ring of truth. The management dealt ruthlessly with employees who stepped out of line, Maria-José knew of several cases. She could expect no mercy from them.

'They can't prove that I knew about the bomb,' she objected.

'In the end they will. They'll probably find out that I planted it. Everyone in Rio knows that you used to be my girlfriend, perhaps still are. You and I, we're the people who struck a blow against the wimps who want to save that bloody awful rain-forest from the march of progress. We have to stick together.'

Hypnotised by this, she had fled with him from one hiding place to another, sheltered by contacts among right-wing underground movements. From somewhere in this dim underworld, Manuel produced a false passport for her in the name of Maria Silva. They slipped across the frontier into Paraguay, then on to Bolivia and Chile. Manuel's parents no longer supported him, they had finally realised that his brand of violence damaged the interests of their class. So he lived by his wits on the uneasy margin between right-wing terrorism and crime.

Maria-José, tagging along unhappily behind him, quickly became convinced that he was mad. Most of his activities seemed to consist of violence for violence's sake. He still made love to her, forcefully and impersonally, but made no attempt to hide a mass of infidelities. She was tied to him, because she had no

173

money. He kept her short, knowing that she would get away if she could.

Then came the day when he came home battered and wounded but triumphant, with the proceeds of a big cocaine deal in his pocket. She bandaged him, then waited till he was asleep and helped herself conscientiously to only half the money. She was away within the hour, and on a flight out that same night. From Asuncion she telephoned her mother, who had heard nothing from her for almost a year and believed that she had died in the bombed plane. Maria-José impressed on her the need for secrecy and arranged to meet her clandestinely in Buenos Aires.

Senhora Beleza was horrified when she heard the full story of the bombing and her daughter's failure of nerve. But she was overjoyed to find her only child alive and remained unshaken in her affection. It was clear that Maria-José would have to stay underground. There had been rumours that she had survived, that she had been seen leaving the plane shortly before take-off. Various lawyers and inquiry agents had called on Mrs Beleza to check that she had heard nothing of her daughter. Some of the inquirers had been representing relatives of people killed in the crash. But at least one, who had behaved very unpleasantly, had been identified afterwards as a senior executive of the airline.

Clearly, both sides in the approaching compensation proceedings were interested in Maria-José, with the airline determined to prove that she was dead, if necessary by killing her. She took menial jobs abroad. Mrs Beleza lived in fear, convinced that her house was watched and her telephone tapped. They dared not meet, in case she led the airline's executioners to Maria-José. It was a miserable, hunted existence which had no future, no purpose.

In the past few days it had become miserable to the point of uselessness. Her mother had been followed from Rio, and once the airline's gunmen knew Maria-José was on the island it was only a matter of time before they found her. She had made no attempt to keep track of their activities, done nothing to save herself. Her life was not worth prolonging, it might as well end.

Then, in the middle of the night, Lúcio Freitas had burst into the cottage, terrified her with stories of gunmen closing in on the quinta, swept her away and given her shelter. How had he known she was in danger? Antonia knew why she was in hiding, and had used the knowledge to make sure she toed the line. Antonia had told Isabel Nielsen, who had known nothing of the story when she recommended Maria-José for the job with Sir Adrian. The horrid truth had shocked her into submitting to Antonia's demands and supplying rarities from her collection to keep him amused. She must also have told Lúcio Freitas, but why? And why had he concerned himself with her, he had hardly spoken a word to her till now. There was something devious yet brutal about his manner, she did not trust him.

Finding no answer to the riddle of his behaviour, she punched her pillow angrily into shape and tried to sleep. It was the hour of despair before the dawn. She dozed, woke, dozed again, then sat up in bed, listening in horror. There was shouting outside, gunfire. She dressed hastily, climbed out of the window and slid to the ground, then began scrambling up the mountainside behind the house. Above her she could hear the rushing water of the levada. This was what Freitas had told her to do if danger threatened. She was to climb up to the levada, and walk along the path to the waterhouse where the levadeiros kept their tools, and wait there for him to come for her.

Woken by the clamour of the bell at the entrance, Celia opened the shutters and looked out. Dawn had just broken. A police car was standing out in the lane, and the driver was ringing the bell and shouting.

She opened the window and shouted down. 'What is it?'

'Come please. Come quickly.'

Had Gerald and the children been found? She pulled on slacks and a shirt and ran down to the gate. 'What's happened?'

'Here is a letter,' said the driver, holding it out to her. Without giving her time to read it, he held open the door and hustled her into the car. To her surprise it also contained Father Rodrigues. Why was he involved?

The speed at which they drove off made it clear that this was an emergency. She opened the note, and read. 'Please come. Miss Beleza threatens suicide and needs your help and comfort.' It was signed Luis Pinto.

As the car sped away, she asked Father Rodrigues what had

happened. But he had no English, so she addressed herself to the driver instead. 'The Brazil woman, she is on the levada,' he replied, 'and she say she will jump.'

So that was it. All the guide books warned tourists that people subject to vertigo should not attempt some of the walks on the maintenance paths beside the irrigation channels which ran along the steep mountain-side, often skirting precipices. She and Father Rodrigues had been summoned to talk Maria-José out of jumping off the levada path.

The road led out of the suburbs and began a twisting ascent into mountains shrouded in the mists of early morning. As they skidded round hairpin bends at break-neck speed, Celia tried to think herself into Maria-José's desperate situation, and concluded that only the religious arguments to be expected of Father Rodrigues had any hope of persuading her to stay alive.

Cars had crowded into a lay-by near a small building at the roadside. Beside it, the levada led off along the flank of the mountain. Urged on by a driver waiting by one of the cars, they started along it, with Father Rodrigues in the lead and Celia close on his heels. As she picked her way along the path, with a steepish drop on one side, and on the other a deep channel cut in the rock which was full of rushing water, she decided that walking the levadas was an overrated macho amusement and not for her. Even without a would-be suicide waiting somewhere ahead, there was no question of admiring the spectacular scenery. The path was narrow and uneven. She had to keep her eyes firmly fixed on it to avoid stumbling into the water or down the slope on the other side.

At an outcrop of rock, a short tunnel took the levada round a bend. Beyond it, Pinto was waiting for them. Twenty yards on, Maria-José stood rigid, at a point where the path overhung a hundred-foot vertical drop. Pinto had a brief exchange with Father Rodrigues, then let him go past. Advancing only a few yards, he crossed himself then began speaking to her.

Pinto addressed himself to Celia. 'Thank you for coming.'

'I'm afraid there's not much I can do, or say to her.'

'It is enough if she sees you. For her, you are a figure of comfort.'

'How long has she been there?'

176

'Over an hour. One of my men saw her from below, standing there. I have told her that the Portuguese Government makes no accusation against her, she can go free. But she is as if deaf. My words made no impression.'

It looked as if Father Rodrigues, preaching the love of God and the sin of self-destruction was faring no better. Maria-José, staring down fixedly at the abyss below her, did not turn her head. 'Do not go closer, or she will jump,' Pinto told him as he took a step forward.

For twenty minutes Father Rodrigues pleaded with her, sometimes uttering what sounded like prayers, sometimes waiting in patient silence for the reaction which did not come. Presently he stood aside and motioned Celia past him, with a gesture which meant: You try, it's your turn. Feeling utterly inadequate to the occasion, she called: 'Maria, it's me, Celia Grant.'

There was no response. She was still staring down into the abyss.

'Do come away from there,' Celia persisted. 'You'll fall if you're not careful.'

Father Rodrigues spoke again, gently. Celia renewed her appeal, and they began calling to her alternately in a kind of litany, with intervals of silence from time to time. The tension became intolerable. Once they thought they detected a slight movement of Maria-José's head. But it proved to be only their imagination.

Suddenly she seemed to be listening. With what looked like an enormous effort, as if her neck was stiff, she was turning to look at them. Then came an expression of horror, as if she had just realised where she was and what was happening. Sinking down on to her hands and knees as if suffering from vertigo, she began crawling along the narrow path towards them.

ELEVEN

Down by the forester's house, Freitas lay dead on a stretcher, with a blanket over him. Detectives questioning the four men they had arrested were getting nowhere. Barton refused even to state his name and the other three, taking the lead from him, maintained an equally defiant silence. They had no identity papers on them and the car's documents showed that it had been legally hired three days before in the centre of Funchal, apparently by someone called John Smith.

Maria-José, shivering in a borrowed blanket, was sitting in the back of one of the police cars beside Father Rodrigues, who was talking to her earnestly. The car was to take them and Celia back to Funchal, but Celia had refused to get into it till she heard from Pinto whether the night's events had thrown any light on the whereabouts of Gerald Hanbury and the children.

'Unfortunately not,' he told her. 'That is to say, not directly. But we have these.' He held out for her inspection four greasy cardboard boxes, which had clearly contained takeaway food. The firm's address was printed on the lid. 'The shop is on the Estrada Monumental, among the hotels. If they shop there regularly, it makes a starting point for our inquiries.'

With this meagre comfort she had to be content.

Maria-José was deathly pale and exhausted during the drive back to Funchal with Celia and Father Rodrigues. When the car stopped outside the gate of the Quinta Coulson she opened her eyes and realised where she was. 'No! I cannot stay here, they will find me.'

There was truth in this. Only four of the mobsters had been arrested. Others might still be at large.

'But where will you go?' Celia asked.

'To my friend Mrs Nielsen. But only till I can book my flight to Rio.'

'Maria has decided to submit to the authorities,' said Father Rodrigues.

Maria-José nodded gravely. 'And after the prison I shall enter a religious order which cares for the poor.'

Celia exchanged glances with Father Rodrigues. Her look said: I suppose this is the best solution in the circumstances. His replied: Anything is better than the awful sin of suicide.

The car drove away and Celia went into the house, to find Teresa mystified by the absence of the senhora at breakfast time, and full of a horror story she had heard from Mrs Freitas about the kidnapping of her Lúcio in the middle of the night.

If I tell her that Freitas is dead, Celia reasoned, I shall have to go with her to break the news to Mrs Freitas. There will be frightful lamentations which I am too bruised emotionally to bear, and when I am asked about the whys and wherefores I shall have to tell the unfortunate woman things about her husband's behaviour which will only make the lamentations louder. Therefore I shall keep callously silent and enjoy my toast and coffee.

Still acutely worried about Gerald and the children, she was also faced with the problem of Sir Adrian, who was due to leave hospital soon. Where was she to find a minder for him, and also someone to give the minder logistical and moral support? In the short term at least, he would have to resign himself to a home for the elderly. She decided to visit him in hospital and prepare him for this fate.

She found him sitting in a chair by the window and looking remarkably spry. He greeted her warmly, and listened carefully when she explained that his Maria had gone for good, with no replacement in sight. For the present at least, he could not go back to his old quarters at the quinta and would have to put up with a rest home.

He frowned and shook his head and became agitated.

'I know it's hard,' she insisted. 'But I'm afraid there's no alternative.'

Even more agitated, he launched out into one of his agonised struggles for speech. She made him repeat the inarticulate noise

179

that came out, and at the third attempt made sense of it. He was saying 'Not . . . quinta.'

'You don't want to go back there?'

An emphatic 'No.'

'A retirement home, then?'

A qualified 'No,' followed by 'Eee . . . Gaah.'

'England?' she cried when enlightenment came. 'You want to go back to England?'

He nodded and smiled, delighted to have been understood.

'But Adrian, what about your orchids?'

He waved them away with a bored gesture of dismissal.

'Adrian, you're quite sure? You've been here for years, it'll be quite a change.'

He was unshakable. Evidently he had decided to die on his native soil.

She left him, with a great weight off her mind. Caring for the elderly was far less difficult if it did not have to be done from a distance by remote control. She would phone Margaret. As his sister-in-law, it was up to her to arrange something. So far she had not done a hand's turn to help.

Meanwhile, Pinto's team of detectives were engaged in humdrum leg-work, a contrast with the alarms of the night. Their starting point was the discovery in the villains' car of the sordid remains of takeaway meals. Their supplier proved to be a small shop in the package-tour hotel area along the coast road to the west of the town, which provided chicken and chips or espada and chips to dwellers in cheap self-catering holiday flats and the like. The bully-boys were among their regular customers, ordering food in quantities which suggested that they were feeding their captives on it as well as themselves. Encouragingly, they had almost always arrived on foot, which suggested a hide-out somewhere near by. But on one occasion, an assistant had carried the order out to a car which could from its description have been the hired car used for the expedition to Maria-José's hide-out up the mountain.

Armed with descriptions of the suspects, Pinto's men fanned out. It soon became clear that similar-looking people had been seen bearing loads of takeaway food up a street leading inland off the coast road into an estate of raw-looking little houses perched on a steepish slope. An agency specialising in letting holiday

180

accommodation admitted having rented one of the houses to a fat blond American and a thin tense-looking man who spoke like a Brazilian. Neighbours confirmed that there had been unusual activity at the house. Cars had arrived and departed very late at night. The inhabitants were all men. Five or six of them had been seen coming and going. At intervals enough takeaway food was brought in to feed an army.

A detective knocked at the door, then crouched to one side as a shot from an upper window hit the doorstep. Pinto summoned police sharpshooters and trained negotiators with loud-hailers and settled down grimly to a house siege in which the lives of two adult hostages and two children were at stake. It took the team two hours to establish that there was only one gunman in the house, and another hour to persuade him that with the place surrounded front and back there was no point in further resistance. But Pinto's hopes of finding the hostages were disappointed. Bettencourt, Gerald Hanbury and the children were not there, though they had been. Among the takeaway boxes in the cellar, one of the detectives found a small boy's shoe.

As an interrogator, Pinto could be terrifying if he wished, and in this case he did. The gunman was told that the penalty for kidnapping under Portuguese law was life imprisonment, and that he could expect no mercy unless he revealed at once where the hostages were. On being told that four of his colleagues were already under arrest for false imprisonment and murder, he crumpled up and murmured something about a boat.

'What boat? Where?' Pinto stormed.

'Down in the marina.'

Aboard the cabin-cruiser *Sunrise*, Ricardo Fernandes wondered gloomily what to do about the hostages down in the chain locker. The timetable had gone badly wrong, it had taken longer than they expected to soften Freitas up and make him tell them where he had got Maria-José Beleza hidden away. But even allowing for the delay, Ed Barton should have been back hours ago with her and Freitas, and with luck the diamond necklace. Something must have gone badly wrong.

What was he to do? The two men had to be disposed of, they had both been asked questions about Maria-José, they knew too much,

181

to be allowed to go free. It was a pity about the children, but that was their bad luck. The question was, should he wait any longer for Ed to arrive with Maria-José and Freitas, who had also to be got rid of? Could he get them on board in broad daylight without a lot of noise and fuss that would attract attention? Probably not.

What if Ed had been arrested? It was a possibility. In that case, Fernandes reckoned, he would be on his own. He would have to tidy up as best he could and get out of Madeira before the same thing happened to him. Killing two men and two children and throwing them overboard out at sea was a tall order for one person, but he was not squeamish. If it was a case of saving his own skin he could manage. Suddenly he gave way to panic. It was time to act. He started the engine, slipped the moorings, and headed out towards the open sea.

Bound and gagged and crowded into the confined space of the chain locker with Bettencourt and the two children, Gerald Hanbury heard the motor start and had no illusions about what was in store. The two children, mercifully, were asleep. They had been sleeping soundly when they were carried aboard, for the kidnappers had been lacing their Coca-Cola with something to keep them drowsy and quiet. They were doing something similar to the instant coffee they produced for him and Bettencourt, but he had managed not to drink the last mugful, administered just before they were driven to the marina. To judge from the effect on Bettencourt, it must have been an exceptionally strong brew. An observer watching him being transferred from the car to the boat late at night would have concluded that a hopeless drunk was being helped to bed by solicitous friends.

When Gerald's turn came to be taken aboard, uncomfortably aware of the gun barrel pressed against his ribs, he took his cue from Bettencourt and played drunk. Four of the kidnappers had been present then to attend to the binding and gagging, but he had heard several of them leave shortly afterwards. Since then he had heard no voices and only one set of footsteps. He was sure there was only one kidnapper on board. Now that the boat was under way he would be far too busy at the helm to investigate what was happening in the chain locker. The time for action had come.

Stiff from his bonds, he manoeuvred painfully in the confined space till he and Bettencourt were back to back with his bound

182

wrists level with Bettencourt's. His hands were too numb to function effectively, and the pain was agonising as he set one of them fumbling with the knot in the rope round Bettencourt's wrists.

Working behind his back and in total darkness, it took him an age to get Bettencourt's wrists free. He was beginning to recover from the effects of the drug, and Gerald managed in the end to prod him into wakefulness. As they were both gagged, Gerald had to explain by nudging that the next item on the programme was for Bettencourt to untie his wrists. When Bettencourt had grasped the point, he shook off his drowsiness and acted with commendable speed, so that they were soon able to remove their own gags and untie their ankles.

The door of the chain locker was fastened on the outside, which made it impossible, even if it was advisable, to come out of hiding and try to overpower the armed man at the helm. They would have to wait till he came to kill them and dump them overboard.

Time passed. Evidently the plan was to wait till the boat was well out of sight of land. Whispering with their heads close together, they planned their tactics.

Sitting on deck at the wheel, Fernandes was also considering his tactics. He was concerned to avoid anything messy and incriminating, such as bullet holes in the hired boat, or blood on the cushions in the cabin. After considering various alternatives, he decided to haul the hostages up on to the foredeck one by one, shoot them through the side of the head and push them overboard. A bucketful or two of sea water would remove any traces of blood. But this could not happen yet. Though Madeira was far away on the horizon, there might be prying eyes on a group of small islands only a few miles away.

When he reckoned it was safe to do what he had come to do, he stopped the engine and went forward to open the door of the chain locker. Inside, the two men tensed themselves as the boat hove to, knowing that the moment of crisis had come.

Fernandes opened the door and started to pull at the pair of feet nearest him, intending to drag their owner out into the cabin. But the feet did not move forward as expected because Bettencourt, to whom they belonged, was clinging with all his might to Gerald, whose feet were braced against the bulkhead.

As expected, Fernandes had to put his head and shoulders into the chain locker to find out what was causing the obstruction. This put him at their mercy. Attacked by a bewildering tangle of aggressive arms and legs he tried to back out of the chain locker, but found this impossible because there was a noose of rope round his neck and both his arms were being sat on. He struggled for a time, but soon became convinced that the two hostages meant what they said when they told him to stop struggling unless he wanted them to twist his neck till it broke.

The children had been woken by the commotion, and cowered back into their corner, whimpering. 'Dad, what's he doing to you?' asked Peter's frightened voice from the darkness.

'Nothing. It's going to be OK,' said Gerald. But this was still far from certain. He could see no way of getting Fernandes out through the narrow doorway into the cabin without giving him a chance to break free and get at his gun. In the end, they had to drag him inside, creating intense overcrowding, and tie his hands and feet before handing the children out and then emerging themselves.

Bettencourt bent over the engine, preparing to get it started. Up on deck, Gerald looked round at the expanse of sky and sea. A motor launch was speeding towards them from the distant port of Funchal.

'Dad, can I steer?' asked Peter.

'No, he's too little,' said Sarah. 'I can, though, can't I?'

Gerald noted with relief that despite the children's horrifying experiences, their reactions were back to normal.

After telling their story in outline to the police, Gerald and Bettencourt were taken off to the Cruz de Carvalho hospital for repairs after the battering the gunmen had given them. Celia, summoned to the marina to take charge of the children, found that they were ravenously hungry and took them off to a restaurant for a gargantuan meal.

'I shall always associate takeaway chicken and chips with crime,' Sarah declared, tucking into her trout meunière. 'We got nothing else, and my stomach heaves at the very thought.'

'Even the Coca-Cola tasted funny,' Peter complained.

Later, when they had reached the ice-cream stage, Sarah said:

'Aunt Celia, we both think you're a fabulous aunt, but would you mind awfully if we went and lived with Dad instead?'

'Of course not, if you want to.'

'Well, we do,' said Peter firmly.

'The point is, he behaved terribly well all through,' Sarah explained. 'Not just getting us out of that hell hole on the boat, Smelly Bettencourt helped with that, and on the whole he behaved quite well too, but not as well as Dad. Right from the beginning Dad kept telling us stories so we wouldn't be afraid, marvellous ones that made us laugh. There was a lovely one about a wicked queen and a yucky princess who was her stepdaughter that she was unkind to, only the silly girl was such a wimp that she deserved everything she got, including being turned into a frog by a prince she made a pass at, it was really good.'

After Peter had told her the plot of the story in full detail, Sarah began to talk about their experiences. 'The most frightening bit in a way was right at the beginning, when the two men came out of the bananas on the far side of the lane and jumped into the car. The thin one got in front to drive and the fat one got in the back where we were. He sat down right on top of me, and he was huge and very smelly. It was like having an elephant with a perspiration problem land on one's lap.'

'He had a gun,' said Peter. 'He made Sarah and me get down on the floor, and Dad had to put his head right down between his knees.'

'They were arguing all the time,' Sarah reported. 'The thin one kept shouting "What do we want with these kids, why don't you throw them out?" And Dad was marvellous and said, "Yes, why don't you?" because right from the start he was trying to make them let us go, and not worrying about himself. But the fat one told him to shut his bloody mouth and keep his fucking head down. I'm sorry about the language, but he was that sort of man.'

'He used worse words than that,' said Peter darkly.

'Anyway, the thin one who was driving kept screaming at the fat one to chuck us out, and the fat one said, "Not here, there are too many houses, they'll get to a phone." And then the thin one said, "What about here?" and the fat one said, "There are still houses. We can't dump them, they'll have to tag along." And when we arrived at the house where we were going to be kept,

185

they put rugs over our heads and took us indoors and put us in a sort of cellar with pipes and things and Dad said we weren't to be frightened because it was all a mistake and he'd get it sorted out quite soon. And it was then that he started telling us stories.'

'And then they took Dad away,' said Peter, 'and we got frightened.'

'Yes, they took him away into another cellar, I think it was, and shouted at him a lot, and we couldn't hear what they were saying. When he came back he had a black eye and a cut on his head and it was bleeding a lot and he put his hankie on it. He said they'd asked him again and again where had he hidden Maria and who knew about her besides him. And when he said he scarcely knew Maria and what was it about her that bothered them they said, "You know damn well what it is," and went on hitting him.

'After that they left him for a bit and he told us some more stories, but we were a bit frightened because it didn't seem to be all a mistake like he said and they'd hurt him and we were getting very hungry. And presently the fat man came back and said had Dad thought it over and was he going to talk. And Dad said yes, he had thought it over and yes, they'd got the better of him and he would tell them what they wanted to know, and perhaps if they talked as one old lag to another they could work something out.

'Peter and I were rather alarmed by all this, because he was being very convincing about being a paid-up member of the criminal underworld. But he gave us an enormous wink, and we twigged what he was on about when he came to the next bit, which was that they had to get one thing straight: he wasn't saying a word unless they let us go first.

'That made them furious, and they said like hell they would let us go to set the police buzzing around after them like flies, and Dad was to tell them what they wanted to know pronto, or else. And of course after that he had to go into reverse and try to convince them that he wasn't a member of the criminal underworld after all. They didn't believe him till they'd knocked him about a lot more, but it was very decent of him, don't you think, to try to make them let us go.'

'So that's why we think we'd like to go and live with him,' said Peter.

Sarah nodded. 'Of course, he shouldn't have done whatever he did about the money, but I think Mum got it a bit wrong.'

That afternoon Celia went to the hospital to collect Adrian, who was to stay at the Quinta Coulson for a day or two before leaving for England with Celia and the children. On the way to his ward she was waylaid in the entrance hall by Dr Mendes.

'I believe, senhora, that you are the executor of poor Mrs Hanbury?'

Celia admitted that this was so.

'I was her doctor as well as Sir Adrian's and I am sorry that I must send you a bill on her account.'

'Oh? You were giving her some treatment?'

'No. An investigation. I have only now received the account from the laboratory.'

'D'you mind telling me what it was investigating?'

'There were symptoms suggesting the presence of a cancer.'

'And was this diagnosis confirmed?'

'No, the tumour was benign. She would have been very relieved to learn this, but unfortunately the results reached me from the laboratory only after she was dead.'

He gave her a look full of significance, and went out to his car. Celia stayed where she was, brought to a standstill by the meaning she read into his look: when a woman is terrified because she thinks she has cancer, no one should be surprised when a half-empty bottle of whisky is found by her bedside.

Adrian was in high spirits and dressed ready to leave. 'You still want to come back with us to England?' she asked.

He nodded emphatically and neighed with pleasure at the prospect.

At the quinta there was more neighing, first at being back in his own house, and then in the drawing-room at the sight of his grandchildren. As a boisterous reunion began, Celia went to the kitchen to brief Teresa about meals, but was not allowed to do so till she had inspected a battered account book which Teresa held out to her. It emerged that Antonia, typically, looked at the book every Friday to satisfy herself that the marketing had been done economically, then doled out money for the following week's housekeeping. Celia looked at the first page of ill-spelt

English, then handed it back. 'I'm sure it's perfectly in order, Teresa.'

'I spend only for the food, senhora. Except only that I pay the account of the *serralheiro*.'

'The *serralheiro*?' Celia queried.

'The one who fit the locks for the houses. Also, he copy the keys.'

'Oh yes. The locksmith. Why did we owe him money?'

'I tell you. Yesterday the *serralheiro*, he ring me to say, the key that the poor Senhora Hanbury leave me to copy, it is ready, the one she give me and the one I make. I say, I take them and I pay you when I come for the marketing.'

'What key was it?'

Teresa pointed meaningfully at the outside door of the kitchen.

'Then . . . she must have given him Maria's key to copy,' Celia concluded, 'the one Maria couldn't find when Sir Adrian had that bilious attack in the night. Why on earth didn't she tell Maria she'd taken it?'

Teresa did not answer. They exchanged significant looks, both knowing who the key was intended for, and why the copying operation had to be managed furtively.

The riddle of the key had been cleared up, there remained only the problem of the whisky bottle. She asked Teresa again about Antonia's drinking habits. 'Normally she drank very little, except at a party, and then only wine, is that right?'

Teresa agreed warily.

'But in the last few weeks of her life, there was a change?'

Taken aback, Teresa made an evasive gesture.

'I know, it was stupid of me,' said Celia. 'Sarah was there when you were asked, and you felt she shouldn't be told the truth. I don't blame you, Teresa. How bad was it?'

'Very bad. The senhora, she had been to the doctor. She was frightened.'

'The terrible thing, Teresa, was that she needn't have been frightened. Dr Mendes told me today that it was a false alarm. If she hadn't been frightened, she wouldn't have drunk too much and fallen downstairs.'

Celia had begun to feel as if the ground was quaking under her feet. How could she have been idiotic enough to nourish dark suspicions of murder? She went hot all over with embarrassment at the thought. Mercifully she had not expounded her humiliating error to anyone. But having been wrong about that spoiled the flavour of everything she had been right about; right through luck, she decided, rather than good management. What would Pinto have thought if she had blurted out her suspicions to him, and been proved wrong?

Pulling herself together, she went back to the drawing-room, where Adrian and the children were still holding high revel, and nerved herself for the next tricky task: explaining to Adrian that he must stop hating his errant son-in-law, who had redeemed himself in the eyes of his children by his bravery; and who, because he had nowhere else to go, would be moving into the quinta till they all left to catch their plane home.

A year later a customs man, searching for drugs in the cabin-cruiser *Sunrise*, found a diamond necklace in the bilges, wrapped in an oily rag. It was not clear whom it belonged to, and he made no effort to find out.